Visit us at www.boldstrokesbooks.com

Date With Destiny

by

Mason Dixon

2013

DATE WITH DESTINY

ISBN 10: 1-60282-878-4
ISBN 13: 978-1-60282-878-0

This Trade Paperback Original Is Published By
Bold Strokes Books, Inc.
P.O. Box 249
Valley Falls, NY 12185

First Edition: June 2013

Credits
Editor: Cindy Cresap
Production Design: Susan Ramundo
Cover Design By Sheri (graphicartist2020@hotmail.com)

Acknowledgments

Thanks to Radclyffe and the entire Bold Strokes Books team for taking a chance on me and my fledgling attempt to tell a story. All the hours spent staring at the blinking cursor on my computer screen finally paid off. I hope this book will be the first of many more to come.

Thank you also to Rashida and Destiny, the main characters who sometimes insisted—often quite loudly and usually in the middle of the night—on telling me exactly how they wanted to be portrayed in the pages that follow. I hope I've done them justice. If not, I'm sure they'll make a point to tell me about it later.

Last but not least, thank you to the readers. Your date with destiny awaits. Fingers crossed it's a good one.

Dedication

To my boo. I couldn't have made it this far without you.
Love you, girl.

Chapter One

Friday, March 3
7:50 a.m.
Savannah, Georgia

Rashida Ivey looked in her bathroom mirror as she prepared for work. She had come to the unwanted conclusion that only people blessed with good genes and even better plastic surgeons looked their best naked. Unfortunately, she had neither. She appraised her five-foot-nine inch body with a discerning eye.

Her shoulders were broad, tapering to a waist that was only one dress size bigger than it had been during her college days. Her arms and legs were toned without being too ripped. Muscular but with a hint of feminine curves. She ran her hands over her stomach. No matter how many miles she walked before work, no matter how many calories she counted during the day, and no matter how many flights she climbed on the StairMaster at night, she couldn't make her stomach as flat as the supermodels she saw strutting across her TV screen.

"Good thing I'm not planning on posing for a Victoria's Secret catalog any time soon."

She rubbed lotion onto her mocha-colored skin. She was thirty-five, but most people said she looked at least ten years younger.

Black don't crack, she thought as she smoothed moisturizer on her face. Save for lipstick, she usually eschewed makeup, preferring the natural look. The aesthetic extended to her hairstyle as well. After tiring of visiting the hair salon every few weeks for a fresh perm or a touch-up, she had cut her chemically straightened, shoulder-length locks short and allowed them to return to their natural state. Now she could swim without worrying about her hair turning green or work out without fearing the sweat would undo what had cost her fifty dollars and three hours of her time.

She rubbed pomade on her hands and moistened her scalp. The two-inch twists she now sported were easier to maintain than her former hairstyle and, in her opinion, even more stylish.

She stepped into a pair of lacy black underwear and slipped on a matching bra. Even though it was casual Friday, which meant jeans and a polo shirt instead of the power suits she wore the rest of the week, she wasn't going to change her routine. Sexy underwear made her feel confident and on top of things, no matter how close her day came to spinning out of control. Some days came closer than others.

She was the district operations manager for Low Country Savings Bank, a privately owned community bank headquartered in Savannah with four additional branches in the surrounding area. As the DOM, it was her responsibility to serve as the liaison between customers, the retail team, and the employees in the operations area, which meant both her customer-facing and behind-the-scenes skills had to be on point.

There were days when customers and employees alike worked her last nerve, but she couldn't let it show. Today had the makings of one of those days, and it hadn't officially started yet. Each time her cell phone chirped, the sound signaled bad news.

Three tellers and one branch manager had called in sick. Two had been legitimately suffering from head colds all week. The other two probably had nothing more serious than an itch for a long weekend. She had already mobilized the three floaters on staff to fill the teller slots, and the assistant branch manager on Wilmington Island could take up the slack for his missing teammate, but if anyone else called in, she might have to bite the bullet and run a window herself. She trained tellers all the time, but she hated being one herself. The pressure to finish the work day without being out of balance made her palms sweat.

She slipped her cell phone into its holster, clipped the holster to her belt, and crossed her fingers she wouldn't get another phone call or e-mail before she left her apartment. She had too many other things on her plate to throw her planned schedule out the window. In addition to drilling an unpaid safe deposit box in the Springfield branch and sitting down for the weekly update session with her boss in Richmond Hill, she and Jackie Williams needed to check the security procedures at the Savannah office and conduct the quarterly branch audit while they were onsite. The time-consuming chore was one she didn't want to be forced to reschedule. But if worst came to worst, she would scrap her original plans and do what she had to do. The branches couldn't run themselves.

Thanks to a hiring freeze brought on by the slow economy, most branch locations were already operating with the bare minimum number of employees. Rashida had to make sure the ones that remained had the support they needed to do their jobs even if it occasionally meant burning the candle at both ends while holding a lit match under the middle.

She groaned when her phone vibrated against her hip. "What now?"

She read the text message on the phone's display. Jackie, who prided herself on being at least ten minutes early for every appointment, was uncharacteristically running late. But at least she planned on showing up, which was more than Rashida could say for the four who had called in sick.

Take your time, she texted back. *I'll handle the security check myself and meet you at the branch at nine.*

I'll make it up 2 U on Sunday, Jackie replied. *The first round's on me.*

Rashida chuckled ruefully. *Depending on how Saturday goes, I might need more than one.*

She headed to the living room and raised the volume on the local morning news show playing on the TV. According to the dorky but accurate meteorologist, the weather was going to be unseasonably warm for the next few days with a chance of rain on Monday. She hoped the bad weather, if it arrived, cleared out before St. Patrick's

Day. The tourists would show up for the annual bacchanalia rain or shine, but the marchers in the parade would be soaked before they made it past Lafayette Square. She had been spared marching duties this year. Jackie, the bank's security officer and her best friend, had drawn the short straw. If it rained, Rashida would be willing to bet Jackie would never let her hear the end of it. She smiled at the image of Jackie trying to keep her hair protected from the elements.

"If Mother Nature ruins Jackie's 'do, there'll be hell to pay."

In the kitchen, she dropped a sliced banana, a pack of vanilla breakfast mix, milk, and several ice cubes into a blender and melded the ingredients into a smoothie. She saved three of the ice cubes for the orchid that sat on top of a pile of cookbooks she had bought with the best of intentions but had yet to use.

"Good morning, Riko."

She greeted the orchid as she placed the ice cubes on the rich dark brown soil that filled a small terra cotta pot.

The orchid had been a birthday present from Jackie. Even though her thumb was decidedly not green, Rashida had somehow managed to keep the plant alive for nearly a year, a personal best. The orchid had been covered with big white blooms streaked with purple when she pulled it out of the box last April. The original blooms had fallen off long ago. Even though the plant's leaves were healthy and its spindly stems were festooned with bright green buds, no new blooms had taken the old ones' places.

"You and Riko are made for each other," Jackie often said, giving herself a figurative pat on the back for picking out the perfect gift. "Both of you are taking your own sweet time to open up again."

Rashida hadn't been completely off the market since she and Diana Vasquez broke up two years ago, but her dates were so few and far between, that certainly appeared to be the case. She blamed work. It was the easiest excuse. Her uncertain hours made romantic entanglements difficult but not impossible. The real culprit was her unwillingness to put herself out there. To risk being hurt again. She didn't want to watch another relationship wither on the vine knowing she was partially responsible for its demise.

The breakup with Diana had been amicable but not painless. Six years hadn't been easy to walk away from, even if walking away had been the right thing to do. In truth, she hadn't completely turned her back on what she and Diana once had. Even though she knew they were over, she hadn't been able to completely let go. To put the final nail in the coffin. Tomorrow, though, she was finally taking hammer in hand and Diana was supplying the nails.

"It's time for closure," Diana had said the last time they talked.

Rashida popped two multivitamins into her mouth and crunched down on the bitter pills. "Closure's for envelopes."

She downed the smoothie, brushed her teeth, and applied a coat of her favorite lipstick. Then she secured her laptop, portable printer, and daily organizer in a pair of sturdy black leather rolling bags. Pulling the bags behind her as she headed to the elevator, she felt like a passenger rushing to catch a departing plane.

Her hectic schedule added to her nomadic existence. Though she was technically based in the newly-opened Richmond Hill branch, she spent so much time on the road shuttling to the bank's other locations, her car felt like her real office. Lunch was something served out of a drive-in window and was inhaled on route. Dinner came out of a box, but at least it was served at home. Usually.

Downstairs, she locked her bags in the trunk of her Prius and pulled out of the parking lot. Her apartment complex was popular with students from all the local colleges, thanks to the units' relatively low rental prices and the building's proximity to downtown Savannah. She valued it for the same reasons. Her apartment was small, but the views were incredible, the residents were colorful, and the carefully preserved beauty of the Historic District was just a few minutes away.

She drove the short distance to the financial district. Johnson Square was Savannah's version of Wall Street. Local, regional, and national banks surrounded the picturesque park on all sides. Low Country Savings Bank's main office was located just off Johnson Square, tucked behind an historic building whose stately lines had caught the attention of more than one movie location scout and across the street from Paula Deen's restaurant. During the spring and summer months, the branch's two accounts representatives spent most of their spare time people-watching as the overflow of tourists waiting to get into The Lady and Sons snaked down Congress Street like a conga line.

Rashida circled the bank to see if any of the employees had arrived. The posted hours were nine to five Monday through Friday, but the geniuses in the marketing department had decided the bank needed to open fifteen minutes early and close fifteen minutes late to make it easier for customers to run last-minute errands before and after work.

And the powers that be wonder why all the tellers have overtime each week.

Rashida checked her watch. Eight fifteen.

The branch manager and the head teller were usually the first to arrive. They probably wouldn't show up for another fifteen minutes or so. That gave her plenty of time to stow her car in the parking garage on Whitaker Street and find a place to see without being seen.

According to the branch's updated opening procedures—each branch's procedures changed at regular intervals to prevent outsiders from sussing them out—no one could enter the bank until at least two employees were onsite. The first unlocked the front door, disabled the alarm, and checked to make sure the building was secure. He or she then gave the all clear by opening the blinds in the branch manager's office and placing a small plastic egret, the bank's mascot, on the windowsill. The second employee was then free to enter. Some people, however, refused to play by the rules, entering the building simultaneously and neglecting to give the all clear to the rest of the staff, who either lingered outside or barged in anyway.

Whether by accident or design, the main branch had the youngest staff and, not coincidentally, was the site of the most turnover and the most security violations.

"Procedures were put in place for a reason," Jackie had said during her last security symposium. "The reason was not to put a crimp in your day but to save your life. Shortcuts, boys and girls, can get you killed."

Now Rashida would see if the employees at the main branch had gotten the message.

She headed to the French Roast Coffee Shop. Starbucks was closer to the parking garage, but everyone and her sister were packed inside to grab their morning doses of caffeine. The French Roast was more expensive than Starbucks but less crowded and gay-owned. Given a choice, Rashida preferred to line the pockets of a fellow member of the GLBTQ community instead of the already bulging purses of an anonymous corporate bigwig.

She pushed the shop's swinging door open and stepped inside. Edith Piaf was playing on a boom box behind the counter. A black-and-white movie starring an impossibly young Catherine Deneuve flickered silently on a flat-screen TV bolted to one wall. The other walls were covered with photographs and paintings of France and its instantly recognizable landmarks.

Rashida took a deep breath and allowed the smell of fresh-baked pastries to permeate her lungs. She felt like she had been transported from Savannah to Paris.

The line at the counter was surprisingly long. The sight pleased Rashida for two reasons. The French Roast was one of her favorite destinations on the weekends. The fact that it was continuing to do well meant she would always have a place to hang out on Saturday mornings and, on a professional note, it meant the small business loan her bank had underwritten had proven to be a sound investment.

She pulled a number out of the dispenser on the counter. The number on the Now Serving sign above the chalk-covered blackboard that served as a menu read seventeen. The slip of paper in her hand read twenty-four. The line was moving relatively quickly—the beret-clad baristas behind the counter were mixing lattes and cappuccinos so fast she could barely keep up—but she was afraid she might miss what she had come downtown for. Eight twenty. Almost time for the branch manager to arrive. She had work to do.

She turned to grab a seat by the window and instantly plowed into a woman who had chosen that exact moment to dart through a break in the line. Black coffee splashed all over the woman's crisp white button-down shirt, trickled onto her starched khaki pants, and dropped on her blue-and-tan saddle shoes. Even the folded newspaper in her hands dripped with the remnants of what had been a nearly full cup of what smelled like Sumatran blend. The only thing that seemed to have remained unscathed was her navy blue blazer—unless the material was too dark to reveal the stain.

"Something told me I shouldn't have worn this shirt today." The woman's voice was deep and commanding. She had the rigid posture of an authority figure, either cop or ex-military.

Rashida swallowed so hard her throat clicked. The woman seemed to be taking what had happened in stride, but she was mortified. "I am *so* sorry." She grabbed napkins off the counter where swizzle sticks and packets of sweetener lay. She pressed the napkins against the slowly spreading stain on the woman's shirt.

The woman's body was firm. Rashida could feel her rippled stomach through the wet cotton of her shirt. The heat that met Rashida's fingers had nothing to do with the coffee dripping from the soaked wads of tissue. She blushed when she realized she was touching a complete stranger in a way that could be considered too familiar.

"Sorry," she said again.

"Don't worry about it."

The woman grinned. Rashida looked up and met her eyes. Then she promptly forgot how to breathe.

The woman's almond-shaped eyes were arresting, so dark Rashida couldn't tell where her pupils ended and her irises began. Her skin was like milk chocolate. As smooth as a Hershey's Kiss and probably nearly as sweet. Her lips were full, the outline begging to be traced with the tip of a finger or a tongue. Her short, side-swept hair highlighted her strong jaw and long neck. One eyebrow arched upward in what could have been amusement or a flicker of interest.

Gathering her composure, Rashida unzipped one of her bags and pulled out the Tide pen she was never without. More often than not, part of her lunch ended up on her clothes. The stain removal pen had rescued her from more than one unwanted dry-cleaning bill.

"I would offer this to you, but I don't think it will do the job."

The woman's smile grew. "Not unless you have four or five more of them in your little bag of tricks." She took the proffered pen, her long fingers brushing lightly over Rashida's. She swiped the pen over a small area of her shirt, but it didn't seem to have an effect. She returned the pen with a shrug. "Thanks anyway."

Rashida blushed again. *Jeez. No one has made me feel this tongue-tied since I was a hormone-addled teenager.*

"What happened was entirely my fault. If you send me a copy of the bill, I'll gladly cover the cost of dry-cleaning your shirt. On second thought, let me give you ten bucks so I can take care of it right now."

The woman held up her hands in a gesture that seemed to say, no harm, no foul. "Not necessary, but thanks for the offer. It was nice running into you. Literally."

She turned to leave, but Rashida wasn't ready to see her go. She rested her fingers on the woman's sleeve. The muscles in her forearm felt like banded steel.

Gorgeous smile, incredible eyes, and a body for days. If she has a brain in her head, she's four for four.

"Let me buy you a cup of coffee," she said. "It's the least I can do."

The woman hesitated as if she had somewhere she needed to be. Or, more likely, someone she needed to meet. No one who looked that good could be single. Could she? Rashida's dwindling hopes flickered back to life when the woman smiled and said, "Sure. I'd love to. I'll grab us a table."

"What would you like?"

"A *café Americain.*"

"Cream and sugar?"

"No," the woman said under her breath. "Hot and black. Just like I like my women."

Rashida turned toward the counter but quickly spun around again. Part of her needed assurance the most striking woman she had ever met wasn't a mirage. The woman caught her staring. She rushed to correct her social faux pas. "Pardon my manners. Or lack thereof. I should introduce myself." She stuck out her hand. "I'm—"

"Number twenty-four," one of the baristas called out.

"That's me," Rashida said.

"Nice to meet you, Number Twenty-four," the woman said, clasping Rashida's hand in her soft, warm palm. "I'm Number Thirteen."

Forget seven. I think I've found a new lucky number.

She ordered a vanilla latte, a *café Americain*, and two chocolate croissants. She paid for her purchases, then dropped one of her business cards into the jar next to the register to enter the weekly drawing for a twenty-five dollar gift certificate.

Gripping both cups of coffee in her left hand and the bag of pastries between her teeth, she carefully maneuvered through the slowly-thinning crowd. The woman stood as she approached the table.

"I'll take those." She grabbed the steaming cups of brew and the bag of croissants and placed them on the table.

"Were you being gallant or were you trying to keep me from spilling something else on you?"

One corner of the woman's mouth quirked upward into a smile. "Let's go with gallant." She blew on her fresh cup of coffee and took a sip. "Is this table okay?"

"It's perfect, thanks."

Rashida had an ideal vantage point. From where she was sitting, she had an unobstructed view of the bank's front door. She watched as Seaton Andrews, the branch manager, cut through Johnson Square and jogged across the street. Megan Connelly, the diminutive head teller, was hot on his heels. Seaton went inside first. Megan remained on the sidewalk, pretending to read the latest edition of the *Savannah Morning News*. Rashida nodded in approval. *So far, so good.*

"Is that where you work?" the woman asked.

Rashida took her eyes off the view outside the window and focused on the one directly in front of her. "Pardon?"

The woman lowered her gaze until her eyes rested on the logo on Rashida's green polo shirt, Low Country Savings Bank printed above a wide-winged egret soaring over grassy marshland. Rashida's nipples hardened as they submitted to the inspection. She had to fight to keep from arching her back and presenting her breasts to the woman's tempting mouth as a gift.

The woman pointed at the logo, then at the branch across the street. "Low Country Savings. Is that where you work?"

"Yes and no. I work for the company, yes, but my office is in another branch. I'm only here for the day."

"Then I guess today's my lucky day. What do you do?"

"Everything," Charles Demery, the owner of the French Roast, answered before Rashida could. "The bank would fall apart without her. Everything would go to hell in a hand basket if she weren't around."

"Don't listen to him," Rashida said, trying to deflect attention away from herself. "Charles is just saying that because I'm one of his best customers."

Charles put his hands on his hips. "I'm saying it because it's true, girlfriend. By the way, congratulations on the promotion, Madam Senior Vice President."

Rashida had worked her ass off to reach the next rung on the ladder of success. Sometimes, though, her reward felt more like a punishment. The official announcement of her leap from vice president to senior vice president had come within the past week, but the designation had been hers for almost two months. During that time, her work hours had doubled, but her salary hadn't kept pace.

"I saw your picture in the business section of the *Morning News* last Sunday," Charles said. "You looked *good*."

"That means the airbrushing was successful."

Charles blew air through his pursed lips. "Every time I see you, you look like you just stepped out of the pages of a fashion magazine. If I looked like you on your worst day, I'd feel like an eleven instead of the perfect ten I am." He tossed his hair over his shoulders as if he were a corn-rowed Bo Derek running on the beach in the movie that made her one of the biggest stars of the '80s.

Rashida laughed at the familiar joke. "Have you met Number Thirteen?" If the mystery woman wouldn't divulge her name, perhaps Charles would do the honors.

"Of course I've met Miss Destiny." Charles patted the woman—*Destiny*—on the shoulder. "She's one of my new regulars.

I'm surprised you two haven't run into each other before now. Now that you have, I'll let you get back to your little love connection. Destiny's looking for a job, Rashida. Maybe you can help the girl out."

Rashida watched out of the corner of her eye as Seaton opened the blinds in his office and placed an eight-inch egret on the windowsill. *Good boy.* She turned back to Destiny and looked at the coffee-stained want ads resting on the table. Several entries were circled. "What kind of jobs are you seeking?"

"Anything." Destiny's hands tightened around her coffee cup. "It's been much too long since I've seen a paycheck. I'm starting to fall behind on some things. If I'm offered a gig that pays, I'll take it, even if it's only temporary. But times are tough, and there are more people looking for work than there are jobs available. I'm competing with people who are way out of my league."

Rashida nodded sympathetically. "I may complain about my job, but I'm thankful to have one to complain about when there are so many unfortunate people who can't say the same."

Destiny brushed the classifieds off the table as if she wished they had never become a topic of conversation. "I have a few leads. We'll see if any of them pan out."

Sensing Destiny's discomfort, Rashida dutifully changed the subject.

"Do you have any idea why your parents decided to name you Destiny?"

"Makes me sound like a stripper or a porn star, doesn't it?" She flashed a grateful smile. "I've heard all the jokes at least once. The one about having a date with destiny continues to be the frontrunner. My friends call me DJ."

"DJ." Rashida cocked her head. "That's nice, but Destiny suits you better."

"Why?"

"Because you feel like something that's meant to be," Rashida said before she could stop herself. "That didn't come out right."

"I don't know. Maybe it did." Destiny ran her index finger along the rim of her coffee cup. Rashida had never been so envious of recycled paper. "You seem like a busy woman so I won't waste your time asking if you're free for dinner tonight. The bank's closed tomorrow. Are you free then?"

"Actually, I'm going out of town in the morning and won't be back until late tomorrow night."

"How about brunch on Sunday? You have to eat sometime."

Rashida grimaced. Her calendar had been free every weekend for months, and the one weekend she plans something she runs into a scheduling conflict. "A friend and I are having a spa day on Sunday. She has a gift certificate that's about to expire so she signed us up for a bunch of services. Manicures, pedicures, massages. The works. I'll be tied up for hours."

"I see."

Some of the light seemed to go out of Destiny's eyes. Rashida hoped she didn't think she was making excuses not to see her because of her job situation. She tried to think of a tactful way to explain that wasn't the case. She normally crossed someone off the list of prospective partners if she didn't have the three G's—the gift of gab, great moves in the sack, and gainful employment. Destiny, for some reason, made her want to revise her selection criteria.

"Sorry I'm late." Jackie squeezed into the booth next to Rashida. "I just couldn't get going this morning." She stared at the two cups on the table as if she couldn't believe there wasn't a third. "Where's my mocha Frappuccino?"

Destiny's eyes darted from Rashida's face to Jackie's and back again. "I see," she said quietly. "Let me save both of us from further embarrassment and get out while the getting's good." She placed her palms on the table and pushed herself to her feet. "Thank you for the coffee. Both cups." Her hand grazed her stained shirtfront. "Have a nice day." She did that back-and-forth thing with her eyes again, indicating she thought Rashida and Jackie were a couple. "Both of you."

As Destiny walked away, Rashida was left with the uneasy feeling she had unintentionally ruined much more than a shirt.

CHAPTER TWO

Friday, March 3
1:45 p.m.
Springfield, Georgia

Rashida sorted the pile of women's accessories on the table by color. She felt a bit like a vendor setting up shop at a flea market.

"Tell me again who this box belongs to," Jackie said.

Rashida checked the name on the lease. "Rev. Gary Isaacson."

"So why does Rev. Isaacson own one hundred women's barrettes and a custom-designed necklace with a stuffed Chihuahua's head on it? On second thought, don't tell me. I don't want to know. Hit me with another shot of the hand sanitizer. I feel a case of the hives coming on."

Rashida squeezed a generous dollop of sanitizer into Jackie's palm. Jackie stared at her over the top of her half-moon reading glasses as she coated her hands with the pungent alcohol-based solution. "What's with the look?"

"Are you finally going to tell me about the tall drink of water with the Rorschach stain on her shirt or do I have to drag it out of you?" Jackie asked.

"There's nothing to tell."

"Yeah and I'm married to Denzel Washington. Come on. Dish. What did I miss this morning?"

"A marriage license, a divorce decree, and three deposit receipts."

"Huh?"

Rashida pointed to the spreadsheet Jackie was supposed to be completing. The audit of the Savannah branch had gone relatively quickly, but inventorying the contents of the unpaid safe deposit box in Springfield was taking longer than expected. The fifteen-by-twenty inch box was packed with dozens of items that had to be meticulously catalogued under dual control. She and Jackie had been at it for over an hour with no end in sight. She was supposed to meet with her boss in fifteen minutes, but she wasn't going to be able to keep the appointment. Not by a long shot. Richmond Hill was an hour away, and she and Jackie had to put in at least another hour here before she could even think about hitting I-95.

"A marriage license, a divorce decree, and three deposit receipts."

Jackie placed her pen on the fourth of what was turning out to be an infinite number of inventory sheets. Soon they would need to make more copies. "Are you going to be this bitchy all weekend or do you plan on getting it out of your system today?"

Jackie was forty-three and the mother of college-age twins. Jade and Jabari were sophomores at the University of Georgia. Jade was majoring in criminal justice, Jabari in business. Both were straight-A students. Jackie loved to boast the twins got their brains from their mama, but their father—Jackie's husband James—was no intellectual slouch either. He was one of the civil engineers in charge of preparing Savannah's infrastructure for the future while remaining respectful of its historic past.

Jackie had seen her through so many hard times Rashida sometimes felt like her third child. She closed her eyes and gave herself a mental reboot. Jackie didn't deserve to bear the brunt of her bad mood. "Sorry. I'm anxious about tomorrow and...other things."

"Such as?"

"The tall drink of water with the Rorschach stain on her shirt?"

"Mmm hmm?" Jackie folded her arms and leaned forward in her seat like she was watching a slow-building movie that had finally gotten to the good part.

"She asked me out."

"Did you say yes?"

"No."

"Why the hell not?" Jackie's voice echoed off the walls of the cavernous conference room. She leaned back in her chair to see if any of the customers in the lobby had heard her. Outside the double doors, business continued as usual. Customers were lined up to make deposits, cash checks, apply for loans, or simply make conversation with their favorite tellers. "Why the hell not?" Jackie repeated in a stage whisper as she pushed the doors shut. "Even though I'm strictly dickly, I could be persuaded to turn over a new leaf for Miss Tall, Dark, and Handsome. That sister was *fine*."

"Tell me something I don't know."

"Then why did you turn her down when she asked you for a date?"

"Because I have to drive to Atlanta tomorrow to see Diana and I'm spending Sunday at the spa with you."

"Did I mention the sister was fine? Your box of crap has been sitting in Diana's closet for two years. It can sit there for another week. As far as the trip to the spa is concerned, my gift certificate doesn't expire this weekend. We have ten more days to play with."

"My 'box of crap,' as you call it, is Diana's excuse for getting me to come to Atlanta, but it's not the reason I'm going. As for Sunday, it's been a long time since I had a good massage."

"It's been a long time since you had a good roll in the hay, too. Which do you want more?"

"Maybe if I toss in a few extra bucks, the masseuse will give me a happy ending. What do you think?"

"I think if you make her an offer like that, I'll end up spending my Sunday afternoon bailing your ass out of jail." Jackie removed her blazer and tossed it on the back of a nearby chair. "I'm going to tell you what I tell my kids. If you ever get into a situation where you're allowed only one phone call, don't waste your quarter on me. I'm not going to come and get you. I'm going to let you sit in a holding cell overnight so you can think about what you did wrong."

"It's good to know I have friends I can count on to be there for me no matter what."

Jackie chuckled, an earthy sound that always reminded Rashida of family reunions and backyard barbecues. "Whether I feel like giving you a hug or wringing your neck, I'll always have your back, girl."

Rashida wished the people in her life who could honestly say the same numbered more than three. Except for her grandmother, who would give her the shirt off her back, the only people she could depend on were Jackie and Diana. Her best friend and her ex-lover. Her relatives could only be counted on to alternately criticize her lifestyle and beg for money. Where were they when she needed them? Conveniently MIA, that's where. In many ways, Jackie was closer to her than most members of her family—and even more loyal. Diana, even though they were no longer an item, was still in her corner, too. She hoped nothing would happen tomorrow to change that fact.

"Refresh my memory," Jackie said. "Why did you and Diana break up?"

Rashida temporarily set work aside as she tried once again to unravel her knotty personal life. "It's hard to explain. The sex was great and I loved her dearly, but I always felt like something was missing. That spark people mention when they talk about the loves of their lives. She was everything I thought I wanted—beautiful, smart, successful, and ambitious—but it didn't work."

"Maybe you're looking for the wrong things. You're looking for someone who's at your level or above it. Maybe you shouldn't be so quick to rule out someone who's a few rungs beneath you on the success ladder but has the potential to move up."

"Are you saying I should lower my standards?"

"Not lower them. Relax them enough to let someone knock the dust off your kitty cat, even if she doesn't make six figures a year or have a fancy title attached to her name."

Rashida immediately thought of Destiny. She was between jobs and, based on the entries she had circled in the want ads, she was looking for something blue-collar. Rashida had never dated anyone so far outside her professional milieu, but she couldn't deny the attraction she had felt to Destiny during their brief encounter.

"If I followed your example," Jackie continued, "I never would have taken a chance on James. When I met him, he was working two jobs to pay his way through school. Neither position was much to brag about, but I could tell he was going places and I wanted to be with him when he reached his final destination."

Jackie spoke with the fervor of a Baptist preacher. Rashida was tempted to raise her hands to the sky and bear witness. Her mind wandered to Destiny again, but she pushed the pleasant diversion from her mind. She had a limited amount of time to reach the goals she wanted to achieve in her career, which meant she needed a partner who was personally and financially secure, not one whose life was in flux.

"I'll remember what you said the next time I hit the McDonald's drive-thru and the cashier gives me the eye."

Jackie picked up her pen and resumed the inventory. "As long as you make sure she has benefits and a retirement plan before you let her get her hands on your Happy Meal."

Rashida laughed for the first time in hours. "Do me a favor." She reached across the conference table and grabbed Jackie's hand. "Don't ever change."

Jackie placed her other hand on top of Rashida's. "You can count on me."

❖

Friday, March 3
4:15 p.m.
Richmond Hill, Georgia

Rashida settled into a plush leather chair in her boss's office. Ted Hollis was a good old boy in every sense of the phrase, from the bottoms of his cowboy-booted feet to the top of his crew cut head. His molasses-thick Southern drawl could lull an insomniac to sleep, but he was more on the ball than his pronounced accent led you to believe, and he was an even bigger tech geek than the head of the IT department.

Dozens of gadgets lined the edge of his L-shaped desk, making his office look more like the display window of an electronics store than a work space. Country music from a free Internet radio station blasted out of the speakers of his souped up computer. He tapped his fingers against his wireless mouse in time to the beat.

Ted stared at the double monitors on his desk while he searched through his e-mail. "Will Jackie be joining us today?" he asked as steel guitars twanged in the background.

"No, she was called back to HQ. There was some kind of incident with the security guard."

"Something happened to Mr. Frank?"

"I don't have any details yet. All I know is he was involved in an altercation. I don't know with whom or what was the outcome. She said Seaton was quite upset when he called, and he reported some of the tellers were in tears."

"That doesn't sound good."

"No, it doesn't."

Frank Redmond—Mr. Frank to one and all—had been a security guard at Low Country Savings for as long as Rashida could remember. When she was a little girl, he used to give her a lollipop each time her grandmother came in to tidy up after hours. Even though he was off the clock, he would watch over them until her grandmother had cleaned the branch from the top to the bottom. While she waited for her grandmother to finish vacuuming the floors and dusting the common areas, Rashida would read a book in the lobby or sit in the CEO's chair pretending she was the one calling the shots. Over the years, their positions of power had gotten reversed. Instead of literally looking up to him, he figuratively looked up to her. In many ways, she preferred their old dynamic to their current one. She'd rather call him sir than hear him call her ma'am.

Mr. Frank was as much of an institution in Savannah as the Waving Girl, River Street, and moss-laden oak trees. The downtown branch had never been robbed, knock wood, primarily because not even the most hardened criminal had the heart to tangle with the gentle man guarding the front door.

Rashida checked her phone to see if she had any new e-mails or text messages. For once, her phone was ominously quiet. A few seconds later, it vibrated in her hand. "That's Jackie now."

"You'd better take it." Ted finally located the e-mail he'd been trying to find for the past five minutes. "When you're done, I have a project for you," he said, hitting the print button. He grinned as he spun around to face her. "I'll tell you right off the bat. You're not going to like it."

"Thanks for the warning." She pressed her phone to her ear. "What's up, Jackie?"

"My blood pressure."

Rashida motioned for Ted to lower the volume on the music wafting out of his computer. Right now, she really didn't care how sexy some chick thought Kenny Chesney's tractor was. "Jackie, I'm going to put you on speaker. I'm sitting here with Ted. As team leader, he needs to hear this, too." She pressed the speaker icon on her phone's display panel. "Okay, Jackie. Tell us what happened."

"Someone held up the Bank of America on Bull Street. Mr. Frank saw the robber running down Congress, forgot he was seventy-two years old, and tried to play hero. The guy ran through him like an NFL running back taking on a peewee team. Mr. Frank slowed him down long enough for the dye pack to go off, but the guy dropped the bag and broke free. The cops have an APB out for a six-foot Caucasian male, twenty-five to thirty, wearing sunglasses, jeans, a Savannah Sand Gnats cap, and a hooded gray sweatshirt. He was last seen driving a late-model brown sedan toward MLK."

Ted shook his head. "I-16's right off of MLK. The guy could be anywhere by now. More than likely, Chatham County's finest will find the getaway car torched in a field somewhere. Unless they get an anonymous tip, chances are they aren't going to find the driver. How's Mr. Frank doing?"

"Not well," Jackie said. "I'm following the ambulance taking him to Candler Hospital. The paramedics say he has a broken collarbone, cracked ribs, a fractured kneecap, and perhaps a ruptured spleen, which means he's going to be out of commission for a while. I've arranged for off-duty cops to stand guard the rest of the afternoon and the beginning of next week, but those guys can be expensive. We have to find a permanent solution."

"I can't picture Mr. Frank coming back to work after he heals," Rashida said. "There's no way he's going to be able to stand on his feet all day, and once word got around that he can't defend himself, the branch would be fair game for anyone with a gun and a stick-up note."

"Everyone's going to be on edge from now until closing," Ted said. "I'll draft an e-mail for all the branch managers advising them to be cautious and alert the rest of the afternoon. Good work, Jackie. Keep us posted."

"Will do."

Rashida ended the call.

"I'll talk to Catherine in HR and see if she wants to offer Mr. Frank a retirement package and go ahead and post his position," Ted said.

"Internally or externally?"

"Both."

"Mr. Frank's backup has made it clear he's happy working only part-time. I doubt he'll take the job."

"I'll ask Catherine to offer it to him and see what he says. We need someone ASAP. Ideally, we'll have a qualified person trained and in place before St. Patrick's Day. The crowds can get crazy once the green beer starts flowing."

"True, but we can't afford to rush the hiring process. After we place the ad, Jackie has to vet each of the applicants and make sure they have all the proper certifications before we can even consider them."

"We'll keep the rent-a-cops in place until we find someone. Yes, they're expensive, but we can't skimp on security." Ted smiled in an obvious attempt to lighten the mood. "Happy Friday, huh?"

Rashida was beginning to think this Friday would never end.

"Almost forgot." Ted reached for the piece of paper on his printer and presented it to Rashida with a flourish. "Your project."

Rashida read the e-mail with a rising sense of disbelief. "Please tell me this is a joke."

"I wish I could."

When Dennis Rawlings, the bank's CEO, came on board three years ago, he had closed the mortgage office in Hilton Head, South Carolina, because he felt the location fell "outside of the company's footprint." Never mind that the housing market in the ritzy resort town had remained strong despite the recession and the mortgage originators there made money hand over fist. Never mind that the bank itself had taken its name from the region along South Carolina's coast, a region that stretched from Beaufort to Charleston and included Hilton Head.

According to the e-mail Dennis had sent Ted, he was reconsidering his decision and she was being tasked with heading up a committee to determine if buying back the mortgage office in the bank's former territory would be an economic boost or a public relations disaster.

"I fought to keep that office open," she said.

"I know you did."

"I said it was a horrible idea to shut it and scrap the plan to expand to Charleston, but I was shot down. A promotion I'd been promised for months was held up for years because I dared to voice my opinion."

"I know." Ted raised one hand in a placating gesture. "At the time, the word from up high was we were getting too big for our britches and needed to downsize. As you can tell from that e-mail, that's no longer the prevailing opinion. The bank has six hundred million dollars in assets. The goal is to get to a billion within five years. In this economy, that's not going to be easy, but you've seen how motivated our corporate lenders are. You've seen how much the mortgage department has added to the bank's bottom line. And I'm not the only one who has seen how valuable you are to this organization. Though he didn't come out and say it, that e-mail is Dennis's way of admitting you were probably right all along. If you prove that you were, I think it's safe to say it won't be long before you'll be ordering a new set of business cards."

"Because I'll be out the door."

"Because you'll be one step closer to running this place."

Rashida had never been ruled by ambition, but she had to admit the idea of eventually becoming the chief executive officer of a bank where her grandmother once scrubbed the floors held great appeal. How many women, let alone African-American women, were heads of billion-dollar corporations? She could be one of a relative few.

She referred to Dennis's e-mail. She was being granted carte blanche to form a research committee, select the members, and hold meetings as she saw fit. She was even free to formulate her own timeline for sharing the results with executive management.

"It's a lot of work," Ted said, "and your plate's already full. Do you think you can do it?"

"Yes," Rashida said without hesitation.

But my long days are about to get even longer.

CHAPTER THREE

Saturday, March 4
12:27 p.m.
Atlanta, Georgia

Rashida normally treated a long drive as an opportunity to clear her head. The drive to Atlanta, in contrast, gave her a chance to think. By the time she parked in front of Diana's house in Roswell, an affluent suburb eighteen miles from the center of Georgia's capital city, she had chosen the members of the exploratory committee she had been tapped to head and even planned their first meeting. She decided on an uneven number of members in order to prevent potential voting deadlocks.

Sitting in her car in Diana's driveway, she dashed off a quick e-mail to the leaders of the mortgage, corporate lending, consumer lending, and marketing departments. She provided a brief overview of the as-yet unformed committee's goals, emphasized the confidential nature of their mission, and invited them to join her team.

All four department heads were married to their smartphones, so she didn't have to wait long for responses. Within minutes, all four had e-mailed their replies. All had just as much on their plates as she did, if not more, but each responded with an enthusiastic yes.

Rashida clenched her fists in celebration. Her Saturday had gotten off to a better start than her Friday. Beginning with her run-in with Destiny, Friday had been one tribulation after another. She didn't expect today to be any different.

Like most people accustomed to success, she didn't handle failure well. And she was about to come face-to-face with her greatest personal disappointment. Her relationship with Diana should have worked. All the ingredients for success were there, but her attempt to blend the components had resulted in a less than palatable outcome.

When she and Diana had met, she had thought the sexy real estate agent would be the love of her life, her very own Princess Charming. But the fairy tale life she had dreamed about had left her feeling strangely unsatisfied. If perfection wasn't enough, what was? She feared the fault lay with her.

"Apparently, happily ever after isn't in my skill set."

She glanced toward the sprawling house. Diana stood in the doorway, her arms folded across her chest. She was wearing a cream-colored silk blouse, a matching mini-skirt that showed off her shapely legs, and a bemused smile. A wide black belt circled her narrow waist. Rashida turned off her phone, climbed out of her car, and prepared herself for what she hoped would be a gentle lecture. When Diana really got going, her withering words could peel paint.

"Do you ever stop working?" Diana asked, opening her arms for a hug.

"Do you?" Rashida gave her the requested hug and a peck on the cheek.

"*Touché*."

Diana's lopsided grin revealed the peach pit dimples that had attracted Rashida to her in the first place. Though the attraction remained, it had cooled from the all-consuming fire it had once been to a faintly glowing ember. Few people were immune to Diana's charms. She was undeniably gorgeous—long, dark brown hair, similarly-hued eyes, skin the color of café au lait, and a gym-toned body that remained a perfect size six despite her lifelong love affair with *medianoches*, the pork sandwiches that came a close second to cigars in terms of prized Cuban exports.

"If I stopped working, I wouldn't have all this." Diana indicated the twenty-room house and the fleet of luxury cars parked inside the hangar-sized garage. "If *you* stopped working, we might still be together."

Rashida grunted in disagreement. "I'm not cut out to be a trophy wife."

Diana was one of the most successful real estate agents in the Southeast. Her annual income had been impressive when she lived in Savannah. After she opened an office in Atlanta, the figure had become astronomical. It wasn't long before she decided to leave her Savannah office in the capable hands of her most successful closer and move where the big money deals were. Rashida had opted not to follow, no matter how hard and how often Diana tried to convince her to change her mind. By then, she had already invested ten years in Low Country Savings and didn't want to start over somewhere else. She had worked too long and too hard to pull up stakes and be forced to prove herself all over again. Like Diana, she wanted to reach the top of her profession, but their respective roads followed different paths.

She and Diana had tried the long-distance thing for a year, talking on the phone every night and seeing each other on the weekends, but the time apart had made Rashida realize the gap in their relationship was more than geographical. They didn't want the same things in life and, aside from successful careers and close relationships with their grandmothers, they didn't have anything in common.

Diana loved the finer things in life, splurging on cars, clothes, jewelry, and her twelve thousand square foot house. Rashida preferred to keep it simple. She had an apartment not a house, bought what she needed not what she wanted, drove a Prius instead of a Lexus, and contributed the maximum amount to her 401K, preferring to save most of her money for a rainy day. She made six figures a year and tucked away five. Thanks to aggressive saving, frugal spending, and a comfortable salary, her nest egg had grown so much she could retire today, but she wasn't ready to pull the plug on her work life. She had a few more career goals she wanted to accomplish first.

She followed Diana into the house. The heels of Diana's designer shoes clicked on the marble foyer, the Louboutins' red soles flashing like moving caution lights. A line of suitcases led into the stately living room.

"Going somewhere?" Rashida asked.

"Nelly and I are flying to Miami for the weekend."

Diana and Nelly Camacho, a twenty-two-year-old model and wannabe actress, had been dating for a little over a year. Rashida had a subscription to *Atlanta* magazine and had seen pictures of them making the rounds of the social scene. She had once been the woman on Diana's arm. Then she had regressed from being a full-time partner to what felt like a part-time tenant. She had gone from sharing a life to a house to a couple of dresser drawers. Now what was she? Nothing more than the owner of a box of tchotchkes she had left behind and could probably live without.

"If you have a plane to catch, I'll take my stuff and get out of your hair." Rashida looked around but didn't see anything that belonged to her.

"You're not getting off that easy. My flight doesn't leave for hours yet. You and I have plenty of time."

Diana curled up on the microsuede sofa. Rashida sat in the matching armchair across from her.

"How was your drive?"

"Not too bad. I got an early start and ended up making good time. I-16 was relatively clear, but 85 was a parking lot as usual."

"How long were you hiding out in my driveway?"

"I wasn't hiding. I was…"

Diana arched an eyebrow as Rashida's voice trailed off. "Working?"

"I was sending an e-mail."

"A work e-mail?"

Rashida finally admitted defeat. "What other kind is there?"

"I still don't know why you keep sticking with that little community bank of yours. With my connections and your skills, you could find a job at a larger bank in Atlanta in no time."

"Perhaps I prefer being a big fish in a small pond rather than a minnow in the ocean."

"No, I think you're too comfortable where you are and you need someone to drag you out of your rut."

"I don't see that happening any time soon."

Diana's voice softened. "You're not dating anyone? It's been two years. I thought you'd be playing the field by now."

"The field won."

Rashida briefly thought of the handful of dates she'd been on since she and Diana parted ways. Encounters that had promised little and delivered even less. No wonder work brought more enjoyment.

"You're quite a catch, Rashida. Take it from me. Any woman would be lucky to have you."

"But now you've got me. Right, *mami*?"

Nelly breezed into the room and sat in Diana's lap. She could easily be mistaken for any of the randy young stars of an MTV reality show. She was wearing so much bling on her ears, neck, and wrists, Rashida feared the metal detector at the airport might short circuit when she tried to pass through security in a few hours.

"You remember Rashida, don't you?"

"How could I forget? She's all you used to talk about until I finally managed to make you see you weren't missing out on much."

"Don't be rude." Diana gave Nelly a smack on the butt that elicited a squeak of surprise. "Say hello."

"Hi," Nelly said brusquely. She wrapped her arms around Diana's neck in a gesture that seemed more possessive than affectionate. "I thought we were going to South Beach."

"Our plane leaves at five thirty. We'll land in Miami two hours later. After we have dinner with my family, *then* we can go to South Beach."

Nelly poked her lower lip into a pout that could have been sexy if it weren't so blatantly manipulative. "Why can't we skip dinner and head straight to South Beach? Your *abuela* doesn't like me, remember?"

Rashida and Diana shared a look. Diana's grandmother Magalys was notoriously hard to please. Rashida knew from experience that getting on her good side was the key to securing Diana's heart.

"She doesn't know you yet. Give her a chance, *azucar*."

Sugar. Rashida felt uncomfortable hearing Diana call Nelly by the term of endearment that had once been reserved for her. She cleared her throat to get Diana's attention. "You have a plane to catch, and I have a long drive ahead of me, so can we get started?"

"Of course." Diana tapped her palm against Nelly's thigh.

Nelly stood but didn't leave. She glared at Rashida. "That's a nice chair you're sitting in, but I wouldn't get too comfortable in it if I were you. You're just visiting. *I* live here now."

"Call me crazy, but I doubt your name's on the lease."

Nelly took a step forward as if she wanted to turn the verbal confrontation into a physical one. Diana stopped her with a firm shake of her head.

"If you want *Doña* Magalys to like you, here's a tip," Rashida said. "Treat her with respect and she'll do the same to you. It always worked for me."

Nelly looked at her as if she were struggling to understand the principles of quantum physics. Rashida chuckled softly. The girl didn't stand a chance.

Diana shooed Nelly away. "Give us some privacy, *azucar*. The grown folks need to talk."

"That's going to cost you," Rashida said after Nelly stormed up the stairs in a jewelry-rattling huff.

"That's okay. I can afford it. Would you like something to drink?"

"Water's fine."

"But whiskey's better." Diana strode to the bar and poured two fingers of bourbon into a pair of crystal highball glasses. She handed one glass to Rashida and resumed her seat. "I know I've asked you before, but I'm going to ask you again. If I had stayed in Savannah, would it have made a difference? If I hadn't pushed for the move, would we still be together?"

Rashida swirled the contents of her glass as she considered the question. She stared into the amber liquid as if it could predict the future. Or, in this case, explain the past. "No. If you had stayed in Savannah, you would have blamed me for holding you back. If I had moved here, I would have blamed you for dragging me someplace I didn't want to be. Either way, I think we'd still be having this conversation."

Diana sighed. "I think you're right. As much as I hate to admit it, I think you're right. Our relationship always felt more like a merger than a marriage." She held up her glass. "Here's hoping you meet someone who makes you reconsider your decision to always put your career first."

Diana's words rang with not-so-subtle hints of accusation—and of truth. Rashida tossed back her drink and pushed herself to her feet. "Where are my things?"

Rashida followed Diana to the room that served as her home office. A cardboard box with her name on it sat on a corner of the desk. Rashida sifted through the box, picking up items with which she had once been intimately familiar but now seemed to belong to someone else. To another life. How could six years of her existence be compartmentalized into something so small? As she tucked the box under her arm, she laid her relationship with Diana to rest and wondered if she would ever have the time or energy to embark on a new one.

CHAPTER FOUR

Sunday, March 5
4:15 p.m.
Savannah, Georgia

Rashida stepped into the elevator on the ground floor of the Bohemian Hotel and pressed the button that led to the rooftop bar. The Bohemian was a relatively new addition to the Savannah skyline, and Rocks on the Roof offered some of the best views of the city.

Tourists crowded the wraparound walkway to take pictures of Bay Street, the Savannah River, and the iconic Talmadge Bridge. Local singles wandered from the indoor high-top tables to the luxe outdoor furniture, trying to see and be seen. Gourmands of all varieties made selections from the sophisticated menu available from the full-service restaurant downstairs.

"I'll get the drinks," Rashida said. "Grab us a table."

"I can handle that," Jackie said.

"What would you like?"

"A Savan Gria Margarita."

"You got it."

The specialty drink combined two traditional favorites, sangria and a margarita, into one deliciously sinful drink. Rashida ordered one for Jackie and a peach martini for herself. After the bartender prepared the drinks, Rashida started a tab and joined Jackie at a table for two overlooking the river.

Jackie raised her glass in a toast.

"What shall we drink to?"

"To ex-lovers."

"If you say so," Rashida said with a frown of confusion. She tapped her glass against Jackie's and took a sip of her drink.

"Don't get me wrong. I love Diana, but she wasn't right for you."

Rashida nodded to the beat of a familiar refrain. Jackie always found fault with someone she was dating after they stopped seeing each other but remained mum while they were together. She was still waiting for her to offer a viable alternative. "Do you have someone in mind for me?"

"Oh, no. There are two things I've sworn I will never do: skydive out of a perfectly good plane and play matchmaker for my friends. If you're not careful, both of those scenarios could end very badly."

"Wise woman."

"My mama didn't raise no fool. So how did things go with Diana yesterday?"

"We were finally honest with each other and ourselves. It was difficult, but liberating in a way." Rashida still didn't feel completely free, yet she couldn't deny a sizeable weight had been lifted from her soul. Until she found the strength to remove the rest of the burden, work would provide a welcome distraction. "How's Mr. Frank doing?"

"Better. When I went to visit him yesterday, half the employees were crowded into his room. He's on some good drugs so he's feeling no pain. I think you're right, though. There's no way he can come back. I know it's still early, but his energy level's nowhere near what it was. It will be a while before he's back to full strength. When he is, I doubt he'll have what it takes to work an eight-hour shift. I was at the hospital for only half an hour or so and he was exhausted halfway through my visit. He said something really odd, though. I'm still not quite sure what to make of it."

"What did he say?"

"He said the robber's face was white but his wrists were black."

"Maybe the robber was wearing black gloves and Mr. Frank mistook the material for his skin."

"That's what I thought at first. Then I thought perhaps it was the morphine talking. Either way, I couldn't let it go. I decided to do some research. I got my hands on a copy of the police report."

"What did you find?"

"According to the lead investigator, the robber *was* wearing gloves."

"Brown or black?"

"Neither. The clear latex variety dentists and hygienists use when they're cleaning your teeth."

"You know what this sounds like? The case in Ohio where all the witnesses said a black man robbed a string of banks and the real culprit turned out to be a white guy in a mask."

"If that's the case here, the real robber could be anyone. Everyone who walked into any of the branches could be considered a suspect."

"Found a new security guard yet?" Rashida asked with a wink.

"I'm working on it. The online ad started running yesterday. The print ad appeared this morning. I expect to have a pile of applications in my inbox when I get to work tomorrow. I want to start interviewing by Wednesday at the latest. Will you be available to help separate the wheat from the chaff?"

Rashida had scheduled the first meeting of the exploratory committee for Wednesday afternoon. She couldn't be in two places at once.

"I trust you. Between you and HR, I'm sure you'll find the right person for the job." She opened the menu. "I'm going to order something to eat. Care to join me?"

"I'd love to, but I'm afraid I'm going to have to sip and run. The early NBA game should be over by now. Even if it isn't, I'm going to drag James out of his man cave and show him what this body looks like polished to a fine, ebony sheen."

Rashida chuckled again. "Have fun."

"I'll be leaving you in good hands. Isn't that your next ex-girlfriend over there?"

Destiny was standing about twenty feet away, one hand on the railing and the other wrapped around a glass of beer. Her eyes were focused on a large cargo ship slowly making its way up the river. Rashida couldn't stop staring. Destiny's regal profile deserved to be cast in bronze and placed in a museum alongside other works of art. She was wearing jeans and a red button-down shirt. The sleeves of a white cable-knit sweater were tied around her neck. Blindingly-white tennis shoes, a new designer model that cost nearly three hundred dollars retail, adorned her feet. Based on the brand name stitched on her back pocket, her jeans had to have set her back nearly as much.

"Didn't you tell me she's out of work?" Jackie asked. "How can she afford such expensive clothes when she isn't bringing home a steady paycheck? And what is she doing here, anyway? This place is many things, but it ain't cheap. It seems to me she'd be better off depositing her unemployment checks in the bank rather than blowing them trying to keep up with the Joneses."

"Before you go on a rant about people content to live off government assistance rather than go out and get a job, at least Destiny is trying to find work. The day I met her, she was looking through the want ads. In the job market, you're judged on every single thing. She has to dress the part. She can't show up for an interview in hand-me-downs and expect to be hired."

"Showing up in three hundred dollar Nikes isn't going to do the trick, either. Being ghetto fabulous is okay for the 'hood, but not corporate America."

"How would you know? Neither of us have been in the 'hood for years."

"And that's a good thing. We have moved on up like the Jeffersons, honey, and I am thoroughly enjoying my piece of the pie." Jackie finished her drink and tossed a five-dollar bill on the table to cover her part of the tip. "See you tomorrow, boss lady."

The term of endearment made Rashida feel slightly guilty about her success. "Each one teach one," her grandmother loved to say. She had worked her ass off to get where she was—hitting her head on glass ceilings and banging her shins as she knocked down racial barriers—but had she done enough to make sure she wasn't the only person of color residing in the upper echelon of the city's banking industry?

She made a mental note to call one of her friends at the local historically black college to see if any promising students in the business departments were in need of a mentor. Then she placed her food order with the waitress and joined Destiny by the railing.

"Come here often?" Destiny whirled around as if she hadn't heard her approach. "I didn't mean to startle you. No spills this time." She took a giant step backward as if she were playing a game of Mother, may I? "I promise to maintain a respectful distance at all times."

Destiny's stern façade cracked into a smile. "Where's the fun in that?" She took a sip of her beer. "To answer your question, this is my first time here."

"What do you think?"

"It isn't the Varsity," she said, naming the Athens greasy spoon that was a favorite of University of Georgia students and working stiffs alike. "A bit too frou-frou for my taste. I prefer dollar value French fries to eight-dollar truffle fries, but it's a nice place. Is this where you hang out when you aren't indulging in flavored coffee and French pastries?"

"I don't get out much. I spend a lot of time at work on the road. When I'm home, I don't usually venture very far."

"Are you meeting your friend here?"

Destiny made the word sound like a pejorative term.

"My friend?"

"The one from the coffee shop. The one I assume accompanied you on the spa trip you told me about the other day."

"That would be Jackie. She was here for a bit. She's heading home to meet up with her husband."

"So you're not…"

"Together? She's my work wife from eight to six. After hours, she belongs to someone else." She smiled at the look of relief that washed over Destiny's face. *So she is still interested. Good to know.*

"She seems so protective of you I thought you had a history."

"Sorry, no."

"Did you get her a job at the bank or did she get hired first and give you the hook-up?"

"Sometimes it isn't who you know but what you know. Jackie and I were hired at roughly the same time, but we didn't know each other until we started working for the same company." Rashida was slightly offended by Destiny's inference she hadn't earned her job on her own merits, a common misperception she had worked diligently to dispel. Diana used to call it the chip that fueled her fire. She took a moment to cool the flames. "I have a table if you'd like to join me."

"I don't want to intrude."

"You wouldn't be intruding. I ordered some food, but as my grandmother always says, my eyes might have been bigger than my belly."

"If you need some help, I'll be glad to do what I can."

"Yes, please."

"Did you have fun at the spa?" Destiny asked as Rashida led the way to their table.

"The spa was an adventure in itself. Let's just say I'm glad I saved the massage for last."

Destiny pulled out her chair for her before settling into her own. "You can't throw out an intriguing line like that and leave me hanging. What happened today?"

Rashida hesitated. The details were almost too embarrassing to share with someone she barely knew. On the other hand, they were too hilarious to keep to herself.

"For their twenty-fifth anniversary, Jackie's husband bought her a gift certificate to one of the local day spas. She didn't want to go alone, so she invited me to accompany her. We looked through the spa's brochure and selected the services we wanted. She signed up for a facial, mani-pedi, herbal wrap, and massage. I chose a facial, a massage, and something called a scotch spray. I had no idea what a scotch spray was, but it sounded good. The brochure offered only a vague description, which should have been my clue right there. In my head, I pictured standing under a refreshing mist or a relaxing waterfall. Not even close. I felt like a civil rights protestor being fire hosed by the police. The spa attendant was cute, but she seemed to derive entirely too much pleasure from her job."

"Sounds painful. In more ways than one."

"It was. I know you want to run out and get one, so let me explain the process. You walk into a large tiled room with excellent drainage—another clue I didn't see. Then you take off your robe and stand naked against a wall while an attendant aims three jets of high-powered water at you. The aim is not to relax you but to 'break up the toxins and cellular blockages in your body.'" She bracketed the words with her fingers, remembering the sting of the spray as it pelted her sensitive, unprotected skin. "It was the longest twenty minutes of my life. By the time it was over, I felt like a side of beef that had been tenderized with a meat mallet."

"Ouch."

"My sentiments exactly."

"You make it sound like so much fun I can't wait to have one."

"Believe me, you're not missing much."

By the time Rashida finished her story, the waitress brought out the food. "One butcher's plate. Can I bring you anything else?"

"An extra set of silverware would be wonderful, thank you."

"Be right back."

Destiny looked at the platter of meat, olives, cheese, and rustic bread that lay between them. "Your grandmother was right about you."

"She usually is."

Destiny quickly filled her plate. "What else does she know about you?"

"She knows where all the bodies are buried, but you'd have to OD her on truth serum if you want to drag the locations out of her."

"Have you always been close?"

"Ever since I was a little girl, yeah. I'm probably closer to her than I am to my mother."

"Why's that?"

"I'm not quite sure. My mother and I have always been like oil and water. My grandmother and I like two peas in a pod. When

I came out, my mother acted like it was the end of the world. My grandmother made me realize it wasn't the end. It was the beginning."

"She sounds like someone I'd love to meet."

"Yeah, I love her to pieces." Rashida imagined introducing Destiny to her grandmother. She wondered what reaction she would receive, the acceptance she was accustomed to or a rare sign of disapproval? But it was much too soon to worry about either. "What about you? Are you and your family close?"

Destiny shook her head. "My coming out story doesn't have the happy ending yours does. I've been on my own since I was seventeen. My father saw me on a date with my girlfriend at the time. When I got home, he had changed the locks on the doors and my clothes were scattered all over the lawn. Both he and my mother made it clear I was no longer welcome in their home or their lives. I haven't seen either of them since."

Rashida paused in mid-chew. Destiny's voice was matter-of-fact, but her eyes glittered with repressed pain. The bonds she shared with her own family were frayed, but she couldn't imagine completely severing the connection. How lost Destiny must have felt being on her own. How lost she must still feel. "What did you do?"

"I stayed at a friend's house for a while. When I stopped feeling sorry for myself, I picked myself up, got my G.E.D., got a job, and never looked back."

In her head, Rashida heard her grandmother's grunt of disapproval. Destiny didn't have a high school diploma, let alone a college degree. There were few things Viola Ivey valued more than education. She had been happy when Rashida graduated from high school. When Rashida had graduated from college, she had been so proud Rashida thought she would carry her across the stage. Everyone deserved a moment like that. She wondered if Destiny had experienced anything similar.

"Do you have friends or other family members with whom you're in touch?"

"I haven't stayed in one place long enough to make many friends. As for my family, I left them in my rearview mirror long ago. It's just me, I'm afraid."

The strength Rashida sensed in her was apparently not just physical but mental and emotional as well. Destiny must have endless reserves of all three in order to mature from a frightened teenager who had been left to her own devices to the confident, self-assured woman sitting across from her.

"What's your work experience?"

Destiny smiled. "You name it and chances are I've done it at least once. I enlisted in the Army after high school and served as an MP for three years. Since I got out, I've been some of everything. Courier, salesperson, security guard. My last job was working guard duty for a small security company in Athens. That was my favorite. The owner was a UGA grad who managed to snag free tickets for all the big games. There's nothing like football Saturday in a college town."

Rashida didn't have to ask if Destiny missed Athens. She could tell by the wistfulness she heard in her voice. "How did you end up in Savannah?"

"I worked for my old company for six years until they went belly up eight months ago. I've been scouring the want ads since then. The owner has a friend who owns a business here and he thought I could latch on. I moved here on a promise, but the promise didn't pan out."

"Where are you staying?"

In Savannah, as in most towns filled with old money and the *nouveau riche*, your address was as much of a sign of success as the kind of car you drove.

"Garrett Walker, an old Army buddy of mine, has a place on Thirty-seventh Street. I've been bunking in his guest room for a while, though his wife keeps finding a way to work the famous Ben Franklin quote into every conversation."

"The one about fish and houseguests stinking after three days?"

"Maybe I can move in with you when Traci kicks me out. What kind of couch do you have?"

Destiny grinned to let Rashida know she wasn't serious. At least Rashida hoped she wasn't serious. Her gut told her she could trust Destiny, but how much did she know about her aside from her name and a few biographical details? Then again, did she need to know someone's entire life story in order to know her heart? Destiny seemed open and honest. A woman of her word. Someone you'd want standing next to you in a firefight or holding your shaking hands after a bad dream. "You and I are practically neighbors. I live a few streets over from you."

"Where?"

Rashida wasn't ready to give her exact address to someone she was still getting to know. "Near the Starland Design District."

"What's a banker doing living among starving artists and struggling musicians?"

"I'm not a banker twenty-four seven."

"So who are you when you're not at work?"

"I'm still trying to figure that out myself."

Rashida's friends and fellow employees constantly commented on how she seemed to have her shit together. If only they knew. She faced the same obstacles they did. To do her job, to live her life, and to be comfortable with who she was at the end of the day. Destiny made her want to share the uncertainties she hid from everyone else. To let down her guard and expose the vulnerable underbelly she didn't dare display to the sharks in her field.

"If you need help, I'm available."

"I'll be sure to keep my options open."

Destiny leaned forward. Her eyes invited Rashida to do the same. "I hope you do."

The timbre of Destiny's voice sent shivers down Rashida's spine. She rubbed her arms to guard against the sudden chill—and the heat she felt beginning to build between them.

"I do have some good news," Destiny said brightly.

"Oh?" Rashida reached for a slice of prosciutto as she tried to regain her bearings. What was it about Destiny that kept her off balance? Her eyes? Her voice? Or the increasing likelihood that their chance meeting two days ago wasn't an accident but fate?

"When I went to the French Roast to buy a cup of coffee yesterday, Charles offered to give me some shifts until I find a permanent gig."

"He's one of the sweetest men I've ever met. That sounds like something he would do." Rashida felt something click into place. "Wait. You said you worked as a security guard for six years. Do you still have your license?"

"I always keep it up-to-date because I never know when I might need it. I can't carry a weapon because I'm not currently registered with a security company, but I could work as an unarmed guard if anyone was hiring. Why do you ask?"

"Because I have an opening you might be able to fill." Destiny's devilish grin made Rashida's temperature rise. "A job opening, that is. We need a guard in our downtown office, and we need someone who can start immediately. We offer the standard benefits. Two weeks' paid vacation, the option to participate in a 401K retirement plan, and medical, dental, and vision insurance. Are you interested?"

Destiny sat up straight. "Damn right I'm interested. Where do I sign up?"

Rashida smiled at her enthusiasm. "There should be a link in the online ad on our website. If not, you can mail a cover letter and a copy of your résumé to our HR department."

"I'll do that as soon as I leave here. Thanks for the heads-up."

Rashida was glad she had removed herself from the hiring process. Even without knowing all of Destiny's qualifications, she doubted she'd be able to offer an unbiased opinion on Destiny's suitability for the job. There was also the matter of the no fraternization agreement. One of the many documents Low Country Savings Bank employees were required to sign once they came on board was one that decreed they weren't allowed to date other bank employees. Dating was considered not only a potential conflict of interest but also a security risk. If Destiny was offered the job and decided to take it, she and Rashida could never be anything more than co-workers. Rashida started to tell her about the agreement but kept quiet. If Destiny wasn't offered the job, the agreement wouldn't be an issue. If she was offered the job, she would have to weigh a sure thing against a possibility.

Either way, the decision would be out of her hands.

The waitress came to clear the table and ask if they needed anything else.

"Would you like another drink?" Rashida asked.

Destiny put on her sweater as the setting sun brought on the evening chill. Temperatures in the lower seventies had given way to those in the upper fifties. "I'd love one, but I think I've monopolized enough of your time."

"You haven't heard me complain, have you?"

"In that case, bring it on."

"Be careful what you're asking for," Rashida said. "You just might get it."

Destiny's lips curled into a teasing smile. "Isn't that the point?" She turned to the waitress. "Another round, please."

"For here or to go?"

"To go."

"I'll be right out with your drinks and your bill."

Rashida gave the waitress her debit card to expedite matters. "Are you done with me so soon?" she asked after the waitress left.

"I haven't even started with you yet," Destiny said in a sexy whisper that would have made Rashida's knees buckle if she hadn't been sitting down. "If you're up for an adventure, I'd like to show you something."

Rashida played it coy. "I don't know if I should go with you. My last adventure didn't turn out as well as I'd hoped. Can you assure me there won't be any water involved?"

"There's water nearby but no high-velocity jets. Is that good enough?"

"I guess it will have to do." Rashida signed the bill and slipped the receipt into the back pocket of her jeans.

"I'll keep you safe. I promise." Destiny pushed her chair away from the high-top table and offered Rashida her hand. "Shall we?"

Rashida grabbed her plastic to-go cup and accepted Destiny's offer of help. Or was she agreeing to something more?

They took the elevator downstairs and walked along the red brick walkway parallel to tourist laden River Street. Restaurants, souvenir shops, and art galleries were on their right, the riverfront to their left. The cool air coming off the water made Rashida grateful she had chosen to wear a sweatshirt today.

"Where are we going?"

"Almost there," Destiny said with a sly smile.

Rashida had no idea what kind of "adventure" Destiny had in mind. She had lived in Savannah all her life, been to River Street hundreds if not thousands of times. She knew the area like the back of her hand. What could Destiny possibly show her that she hadn't already seen?

"You don't like surprises, do you?" Destiny asked.

"If I know what they are."

"That goes against the concept of a surprise, doesn't it?"

"I'm like a Boy Scout. I like to be prepared."

"No, I think you like to be in control. But when you're with me, you need to let me be in charge every once in a while."

Destiny tossed their empty cups in a trash bin and stopped in front of a spot across from a T-shirt shop. The spot was shaped like a circle. The brick tiles inside the circle formed an X.

"You don't always have to lead, Rashida. Sometimes it's better if you follow."

As Destiny nudged her toward the center of the circle, Rashida forced herself to stop anticipating what Destiny had in mind and allowed her to take control.

"Stand in the middle. Place your feet on the X."

Destiny held her by her shoulders as she maneuvered her into position. Rashida smelled the scent she had already come to associate with Destiny, a mix of citrus and cinnamon. She smelled like a warm fruit punch that made even the largest house feel cozy on a cold winter day. She dropped her hands and took a step back. Rashida missed her already.

"Now say something."

"Something like what?" Rashida was startled by the sound of her own voice. "God, that's weird. It sounds like I'm standing in an echo chamber."

"They call this spot Echo Square. Garrett showed it to me shortly after I moved down here. At first I thought I'd had one too many frozen daiquiris from Wet Willie's, but the same thing happened each time I came back, whether I'd been drinking a Call a Cab or a glass of sweet tea."

"This spot isn't in any of the city guidebooks or tourist brochures." Rashida couldn't get used to the sound of her voice echoing in her ears. She felt like she was standing on the edge of the Grand Canyon without the steep drop-off in front of her. "I never knew it was here."

"Most people don't." Destiny smiled triumphantly. "How do you feel about surprises now?"

"Like I'd better get used to them if you're around."

Destiny offered her arm. Rashida had never dated anyone who so clearly identified as butch. Her former lovers were high femmes, which occasionally meant high maintenance. She wasn't used to having her car door opened for her or her chair pulled out to make it easier for her to sit down. Things she suspected would be common occurrences as long as Destiny was around. She was surprised to discover she liked the ideas of being treated like a lady and of having Destiny around to do it. She placed her hand in the crook of Destiny's elbow as they continued their journey down River Street.

"I guess I'd better get used to a lot of things."

CHAPTER FIVE

Tuesday, March 7
2:46 p.m.
Richmond Hill, Georgia

Rashida's desk phone rang while she was in the middle of reviewing newly opened accounts. Part of her job function was to review the opening deposits, determine if the appropriate holds had been placed on the funds, and assign each customer a risk rating. Certain retail customers constituted a higher risk simply because of their line of business. She flagged an account for a check cashing company and sent an instant message to the Assistant Bank Secrecy Act Officer to remind him to conduct the necessary due diligence. She answered the phone on the third ring, fielding the call just before it would have gone to voice mail. "Rashida Ivey," she said automatically.

"I know you told me you didn't want to be involved in the hiring process," Jackie said, "but I thought you'd want to hear how Destiny's interview went."

Rashida drew her attention away from the reports on her computer screen and focused on Jackie's voice. She didn't know whether to root for Destiny or against her. Should she be selfish or selfless? "How did she do?"

"She knocked it out of the park. She aced the interview and passed the online skills test with flying colors. At the moment, she's the leading contender. I'd offer her the job right now if I didn't have an interview scheduled with an internal candidate tomorrow."

Jackie sounded surprised Destiny had performed so well. Rashida wasn't surprised at all.

"That's great," she said tonelessly.

"I thought you'd be turning somersaults. You sound like I just told you your dog died. What gives?"

"I'm glad Destiny interviewed well, and I'm sure she'd make a wonderful addition to the team, but if she joins the staff, I won't be able to date her."

The complaint sounded much different when she gave voice to it than when she had kept it locked inside. In her head, it made perfect sense. Out loud, it sounded petty and small.

"I'd forgotten about that silly rule," Jackie said. "Other people break it all the time and nothing happens to them. Why can't you join the crowd?"

Rashida was reminded of the famous quote more often attributed to Spiderman's uncle Ben than its rightful author. *With great power comes great responsibility.* She eyed the new pack of business cards she had recently received via interoffice mail. Her name, contact information, and new title were printed beneath the bank's logo. She ran her finger over the embossed letters.

"As a member of management, I'm supposed to lead by example, not become an example of what not to do."

"I knew you'd say that. Do you want me to make it easy for you and take her name off the list?"

"No, of course not. I'm not that shallow. At least I hope I'm not. If Destiny turns out to be the best person for the job, by all means offer her the position. Don't give me a second thought. Have you vetted her yet?"

"Everything checks out. Her work history is as clean as a whistle and all her personal and professional references provided glowing testimonials to her character and work ethic. Like I said, the job is hers to lose. Tony will have to show me something special to beat her out. Based on what I've seen from him so far, that isn't likely. His out of balance numbers are troubling. He's close to crossing the threshold that would result in automatic termination, which is probably why he wants to move on to something else. After being a teller for so long, I'm not sure he has the proper mindset to be a guard. He's used to treating customers as friends. I need someone who sees them as possible suspects."

Rashida felt a mixture of excitement and trepidation. Destiny's long drought appeared to be almost over. Hers, on the other hand, seemed likely to continue. "I've got to go. My other line's ringing."

"Not a problem. I'll talk to you later."

Rashida hung up and fielded the incoming call. "Rashida Ivey."

"Hey, it's Destiny. How are you doing?"

"I'm well. You?"

"Things are looking up. Thanks again for the tip on the job."

"You're welcome," Rashida said, wondering how Destiny had gotten the number for her direct line. Destiny had asked her for her phone number before they went their separate ways on Sunday, but she had provided the one to her cell, not her office.

"You sound out of sorts. Is everything okay?"

"Of course." Rashida tried to inject some levity into her voice. "I'm busy with work, that's all."

"I understand. I won't keep you long, especially since thanking you isn't the reason I called."

"No?" Rashida's heart raced in anticipation. Was Destiny about to ask her for another date? If so, it had to be tonight. Tomorrow could be too late.

"I'm calling to let you know your business card was selected in last week's drawing at the French Roast. You won the gift certificate."

"Oh." Rashida tried to keep the disappointment out of her voice. "That's fantastic."

"Would you like me to mail you the certificate or would you prefer to pick it up yourself? We're open until ten if you want to drop by one night after work."

Rashida tried not to order takeout for dinner during the week to avoid the unnecessary expense, but she had a lot of prep work to do in advance of tomorrow's meeting, and she could use a caffeine boost to help her power through. A bowl of soup and a side salad wouldn't hurt her bottom line too much. "I'll pick it up tonight."

"Yeah?"

"Yes, I'll be there around seven."

"Great. I'll see you then."

The rest of the afternoon dragged by the way it always seemed to whenever Rashida had something to look forward to after closing. At five thirty, she packed the reports she needed into her briefcase and headed out. Traffic on I-95 was brutal as hordes of commuters tried to head home at the same time. I-16 was only marginally better. By the time she got to Savannah, she was ready to pull her hair out. She left her car in the bank's parking lot and walked to the French Roast.

Most of the tables were filled with students from the local art school, many doodling in notebooks filled with sketches of people, landscapes, and design projects. Destiny was taking orders at a booth filled with four baby dykes. Rashida caught her eye before heading to a table in the back of the restaurant. Destiny held up a hand to indicate she'd be with her as soon as she could. While she waited, Rashida booted up her laptop and plugged in the device she used to protect her computer from spyware before she logged on to the shop's wireless network.

"Coffee, tea, or me?"

Rashida looked up at the sound of a now-familiar voice and smiled despite herself. "You don't really want me to answer that question, do you?"

"Actually, yes, I do."

Destiny slid into the opposite side of the booth. She was impeccably dressed as usual. Her black beret was tilted at a jaunty angle. A black vest and matching slacks were paired with a crisp white shirt, the sleeves of which were rolled up to her elbows. A loosely knotted red tie added a pop of color to her ensemble. She was wearing the standard night uniform issued to all French Roast employees, but she somehow made the look her own.

"You seemed distant when I called you this afternoon to tell you you'd won the gift certificate. I didn't interrupt anything, did I?"

"No." Rashida didn't feel like getting into it. What was the point? "Just the same old, same old."

"Then did I do something to scare you off?"

"No, I did."

"I don't understand."

Rashida wasn't eager to have this conversation—or to put an end to something that had barely begun—but Destiny's earnest expression made her want to come clean.

"If you're offered a contract with Low Country Savings, there's a clause you need to be aware of before you sign." She told Destiny about the no fraternization caveat that had been occupying her thoughts since Sunday.

"So by telling me about the job, you might have ended our chance to see each other?"

"It would appear."

Destiny was quiet for a moment. Rashida could hear her wheels turning but couldn't tell what direction they were headed.

"Do you think I'll get the job?"

"I'm not part of the decision-making process, but from what I hear, your interview went well and you're one of the top contenders."

Destiny tossed her order pad on the table and stuck her pen behind her ear like a sassy waitress in a greasy spoon. "Let me see if I understand what you're saying. If I take the job, I'd earn a steady paycheck for the first time in months, I'd have insurance and benefits, but I'd never get to kiss you or know what you look like when you come."

Rashida felt a rush of liquid heat pool between her legs. "You're being a bit presumptuous, aren't you? How do you know we were ever going to be more than friends?"

"Were? Now who's being presumptuous?"

Destiny reached across the table and trailed a finger across the back of Rashida's hand. Rashida felt the sensation shoot up her arm and spread throughout her body. If Destiny kept it up, she might get her wish.

"I want the job," Destiny said, "but I want you, too. Another job will come along. I don't think I'll be lucky enough to find another you."

Rashida reluctantly pulled her hand away, even though Destiny had just said something she had always wanted to hear. "I can't ask you to choose me over your livelihood."

She had grown up straddling the poverty line. She knew how it felt not to have enough money to make ends meet. Sometimes getting them close enough to wave at each other was the best her family could do. Her parents had worked hard for everything they had, making sure she and her brother and sister never went without. Even though they didn't always get the bright, shiny new toys or fly designer outfits they asked Santa to bring them, there was always something under the tree. That had been enough for her but not for her brother and sister. Derek and Gail had found relief from their disappointment with their respective lots in life by seeking solace in the easy thrills found in the streets. She had found escape in books, using the knowledge she gleaned from them to escape the dreary world in which most of her relatives remained hopelessly mired. The more successful she became professionally, the farther away that world seemed. She had never felt as if she belonged in it in the first place and there was no way she would ever willingly return.

"Would you rather I take the job or would you rather see where this leads?"

Rashida's cell phone rang, saving her from having to respond to a question she didn't quite know how to answer. Jackie's number was printed on the display. "One second. I've got to take this. Yes, Jackie?"

"It looks like your girl wins. Tony just called me. He and his wife have a baby on the way, which explains why he's been so distracted recently. Jeannine convinced him the security guard job was too dangerous and he pulled his name from contention. The job's Destiny's if she wants it. Do you know where she is? I'd like to make her an offer, but she's not answering either of the numbers she provided on her application."

"Hold on. She's right here." She offered her phone to Destiny. "This call's for you."

"Are you sure you want me to take this?" Destiny asked.

"Jackie wants to make you an offer. I think she deserves to be heard. Whether you accept her offer is up to you."

She watched as Destiny listened to what Jackie had to say. Destiny's expression slowly changed from shut down to skeptical to disbelieving. Then she said the words Rashida suspected would change their lives forever.

"When would you like me to start?"

Destiny listened for a minute or two, then ended the call. "Thank you," she said, returning Rashida's phone.

Rashida dropped the phone into her purse. "Welcome aboard," she said without taking her eyes off her computer screen.

Destiny examined her face. "I'm sorry," she said with a helpless shrug, "but I've got bills to pay."

Rashida gave her a quick glance. "Believe me, I understand."

Destiny continued to linger at the table even after she'd taken her order. "Are we okay?"

"We're fine." Rashida tried to put the required distance between them now that they were going to be working together. "Please make sure the kitchen puts my dressing on the side."

"Yes, Miss Ivey."

Rashida stiffened at the formal term of address. A term she would have to get used to. She pulled her reports from her briefcase and went back to work. Focused on completing her presentation for the committee meeting, she stayed at the French Roast until closing time. When she finally looked up from her computer, the doors were locked, she was the last customer, and most of the staff was looking at her like she was keeping them from something.

"I didn't realize how late it was."

She gathered her belongings and tossed enough money on the table to cover the cost of her order and leave a sizeable tip to compensate for any inconvenience she had caused.

"Wait up," Destiny said as she headed for the door. "Give me a second to clock out and I'll walk you to your car."

Rashida started to argue she was fully capable of walking the short distance from the coffee shop to the bank's well-lit parking lot, but she could tell by the determined set of Destiny's jaw that protesting wouldn't get her very far.

They made the journey in silence, Rashida already uncertain how to cope with the sudden sea change in their burgeoning relationship. After locking her computer in the trunk of her car, she broke the discomforting quiet. "I seem to have misplaced my manners. Let me be the first to offer my congratulations. In a few hours, we'll officially be co-workers." She stuck out her hand. "Welcome to Low—"

Destiny moved forward as quick as a cat, pinning her against her car. Rashida was unable to suppress a gasp of surprise. Then Destiny kissed her. Long and hard and deep. The kiss was passionate and fierce but unbelievably tender. Rashida's first instinct was to push Destiny away, but her hands, as if acting of their own volition, tangled themselves in the lapels of Destiny's vest and pulled her closer.

Destiny's tongue explored her mouth, asking a series of questions. Rashida's unspoken response to each was a resounding yes.

God, how she wanted this. How she wanted this woman who was so wrong for her but felt so right. She wanted more. The kiss was just the beginning and she didn't want it to end. But end it did. Much too soon yet much too late. Destiny lit a match, a fire started, and Rashida couldn't put it out. Nor did she want to.

"I'm sorry," Destiny said, "but I couldn't go another minute without feeling your lips pressed against mine."

And Rashida couldn't go another second without feeling Destiny's hands sliding over her bare skin. "Get in the car," she growled.

Destiny climbed in the passenger seat and Rashida sped out of the parking lot. Her apartment was only a short distance away, but they didn't make it that far.

"Pull over," Destiny said when they reached a tree-lined residential neighborhood. Her hand slipped under Rashida's skirt, skimming past her knee and sliding up her thigh.

"We're almost to my place."

Keeping both hands on the wheel and her eyes on the road, Rashida was all too aware of but didn't put a stop to Destiny's inexorable progress.

"I don't care. Pull over."

Rashida parked on a residential street in the Victorian District. Expensive condos, apartments, and townhouses lined both sides of the road.

"Now come here."

Rashida unbuckled her seat belt, climbed over the center console, and straddled Destiny's lap. The headlights of a passing car briefly snapped her back to reality. Then Destiny's mouth found hers and reality—reason—flew out the window. Her inhibitions quickly followed. The fear of getting caught in a compromising position disappeared, replaced by the fear of never knowing how it felt to have Destiny's body moving against hers.

Destiny unbuttoned her coral suit jacket and tossed it aside. Then she went to work on her blouse, pulling it out of her skirt and reaching for the buttons. The blouse was one of her favorites, but the oversized buttons made it impossible to get into or out of in a hurry.

"Just rip it."

Destiny effortlessly tore the blouse apart. The buttons pinged off the passenger's side window like stray gunfire. Destiny unhooked her bra. Then her mouth, hot and wet and eager, closed around her nipple.

Rashida tried to muffle her cries, but Destiny's skilled tongue drew noises from her that sounded more animalistic than human.

Destiny reached for her underwear and she lifted her hips to allow her access. Destiny slipped two fingers inside her and she moved against them, bracing herself with one hand against the window and the other against the windshield. For a brief moment, she wondered what she looked like half-naked and crazed with lust. Then Destiny told her.

"You are so fucking sexy."

The comment, combined with the sensation of Destiny's breath kissing her skin, sent her over the edge.

"Any regrets?" Destiny asked after she finally came back down to earth.

"Just one," she said as Destiny joined the halves of her ruined shirt, covering her exposed breasts. "Why couldn't we have done this sooner?"

Destiny smiled up at her as porch lights flared to life all around them. "We've got ninety minutes left. Let's not waste any of them sitting here."

Rashida drove Destiny to her apartment, where they made love for hours. Though "making love" was too tame a phrase to describe what transpired between them. Rashida had never felt so reckless. So out of control. She felt like a stranger and, yet, thoroughly—finally—herself.

Destiny summed up the experience perfectly. "I can't get enough of you," she said as they caught their breath between rounds.

"And that's a bad thing?"

"Under the circumstances, it's a very bad thing." She trailed a finger down Rashida's back, leaving goose bumps in its wake. "I never thought I could pull a woman like you."

"We aren't so different."

The revelation, which occurred the first time Destiny kissed her, had come as a bit of a surprise. Yes, she made more money than Destiny, and her job responsibilities were vastly different, but in the end, she and Destiny had one very important thing in common. The only thing that mattered. They both loved the heat that only two women could produce. Rashida knew she was playing with fire by allowing Destiny to get so close. Lying next to her, her body could still feel the flames.

Destiny scoffed. "Look around." She plucked at the high-end bedding. Since sleep was so important and often came so rarely, designer sheets were the one indulgence Rashida allowed herself. "I bet it would take my entire first paycheck to score sheets like these. You are far above my pay grade, Rashida Ivey, but at least I know I don't have to buy you fancy things to make you happy."

Rashida squirmed as Destiny kissed the side of her neck. "Tonight was the best sex I've ever had," she said, running her hands through Destiny's short hair.

"We can have more."

Destiny moved to top her, but Rashida fended her off. "No, we can't. Only if you quit your job or I lose mine, a Catch-22 in any economy let alone one that's improving in tiny increments instead of leaps and bounds."

Destiny slowly dragged a finger across Rashida's lips. "I'm not willing to settle for only one night. Are you?"

Destiny had convinced her to break the rules once, but Rashida couldn't cross the line again. Her professional ethics wouldn't allow her to heed the insistent drumbeat between her legs no matter how enticing the call. She reluctantly pushed Destiny's hand away.

"It will have to be."

Chapter Six

Wednesday, March 8
10:58 a.m.
Savannah, Georgia

Low Country Savings' main office was divided into three floors. The vault, teller windows, new accounts desks, and branch manager's office were on the ground floor; the executive offices were upstairs, and the meeting rooms were in the basement.

Rashida pressed the down button on the elevator and waited for the car to arrive. When the doors opened, she wished she had taken the stairs. Jackie and Destiny were standing in the elevator. Destiny had a sheaf of papers and a copy of the employee handbook tucked under her arm.

"Perfect timing." Jackie pressed the button that locked the elevator doors in an open position. She introduced Destiny to the people who flanked Rashida on either side. "Destiny Jackson, I'd like you to meet Daniel Parker and Harrison Collins, the heads of the marketing and mortgage departments. Daniel makes us look good in the press, and Harrison could sell an igloo to an Eskimo."

"Provided the rate's not too high," Harrison said with a broad smile that matched the twinkle in her sky blue eyes. "Call me Harry."

"And I'm Dan."

Destiny shook both their hands. "It's a pleasure to meet you both."

"What will you be doing here at LCS?" Dan asked, tapping his fountain pen against the leg of his Brooks Brothers suit.

"Destiny's our new security guard," Jackie said. "She's replacing Mr. Frank."

"That means you have some pretty big shoes to fill."

Destiny held up a cautioning hand. "From what I hear, there's no replacing Mr. Frank. I'm simply hoping to follow in his footsteps."

"Well said. Mr. Frank will be greatly missed by one and all, myself included."

Rashida mentally applauded Destiny's tact as she ingratiated herself with two of her fellow employees.

"And, last but not least," Jackie said, "let me formally introduce you to my boss and yours, Rashida Ivey."

Destiny stuck out her hand. "A pleasure to finally meet you as well."

Destiny's voice was even, but her eyes issued a come-hither command Rashida could no longer heed. Fighting to maintain her professional distance, she clasped Destiny's outstretched hand. She stiffened when Destiny's index finger grazed the inside of her wrist.

"Welcome aboard. I look forward to working with you." She reluctantly retrieved her hand. "Is Jackie showing you the ropes?"

"She made me sign my life away." Destiny indicated the pile of papers under her arm. "She brought me upstairs so I can open a checking account to direct deposit my payroll into. After we take a tour of the building, she says she *might* take me to lunch."

"We're going to the South African place you like," Jackie said after the polite laughter died down.

"Would you care to join us?" Destiny asked.

Rashida's heart ached at the expectant look in Destiny's eyes. "Thank you for the offer, but I'm afraid I'll have to pass."

"That's a switch," Jackie said. "I've never known you to turn down a trip to Zunzi's."

"Harry, Dan, and I, among others, will be having a working lunch in the conference room. Maybe next time."

"I'm going to hold you to that."

Destiny held Rashida's gaze until the elevator's closing doors broke the connection. As the car descended to the basement, Rashida allowed her mind to drift back to last night. She remembered the feel of Destiny's body against hers. The taste of her kiss. She closed her eyes, basking in the last dip from the well of memory.

Work, as usual, offered her a safety net. When the elevator reached the basement, she led the way to the conference room. She made small talk with the four people she had invited. Then she called the meeting to order.

"Okay," she said, grateful her peers had answered her call. "Let's begin."

CHAPTER SEVEN

Thursday, March 9
5:26 p.m.
Savannah, Georgia

Rashida sent an e-mail to all the head tellers reminding them to increase the dollar amounts of Friday's money orders from the Federal Reserve. Each branch's vault would be overflowing on Tuesday when the shipment arrived via armored car service, but they wouldn't remain that way for long. Most of the bank's commercial customers would need to have extra cash on hand to accommodate the influx of tourists in town for St. Patrick's Day. By Thursday, the day before the big event, the vault totals would probably be down to the bare minimum.

She glanced at the clock as she shut down her laptop. She was actually going to be able to leave work before six o'clock for the first time in weeks.

"Hallelujah."

She packed her bags and turned off the lights in the office she used whenever she visited the branch on Savannah's Southside. Her cell phone rang before she made it out the office door.

"So close."

Her heart sank when she saw Jackie's number printed on the display. Too soon for a personal call but not too late for a work-related disaster.

"What's going on, Jackie?"

"We have a problem."

"Why does each call I receive from you at work begin with those words?"

"Because I never call you at work unless I have a problem."

When she reached the lobby, Rashida watched the tellers in the Mall Boulevard branch lock their money drawers in the vault and prepare to leave for the day. "What's wrong this time?"

"The vault in the main branch is out of balance."

"Again? That's the fourth time since January. How much is it out this time?"

"Twenty thousand."

Rashida's stomach dropped to her feet.

"Fuck." The expletive slipped out before she could stop it. A few of the employees looked her way and laughed behind their hands. She had a reputation for keeping her cool no matter how serious the crisis. A few more f-bombs and she'd blow that image all to hell. "The other outages were small amounts we attributed to improperly-wrapped bands of money shipped from the Fed. This amount can't be written off so easily. Have you recounted the money in the vault?" she asked as the security guard let her out the front door.

"Twice. And everyone's cash drawers, too. Seaton and I have also checked the cash in and cash out tickets to verify they were cut correctly. No ins on an out and vice versa."

Cash tickets were used by tellers to sell money to or buy money from the vault. After the tellers received or sold the cash, the tickets were "cut" in their teller machines, which kept a running tally of their daily transactions.

"Everything checks out," Jackie said. "None of the tellers are out of balance. Only the vault."

"Which is out twenty fucking thousand dollars." Rashida unlocked her car, stowed her belongings, and climbed into the driver's seat. She pushed the button that acted as the hybrid car's ignition switch. "No one leaves until we find the money. No excuses this time."

"What about overtime?"

As part of a company-wide cost-cutting initiative, all managers had been tasked with finding ways to keep expenses low. The largest expenses of all weren't supplies or utilities but employee salaries. Branch managers were encouraged to keep tabs on their employees' hours and send someone home early if they came close to surpassing forty work hours in a week. As a salaried employee, Rashida was exempt from such limitations. Counting Saturdays, when she made herself available to the tellers by cell phone and laptop for operational support, she routinely racked up sixty- and seventy-hour weeks. And there was no relief in sight.

"Which expense would you rather explain to senior management, a few hundred dollars that may or may not have been a result of internal fraud, or a twenty thousand dollar loss that can be attributed to nothing but?" she asked rhetorically.

"I'll interview the employees and see if I can get one of them to break. How quickly can you be here?"

The trip from Southside to downtown usually took twenty to thirty minutes depending on traffic.

"I'll be there in fifteen minutes."

Rashida sped across town, breaking a slew of traffic laws along the way. She parked in the bank's lot and approached the branch's front door. Destiny peered through the thick, reinforced glass before unlocking the door and ushering her inside.

Mr. Frank always looked slightly rumpled, in uniform or out. Destiny looked crisp and starched. Like a soldier submitting to inspection during morning roll call. The tellers, on the other hand, looked like they'd been put through the wringer. How was she supposed to determine which was the guilty party when all four looked equally nervous?

"May I talk to you for a second?" Destiny asked. The large ring of keys attached to her wide black patent leather belt jingled as she locked the door.

"About?" Rashida unbuttoned her suit jacket, preparing to roll up both her literal and figurative sleeves. She didn't have time for a personal conversation that shouldn't be taking place at all. She needed to get to the reason she was here in the first place: finding the outage.

"I want to talk to you about the missing money." Even though Destiny spoke in a whisper, her voice echoed off the marble columns lining the entrance to the lobby. She took Rashida's arm and led her back toward the door.

The touch, though innocuous, sent Rashida's pulse racing. She was inundated by memories of their one and only night together. Memories that haunted her dreams and left her waking hours filled with need. A need that could never be fulfilled.

"I've seen a case like this before," Destiny said. "When I was in Athens, I pulled holiday duty at a bank to earn some extra money. Like here, the vault was out of balance a few times. Small amounts at first, then a large number. Five thousand, I think it was. We found the money in the teller's trash can. She'd take the money on a day after the cleaning crew had visited the bank. She'd place the bills in the bottom of the trash can, cover them with pieces of scratch paper, and use the can as her personal ATM, making withdrawals as needed until she burned through the stash. By the time the cleaning crew came through again, the can was full of nothing but legitimate trash and the money was gone. We only caught her because she bragged about it to one of the other tellers, who had the good sense to relay the information to her manager. The cleaning crew comes here on Mondays, Wednesdays, and Fridays. On what days did the other outages take place?"

Rashida scanned through the notebook she carried to document situations like this one. "Two Tuesdays and a Thursday. I remember thinking that was odd because unless they occur before or after a holiday, Tuesdays, Wednesdays, and Thursdays aren't our busiest days. Tellers are more apt to be out of balance on a Monday or a Friday because they're so slammed with customers they barely have time to breathe. On a Tuesday or a Thursday, they have more time to concentrate on what they're doing. Have you told Jackie or Seaton what you just told me?"

"No. In all honesty, I didn't remember it until I saw you walking up." Destiny looked abashed, an endearing expression that made her look so adorable Rashida wanted to kiss her. Again. "You remind me of the teller who was caught. She was an angel on the surface but a devil underneath."

Rashida was reminded of the old adage about the perfect woman being an angel in the streets and a whore in the sheets. Destiny was one of the few women who had seen firsthand she could be both.

"Thanks for the tip. Sometimes you stare at a problem so long you need a pair of fresh eyes to help you find the solution. If the information you gave me bears fruit, it will cost someone her job, but I'll owe you a drink."

Destiny puffed out her chest with pride. Only two days on the job and she had already proven herself to be a valuable asset. Even if her tip didn't pan out, Rashida expected her knowledge and expertise to come in handy during her tenure. She was a good hire, even if her presence on staff meant her absence from Rashida's bed.

Rashida strode across the lobby and signaled for Jackie and Seaton to meet her halfway.

"What have you found out?"

Jackie spread her arms in frustration. "I couldn't get anything out of them. Four interviews and four denials. Either they're all guilty or none of them are."

"Have you watched the security video?"

"Yes, but we weren't able to see much," Seaton said. "The cameras are aimed at the customers, not the tellers. Before you say it, yes, I know we addressed that at the branch manager meeting on Monday, but I've been too busy making sales calls to fix the problem."

Rashida counted to ten to stop herself from biting his head off. This wasn't the first time Seaton had dragged his feet on something she had asked him to do, but it would damn sure be the last. He had been given the job as branch manager primarily because his father was on the board of directors. He had the rah-rah enthusiasm of the recent college graduate he was, but his frequent inattention to detail was troubling. His lack of follow through on her request wasn't egregious enough to warrant disciplinary action, but she made a mental note to give him a stern talking-to. As soon as she found the missing twenty thousand dollars.

"Reposition the cameras before start of business tomorrow."

"I'll have Megan take care of it as soon as she clocks in."

"Not Megan. You."

Seaton lowered his eyes. "Yes, ma'am."

Rashida considered her options. Without video evidence, they would need someone to crack, either by confessing or acting as a whistleblower. She decided to put Destiny's theory to the test. "Have you searched their work areas?"

"I did before you arrived," Seaton said eagerly, obviously trying to regain the ground he had lost.

"Did you look through their trash?"

Seaton and Jackie exchanged a look that seemed to indicate Jackie had delegated the job to Seaton and he hadn't performed the task he had been assigned. Surprise, surprise.

Seaton scrambled to cover his bases. "Tony told me he'd already looked through everyone's trash, and I didn't want to undermine him."

"This isn't about undermining anyone's authority or making him look bad in front of his fellow employees," Rashida said. "It's about solving a potential felony."

The dollar amount of the missing funds tipped the crime from misdemeanor status to felony offense. In addition to being terminated, the culprit could face jail time if executive management decided to press charges.

Rashida turned to address the tellers. "Everyone, I need you to dump the contents of your trash cans on the floor."

Three tellers immediately reached for the metal containers located in their work stations, but Tony was slow to comply.

"Is this really necessary? I already searched the cans myself."

"I'm sure you did." Rashida noticed beads of sweat forming on his forehead. He immediately shot to the top of her list of suspects. She smiled to gain his trust. "Humor me, okay?"

She headed for Tony's window while Jackie and Seaton sifted through the other tellers' trash.

"See, I told you," Tony said when Jackie and Seaton found nothing more than the normal detritus typically left behind—coffee-stained Styrofoam cups, empty soda cans, and discarded adding machine tapes.

"Now yours, please."

Tony tightened his grip on the edge of the bin as if he intended to force her to pry it out of his hands. "I ask you again. Is this really necessary?"

"It's an inconvenience, I know, but I'm simply following procedure. We have to discount every possibility before we can write off a loss of this magnitude. I understand how you feel, Tony. I'm tired and ready to go home. I'm sure you are, too. But the sooner you do what I ask, the sooner we can all get out of here. Empty your trash, please."

Out of the corner of her eye, Rashida saw Destiny take a step forward. Destiny stood with her hand on the nozzle of a canister of pepper spray as if she expected Tony to do something rash. Rashida smiled inwardly. She didn't think the situation would spiral that far out of control, but it felt good to know Destiny had her back if it did.

With a sigh of resignation, Tony turned his trash can upside down. Three crushed Coke cans, two empty bags of Skittles, and several crumpled Post-it notes fell to the floor—along with two packs of strapped one hundred dollar bills and a ripped-up cash ticket. The amount on the ticket read fifty thousand dollars but it hadn't been run through a teller machine. Rashida compared it to a ticket that had been run for twenty thousand dollars less and she was immediately able to determine what had taken place. She confronted Tony with her findings.

"You're in charge of the vault when Megan goes to lunch. Based on the time stamp on the front, this ticket for thirty thousand was written by you while Megan was on break. You intended to buy fifty thousand dollars from the vault but only thirty thousand made it to your drawer. Am I right?"

Tony's eyes widened. Rashida prepared herself for an imaginative excuse or even the typical "I don't know how that got there." Surprisingly, Tony came clean.

"My wife and I already have two kids," he said as tears began to stream down his cheeks. "Now we've got another one on the way.

We need the money, but I don't have time to work a second job, and Jeannine wants to stay home with the kids."

Rashida's heart went out to him, but a crime was a crime. She sent the other tellers home then placed a call to Dennis Rawlings so he could decide Tony's fate. She would terminate Tony for the attempted theft, but the decision to prosecute was out of her hands. She could only offer her recommendation, not decide the final outcome.

Dennis listened to her description of the events that had taken place. Rashida could feel him hanging on her every word. His response was measured. "Normally, if something like this happened, I'd advise you to throw the guilty party under the jail. But this is a special situation. We recovered the money, so there's no loss to the bank. The negative publicity we would engender by pursuing this case through the court system would greatly outweigh any positives. Tony's an expectant father who made a stupid mistake in an attempt to support his family. He'd likely gain both the public's and a jury's sympathy. We wouldn't be as fortunate. Terminate him and file a Suspicious Activity Report with all the appropriate agencies. When the FBI and the Department of Banking and Finance finish processing it, he'll never be able to work at another bank again. I think that's punishment enough."

"I agree."

"Good job, Rashida."

"I can't take credit for this one, sir. It was a team effort."

"You and your team have my thanks. I'll make sure the board of directors hears about your efforts as well."

"Thank you, sir."

Rashida's self-esteem soared at the vote of confidence. Her promotion should have provided all the evidence she needed that she was a valued member of the bank's management team, but part of her harbored lingering doubts she had been bestowed with her new title not because she deserved it but to placate her enough to prevent her from jumping ship. The positive reinforcement allayed some of her fears, but not all of them. Preventing a five-figure loss was enough to earn anyone's gratitude. How long, however, would she keep it?

She ended the call and prepared herself to perform a task that never failed to leave a bad taste in her mouth.

"Tony, we've decided not to prosecute, but I'm afraid we're going to have to let you go. I need your keys, your ID badge, and your parking pass."

"I'm sorry." Tony couldn't meet her eye as he handed over the requested items. "I don't know how I'm going to explain this to Jeannine."

"How did you intend to explain coming home with twenty thousand dollars in your pockets?"

He shook his head disconsolately. "I don't know. I was desperate. I wasn't thinking."

That much was obvious.

"Someone from HR will contact you to arrange an exit interview. At the moment, though, that's the least of your worries. Your family needs you. Go home to them."

"Thank you for not sending me to jail."

She couldn't tell if he was more relieved he had gotten caught or that he had survived his near-brush with the law without becoming some hardened criminal's prison bitch. "Good luck finding another job. Wherever you end up, don't ever try anything like this again. If you do, you might not be as lucky as you were this time."

"Understood."

After he gathered his belongings, Destiny escorted him out of the building. Rashida watched him pull out his cell phone and presumably call his wife to let her know he had been fired.

"Some days I hate my job," Rashida said when Destiny returned.

"You did what you had to do," Destiny said softly.

"But that doesn't make it any easier to deal with."

"Let's grab some dinner and put the whole thing behind us."

"That's not a good idea."

"Grabbing dinner or putting today behind us?" Destiny flashed a crooked grin.

"When we ended our conversation last night, I thought it was with the understanding our relationship would be strictly professional."

"It has been."

"Your invitation to dinner didn't feel like a casual request."

Another of those crooked grins. "What did it feel like?"

It felt like an invitation to another night of ridiculously hot sex. An invitation Rashida couldn't accept.

"Being with you was nothing less than amazing," she said, trying to keep Destiny at bay once and for all. "What happened between us was something I will treasure for the rest of my life, but it can never be repeated."

"I don't believe that."

Destiny was standing firm. Rashida had expected as much. When was the last time she had encountered such resistance? And why should she keep fighting when giving in was so damn tempting?

"I'm paid to enforce the rules, not ignore them."

"But breaking them is so much more fun. Don't you agree?"

"Did you read the employee contract before you signed it? When you put your name on the dotted line, you guaranteed what happened Tuesday night will not happen again as long as we work for the same organization."

"I know what I signed. I know what it meant." Destiny took a step forward. "But I want you, Rashida. I can still taste you."

Rashida ignored the intense satisfaction those words provided. She ignored the way her body responded to Destiny's voice. The memory of her touch. She resorted to professional detachment to guide her along the most uncertain path she had ever tread.

"I could write you up for sexual harassment, which is a fireable offense."

"I know. I read that contract, too." Destiny's tone softened. "You *could* write me up, but you won't. Not when you'd rather take me home so we can pick up where we left off the last time we were there. Am I right?"

"No," Rashida said, even though every fiber of her being was compelling her to say yes. "Please don't make this any harder than it has to be. Promise me this line of questioning ends tonight."

Destiny squared her shoulders. "You're going to have to fire me, because I can't promise you that. Can you?"

Jackie rushed over before Rashida could respond.

"Quick," Jackie said. "Pat me on the back."

"For?"

"Having the good sense to hire this woman right here." Jackie pinched Destiny's cheeks like a proud mother. "You saved our bacon, girl."

"I was simply doing the job you hired me to do."

Destiny looked vaguely uncomfortable. Was she embarrassed by Jackie's effusive praise or her own insubordination?

Jackie gazed at both of them intently. "Did I interrupt something?"

"No," Rashida said quickly. In order to avoid a lecture about bad decisions, she hadn't told Jackie she and Destiny had slept together. Why should she? It was a one-night stand. Something to be remembered fondly but not repeated. No matter how much she longed for an encore.

"Actually, yes, you did," Destiny said with another of her knee-buckling grins. "Miss Ivey and I were trying to decide where to go for dinner. She wanted to thank me for the tip I gave her on how to locate the missing money."

Rashida clenched her teeth and kept her mouth shut. Protesting would draw attention, not deflect it. At the moment, attention was the last thing she needed.

"Whatever you do, don't let Rashida decide," Jackie said. "She always eats sushi when she's stressed. I like my fish battered in buttermilk and fried to within an inch of its life, not raw and flopping on the plate."

"What is it about sushi that relaxes you so much?"

Rashida found Destiny's desire to get to know her hard to resist. Instead of walking away after getting what Rashida thought she wanted, Destiny kept coming back. What she wanted was apparently more of the same. How long would it be before Rashida gave in to a desire that mirrored her own? A desire she had to keep in check, no matter how great the personal sacrifice.

"It's impossible to be in a hurry when you're eating with chopsticks. Eating Asian food forces me to slow down. It helps me find my moorings when I feel I've been set adrift."

She had felt something similar the first time she'd looked into Destiny's eyes. Like she'd found shelter during a storm. She and Destiny were consenting adults. Who would it hurt if they formed a relationship? Who would have to know? She would, that's who. And that was one too many. She had advanced to this stage in her career by following the rules both written and understood. She wasn't about to change now.

"If chopsticks were all I had to eat with, I'd probably starve to death," Destiny said with a self-effacing laugh.

"Rashida could teach you. She's a wiz with those things. She could probably snag a fly out of the air like they do in all those old kung fu movies. In fact, I keep expecting her to pack up one day and leave her life here behind like the adventure seekers on *House Hunters International*. I can be the best friend who tags along just to get free face time on TV."

"When I begin looking for a place to retire, I'll be sure to keep *your* comfort in mind," Rashida said.

"You'd do that, leave the only life you've known to start fresh somewhere else?"

There it was again. That desire to know what made her tick. Did she want Destiny inside her head when she was already making inroads into her heart? Too late. She was already there.

"She'd do it in a heartbeat if she could decide which country she wants to live in besides this one."

Once more, Jackie answered for Rashida before she could answer for herself. If this kept up, she would have to hire Jackie as her official spokesperson.

"Don't make it too exotic, okay?" Jackie said. "I'd like to be able to sample the local cuisine when I pay you a visit. I'm not trying any chocolate-covered crickets or beef tongue. I don't want to eat anything that can be used as bait or can taste me back."

"In my humble opinion," Destiny said, "there's something to be said for both."

Rashida couldn't look Destiny in the eye. If she did, she thought she might spontaneously combust. "Are we actually going to have dinner or are we going to stand here all night talking about it?"

"It's your night, Destiny," Jackie said. "Where do you want to celebrate?"

"There's a barbecue place on MLK I've heard raves about. What do you say we give it a try?"

"Sounds good to me," Jackie said. "What do you say, Rashida?"

Rashida wanted to pick up some takeout and head home so she could begin putting yet another long day behind her, but she knew she was outnumbered. She used her company credit card to pay for dinner, an expense she didn't think she'd have much trouble getting approval for from the pencil pushers in the accounting department. By thwarting Tony's attempted theft, Destiny had saved the bank much more than the sixty bucks she forked over for appetizers, dinner, and drinks.

After the meal, Destiny walked Rashida and Jackie to their cars in the unpaved but well-lit parking lot. Rashida could tell Destiny wanted to pick up their conversation where they'd left off before Jackie interrupted them, but Jackie's lingering presence made that impossible.

"Good night, you two. Good job today," she said before she escaped to the safety of her car. Her cell phone rang before she barely made it to the intersection of MLK and Bay Street. She punched the hands-free controls as she turned right at the traffic light. "Rashida Ivey."

"How was it?" Jackie asked.

Rashida maneuvered into traffic on downtown Savannah's main artery. "I told you that was the best brisket I've had in years."

"I'm not talking about the food and you know it. You had sex with Destiny."

Rashida stomped on the brakes to keep from running into the back of a Honda Accord with out of state plates. "What?"

"Don't you dare try to deny it. Every time she licked barbecue sauce off her fingers tonight, I thought I was going to have to peel you off the ceiling. Did you sleep with her before or after I hired her?"

Rashida reluctantly revealed her secret. "After you made the offer but before she signed the paperwork."

"So she was technically an employee but not officially. That argument might hold up in the court of public opinion. I'm not so sure about a court of law. Have you slept with her since Tuesday?"

"No. I've made it clear it was a one-time thing, but she doesn't seem to be taking the hint."

"Do you want her to?"

The question caught Rashida by surprise. "Why wouldn't I?"

"Rashida, it's me. I'm not your boss. I'm your friend. You can talk to me. I'm on your side no matter what, remember?"

Rashida closed her eyes, wishing she'd never allowed herself to end up in such a compromising situation. But hadn't the pleasure been worth the pain? "There's nothing to talk about, Jackie."

"Is that why you didn't tell me what happened between you?"

"It was just one night. It didn't mean anything."

"Are you sure?"

"I was just taking your advice—letting someone knock the dust off."

"I never thought you'd actually go through with it."

"Neither did I."

"Are you glad you did? How was it?" Jackie asked the questions in rapid-fire succession as if she were living vicariously through Rashida. "You looked so sprung in the restaurant she must have really put something on you."

Rashida squeezed her legs together as pleasurable memories flooded her body. "You have no idea."

Jackie grew characteristically pragmatic. "You're not going to continue seeing her, are you? Surely you aren't willing to risk your career for great sex."

"I could buy a vibrator if all I wanted was to get off." Talking with someone she knew she could trust, Rashida allowed herself to be completely honest. "For a few hours, she made me happy. Happier than I've been in a long time. I liked the feeling."

"You don't sound happy about it."

"Because I'm not." She bit her lip as the impossibility of the situation hit home. "The question is, what do I do about it?"

CHAPTER EIGHT

Friday, March 10
4:15 p.m.
Savannah, GA

"Ready to go?" Harry Collins ran a hand through her short auburn hair. The thick tresses lifted away from her face and fell perfectly back into place. Harry wasn't what most people would call conventionally beautiful, but her raw-boned looks were striking. She used them to charm business associates and paramours alike. She was using them now. Or trying to. "If we leave now, we can just manage to beat the five o'clock traffic."

"Martin isn't expecting us until six," Rashida said. "We have plenty of time. And I have a report to finish."

Harry reached across the desk and snapped Rashida's laptop shut. "The report can wait. When was the last time you let your hair down and had some fun?"

Tuesday night when I rutted like a horny teenager in the front seat of my car.

She needed to put that night out of her mind. Harry was the perfect person to help her do it. Harry had raised casual sex to an art form. Rashida didn't know her well enough to confide in her about her own foray into the medium, but she hoped by spending time with her away from the office, she could learn how to put her night with Destiny behind her. She reached for her phone. "Give me five minutes. I need to make sure Jackie can cover for me if I leave early."

"Don't take too long. You know Highway 278 can turn into a parking lot in a heartbeat."

The main road onto Hilton Head Island was a congested four-lane highway that should have been at least two lanes wider. Depending on traffic, the forty-mile journey from downtown Savannah could take anywhere from forty-five minutes to twice that number.

"Call Martin and let him know we're going to be early," Rashida said while she waited for Jackie to pick up. "See if he can meet us in Bluffton instead. That will buy us some time for the drive home."

"Good idea."

Harry pulled out her cell phone. While she told Martin about their change in plans, she crossed her legs at the ankles and propped them on the edge of Rashida's borrowed desk. The hem of her skirt rode halfway up her curvy thighs. Even on casual Friday, Harry was dressed to the nines. Her black pencil skirt was paired with patent leather stiletto heels, a set of pearls, and a light blue button-down shirt with the bank's logo embroidered above the left breast.

Rashida, who had nixed her usual Friday jeans and tennis shoes in favor of khaki pants and loafers in order to look presentable at their meeting with Martin, kept her eyes focused on Harry's face, a view equally as appetizing but decidedly less dangerous. Harry was forty-two, successful, and involved in a twenty-year marriage of convenience with her brother's best friend, a union that softened Harry's hard-edged image while simultaneously butching up her husband's. Rashida had never professed to understand their relationship but couldn't deny it seemed to work for them. Both Harry and her husband, Jared, had wildly successful careers while keeping their extramarital activities hush-hush.

Harry covered her cell phone with her hand. "Is Pepper's Porch good for you?"

Rashida nodded. The little out-of-the-way restaurant looked like someone's house, but the food that came out of the kitchen was practically five-star. She loved the dichotomy between the place's down-home exterior and uptown menu—and the local musicians who provided entertainment in the Back Bar and Dining Room were all incredibly talented.

"What's up, boss?" Jackie asked.

"My six o'clock has been moved up an hour. Can you handle any emergencies that crop up between now and closing?"

"If I say yes, will you promise to clue me in on all the extra meetings you've been attending lately? That's two this week alone."

Rashida and Harry were meeting with Martin Foster to discuss the potential buyback of the mortgage office Low Country Savings once owned and Martin now managed. She hated keeping Jackie in the dark, but it was still much too soon to bring her into the loop. "You'll be the first to know."

"I don't need to be the first. Just make sure I'm not the last. And don't forget to give me a heads-up if I need to start polishing my résumé. I don't want to be caught by surprise if some company swoops in and wants to buy us out."

If everything went according to plan, Low Country Savings would be the one doing the buying, not the other way around. "It's a deal."

"Do I need to cover for you tomorrow, too?"

Rashida was tempted to say yes simply to avoid beginning yet another weekend tethered to her phone for four hours. "No, I can manage."

"In that case, enjoy your meeting. I'll see you next week."

"Jared has plans tonight," Harry said when she finished her own conversation. "Which means I'm footloose and fancy-free for the evening. Our dinner with Martin shouldn't take more than a couple hours, three if he gets really long-winded. The sooner we finish taking his temperature, the sooner we can go to Club One and unwind."

When Rashida was in college, Club One was the go-to gay bar in Savannah, the place where she'd broken out of her cocoon and first tested her wings. Where she'd first danced with a woman without feeling awkward or out of place. It was where she'd first kissed one without worrying who might be watching.

Like so many establishments in the Hostess City, Club One became a tourist attraction after the publication of John Berendt's infamous tell-all *Midnight in the Garden of Good and Evil*. Gay Savannahians of all ages still went to see The Lady Chablis and her fellow female impersonators strut their stuff during the twice-nightly drag shows, but they had to fight through crowds of curious, camera-wielding heterosexuals to do it.

Rashida preferred the old days when Savannah's most popular dance club was a well-kept secret. She was all for inclusion, but there was something to be said for exclusivity, too.

"Do you want to take your car or mine?" she asked as she and Harry rode the elevator downstairs.

"I'll drive, but we'll need to stop by your place after our meeting. I want to get out of these heels before we go dancing tonight."

"Do you always keep a change of clothes in your car?"

The elevator doors slid open and Rashida stepped into the lobby, which was filled with hourly workers cashing their paychecks. She felt a twinge of guilt for leaving early when everyone else was so busy. Harry grabbed her arm and pulled her forward before she could change her mind.

"It pays to be prepared," Harry said with a wink. "You never know when an opportunity might present itself. And there's one opportunity I hope presents itself real soon."

Destiny, her arms folded behind her back like a soldier standing at ease, nodded in their direction. "Ladies."

Harry's eyes crawled over Destiny's body. The hungry look in them matched the ravenous expression on her face. Rashida fought to dispel what felt like jealousy as Harry sidled up to Destiny's side.

"I hear you've had an adventurous first week," Harry said. "I hope the excitement hasn't scared you off."

"I don't scare easily, Mrs. Collins."

"That's good to know. Let me give you one of my cards. If you ever need anything, day or night, give me a call."

Destiny perused the business card before slipping it in the pocket of her uniform shirt. "I can barely afford rent, let alone a mortgage. When I'm in a better position, I'll be sure to get in touch with you."

"You'd better."

Rashida rolled her eyes. Harry was practically purring. Time to drag her out of the building before she made a spectacle of herself—and everyone else. She tapped her watch. "We're going to be late."

"Nonsense." Harry waved her off. "We've got plenty of time."

"And Destiny has a job to do."

"Okay, spoilsport, you win. Let's hit the road. Keep up the good work, Destiny." Harry clapped Destiny on the shoulder, but she looked like she would have preferred placing her hand much farther south.

Rashida lowered her gaze to Destiny's hips. She remembered stroking that muscular ass, squeezing it as Destiny moved against her.

Destiny caught her staring. "Thank you, Mrs. Collins." Then she added with a twinkle in her eye, "Have a good evening, Miss Ivey."

Rashida felt the blood rush to her cheeks. She tried to keep her composure despite how embarrassed she felt. "Thanks. You, too."

"I hope to hear from you," Harry said. "Sooner rather than later."

Rashida wrapped her arm around Harry's and led her outside. "Interesting combination of coquettishness and hard sell. Does it work for you?"

"What do you mean?" Harry asked with mock innocence. "It's called networking, Rashida."

"Oh, is that what they're calling it these days?"

Harry's guileless façade collapsed into a wicked smile. "You should try it sometime."

"Maybe I will."

"No, you won't, but I'm going to keep hammering away at you until I take that stick out of your ass once and for all. Tonight's the night. After we meet with Martin, I'm going to loosen you up if it kills me."

Rashida stopped walking. "I don't think I like the sound of that."

"But I guarantee you're going to love the feel of it."

"Do I need to remind you about the no fraternization clause in the employee contract?"

Harry groaned. "Whose idea was that, anyway, some fifties-era housewife who wanted to make sure her husband didn't spend his afternoons bending his secretary over his desk while giving her dictation?"

"I think it was your mother's."

"I rest my case."

Harry's mother was one of Low Country Savings' founders. Her father was a former president and now served as chairman of the board of directors. Harry could have been given a position on staff simply by virtue of her maiden name, but she had chosen to earn her way. Her sales numbers guaranteed she would be employed for years to come.

As Harry dragged her toward the parking lot, Rashida hung on for dear life. "What have I gotten myself into?"

Harry pressed the unlock button on her key fob. The headlights on her dark gray Hummer flashed twice. "You'll see."

Rashida climbed into the passenger's seat of the oversized SUV. As Harry sped toward the interstate, Rashida felt like she was riding shotgun in a tank. Harry, with her dark sunglasses and firm jaw, looked like General MacArthur wading through the Pacific during his triumphant return to the Philippines.

She and Harry had worked together for almost seven years, but they weren't especially close. They had met for lunch a few times during work hours and Rashida had even attended a handful of dinner parties at Harry's house, but each occasion had felt like a performance. One from which she hadn't come away with a deeper understanding of either of the main players.

She looked sidelong at Harry after they merged onto I-16. Harry smiled but didn't take her eyes off the road. "You want to ask me something."

"You'll probably say it's none of my business."

"I doubt it. My life's an open book. So, some would say, is my bedroom door. You can ask me anything. Go ahead. Fire away."

Rashida hesitated. The question on her mind was one she wouldn't ask her best friend, let alone someone who was barely a work acquaintance at best. "I can wait until you're not driving seventy-five miles an hour on a busy highway."

"I wouldn't have made it this far in life if I didn't have the ability to multitask. Let me guess. You want to ask me about Jared. You want to know why, even though gay marriage is legal in several states, I'm still married to a man. I'll take your silence as a yes. Easy answer? I'm married to him because I want to be. He's more than my brother's best friend. He's mine as well. Like the old joke says, a true friend isn't someone you can count on when you need to be bailed out of jail. A true friend would be sitting in the cell with you laughing about what a great time you had. That's who Jared is to me. He's someone who makes me laugh, understands me, and loves me unconditionally without expecting anything in return. I hope I do the same for him."

"Have you ever—"

Harry wrinkled her nose in disgust. "No, never. I've never slept with a man and he's never been intimate with a woman. We both see other people, but our relationship—our friendship—remains our central focus. I married him to get my parents off my back. I stay married to him because divorce would be impractical for many reasons, the least of which is monetary. We stupidly didn't sign a prenup, which could result in a battle over division of assets if we ever had a falling out. But the main reason we're still together is peace of mind. People may assume one or both of us is gay, but as long as we have these rings on our fingers, they'll never accuse us of it. Even though this is the twenty-first century, we're still in the Deep South in a state that's as red as they come. We've made progress in our neck of the woods, but some things haven't changed. As a woman of color, I shouldn't have to tell you that."

For Rashida, the past was a catalyst to change the future, not an excuse to allow the present to remain static. She could have taken the path of least resistance in order to meet society's expectations, but she had opted to be true to herself. Though her life hadn't been easy, she hadn't regretted a single moment. Could Harry say the same? Even though she seemed to have everything money could buy, she seemed to be missing a few things it couldn't.

"It's obvious Jared makes you happy. I assume you do the same for him. But I have to ask. What would happen if you met someone who swept you off your feet?"

"I have. More than once, in fact."

"And?"

Harry gripped the steering wheel so hard her knuckles cracked. "I'm still married, aren't I? That should tell you something."

"It tells me you're willing to live half a life, but it doesn't tell me why."

Harry stared straight ahead, her eyes focused on the dozens of cars and trucks sharing the road with them. "Maybe I'm too set in my ways."

"Or maybe you're afraid."

Harry smiled as if she'd finally been thrown a pitch she could hit. "Me? Afraid? I'm the one who brought K-Y jelly and a box of condoms to last year's White Elephant party."

Rashida chuckled at the memory of the Bible-thumping head of accounting unwrapping the unexpected gift at the annual exchange of intentionally tacky Christmas presents, but she didn't let Harry distract her from the conversation at hand. "Doing that took balls, but so does falling in love. When was the last time you did that?"

Harry was quiet for nearly a mile. "When I was too young to realize lightning doesn't strike the same place twice."

"Who was she?"

"Her name was Emily Colton. She was someone I'd known since we were eight years old. In high school, our seats were arranged alphabetically so Emily sat behind me in practically every class. My hair was longer then. On the days I wore it up, I could feel Emily's eyes on the back of my neck. I would sit in class imagining her fingers trailing across my skin. She used to call me Redneck because I was constantly blushing whenever she was around."

Rashida chuckled. Harry's childhood nickname was at odds with the sophisticated woman she had grown into. "Or maybe she realized the effect she had on you."

"Maybe."

"Did you ever tell her how you felt?"

"I spilled my guts to her on graduation night after I fortified myself with half a bottle of Boone's Farm Strawberry Hill. She listened patiently, then didn't say anything for the longest minute of my life. When she finally spoke, it was to ask what took me so long. I tried to play it cool despite the gallons of adrenaline and cheap alcohol coursing through my system. I shrugged and said I was trying to be patient. She kissed me and said, 'In this case, patience is definitely not a virtue.'" She shifted into a Southern accent even richer than her own.

"How long were you together?"

"We weren't. The kiss was as close as we ever came. Most of our senior class went to college at the University of Georgia. Emily was one of the few holdouts. She bypassed Athens and chose to study drama at Juilliard. She moved to New York and never came back."

"Is she still there?"

Harry smiled ruefully as she turned onto I-95. "I'll say. She's been up there so long she's practically a Yankee. A few years ago, she won an Obie—Off-Broadway's version of a Tony—for an autobiographical one-woman show she produced, directed, and starred in. Jared and I went to see the play on opening night. The show and her performance in it moved me to tears even before she got to the part about me. I sent her a dozen roses backstage. My only regret is not signing the card."

Rashida placed a comforting hand on Harry's forearm. "It sounds like not signing a card isn't your only regret."

A matching set of tears slowly slid down Harry's cheeks. She knuckled them away. "You're going to make me ruin my makeup. Fortunately, Martin won't notice. He has a crush on you instead of me."

Rashida did a double take. "Excuse me?"

"Haven't you ever noticed how attentive he is toward you?"

"I thought he was simply being courtly."

Harry emitted a sharp bark of laughter. "Courtly, my ass. He wants to fuck you five ways to Sunday."

"Thanks for telling me that twenty minutes before I sit down to dinner with the man."

"You're welcome. Who knows? It might get us a leg up during the negotiations. So to speak." Harry switched the radio to a GLBTQ station, where the rowdy hosts of a call-in talk show were profanely holding court. "God, I haven't thought about Emily in ages. I wonder if she remembers me."

"There's only one way to find out."

"Send her a friend request on Facebook?"

"Or show me those big balls you're always bragging about and go see her."

"I can't do that."

"Why, because you're scared if you embarked on a real relationship, you'd have to come out to your family?"

"No. I'll come out to my family after I finish polishing the final draft of my big speech. I'm sure I'll be cut out of the will as soon as I reach the end, but if I wanted relics from the Civil War, I'd buy them at auction."

Rashida noticed the trace of bitterness that crept into Harry's voice, a trace her ribald jokes sometimes failed to hide.

"As much as I might like to," Harry said, "I can't make some grand gesture to win Emily's heart because she's already spoken for. She and her partner were one of the first to head to the altar when gay marriage became legal in New York."

Rashida tried to be considerate without being condescending. "I would say I'm sorry to hear that, but it seems wrong to denigrate someone's happiness, even at the expense of a friend."

Harry nodded in agreement before literally shaking herself out of her doldrums. "How did we get on this subject anyway? Let's talk about a more pleasant topic, namely our sexy new security guard. Where in the world did Jackie find her?"

This time, there was no doubt in Rashida's mind. The burning sensation in her gut was unmistakably jealousy. "So Destiny's your type?"

"Tall, dark, and handsome with a body that won't quit. Hell, yeah, she's my type. What's yours?"

"I don't have one."

Harry looked at her as if she begged to differ then seemed to think better of the idea. "I'll give you that. You were in a long-term relationship with a sexy Latina. Before that, your bedroom looked like a cross between a United Colors of Benetton ad and the lobby of the U.N."

Rashida turned to face her. "How is it you're more aware of my dating history than I am?"

"Like it or not, Savannah's a small town. Everyone knows everyone else's business."

"Everyone except me."

"That's because you're not trying hard enough."

For a brief moment, Rashida wondered how much of her private life was public knowledge. Did someone other than Jackie know she and Destiny had been intimate? If so, her indiscretion—her moment of madness—might cost her her job. Harry's next question put her fears to rest. Temporarily, anyway.

"Do you think Destiny's seeing anyone?"

"You'll have to ask her that, not me." She quickly changed the subject. "Shouldn't we be prepping for the meeting?"

"I figured we'd play it by ear." Harry visibly switched into business mode. Her posture stiffened and her voice became less empathetic, more matter-of-fact. "Let Martin make an offer before you do. Then, no matter what the number is, act as if it's too high."

"Martin's a former colleague. I don't want to lowball him."

"You don't want him to rob us blind, either. I'm familiar with his portfolio. I know how much it's worth. If he tries to throw out a ridiculous number, I'm going to call him on it."

"That's why I brought you along."

"I thought it was for my good looks and winning personality."

"Two out of three ain't bad."

Harry turned off Highway 278 onto less-traveled Highway 46. A few minutes later, she pulled into a tree-lined parking lot. She switched off the Hummer's engine and set the parking brake. She and

Rashida simultaneously reached for the visors over their respective seats. Peering into the small, rectangular mirrors, Rashida touched up her lipstick and Harry fixed her makeup.

"Martin said he'd meet us in the Dining Room," Harry said as they walked toward the restaurant. "Hopefully, he's halfway through his second Bloody Mary and is willing to agree to anything we propose. If you free up another button or two, you'll have him eating out of the palm of your hand. Or anywhere else you have in mind."

Rashida gave her a playful nudge with her elbow. When Harry pinned her arms against her sides to ward off further blows, Rashida felt the thrill of a burgeoning relationship. She'd had no idea when she'd woken up that morning she'd end the day making a new friend. One she'd known for years but felt like she was meeting for the first time.

Inside the restaurant, Martin rose to greet them when they approached the table. He looked the same as he had the last time Rashida had seen him. His expensive clothes, designer watch, and hundred-dollar haircut trumpeted his success. His bulging belly advertised he hadn't skipped many meals. His deep tan suggested he hadn't missed many rounds on the golf course, either.

Rashida extended her hand. "Martin. A pleasure as always."

Martin raised the back of her hand to his lips. "The pleasure, I assure you, is mine."

"Told you so," Harry said under her breath. She held out her hand. "Thank you for agreeing to meet with us, Martin."

"How's your handsome husband?" he asked after a perfunctory handshake.

"Fine."

Martin looked toward the door. "Will he be joining us this evening?"

"I'm afraid not. He's hunting white tail tonight."

"I didn't think white tail was in season," Martin said with a frown.

Harry spread her napkin in her lap. "Believe me, it's always in season."

Rashida swallowed slowly to keep from choking on her glass of water. She placed her drink order with the waitress and read the menu while she listened to the woman playing blues guitar on the small stage at the front of the room.

"We could keep beating around the bush or we can get right to the point," she said after the salads arrived. "How much would it cost to purchase Hilton Head Mortgage Company? Name your price."

"HHMC's not for sale. Not at any price."

Rashida splayed her fingers to appear unaffected by his apparent rejection. "It never hurts to ask."

Martin leaned forward in his chair, a shark-like grin on his face. "That depends on who's asking." He wrote two numbers on a cocktail napkin and pushed the tiny paper square toward her. He tapped his index finger against the top figure. "Here's my number if you're the one doing the asking."

Rashida glanced at Harry, who nodded to indicate the price seemed reasonable.

Martin tapped his finger against the second figure. "Here's my price if the idea to meet with me was Dennis's instead of yours."

The second number was twice the size of the first. Rashida nearly whistled in astonishment.

"Dennis needs me. I don't need him," Martin said. "Feel free to tell him I said so." He sat back in his chair, fully aware he was in the driver's seat. "I'd love to do business with you, Rashida. Unless there's a change at the top of your organization, I don't see that happening."

Rashida felt the meeting begin to slide off the rails and, with it, her hope of advancement. She was in the middle of a cockfight and she didn't have the proper equipment. "Let's not be too hasty. I'll take these numbers back to Savannah and send them up the chain."

Martin stirred his drink with a stalk of celery. "Dennis would be crazy not to buy my company. He'd be crazier still to pay my asking price. I've got him between a rock and a hard place. The same position he had me in three years ago when he swooped in and cut me and the rest of my employees loose because we didn't fit into his strategic plan. I wish I could see the look on his face when he sees your report. I trust you'll describe it for me in detail when next we meet." He signaled for the waitress. "I think I'll have another drink. Dennis is picking up the tab, isn't he?"

In more ways than one.

"That was brutal," Rashida said during the drive back to Savannah.

"Did you expect any less?"

"I can't blame him for being pissed after being unceremoniously shown the door. I would be, too."

"But you wouldn't let your emotions cloud your judgment."

That's what you think.

"Tonight Martin was toying with us to get Dennis's goat," Harry said. "You have to figure out a way to bring both of them to the table without touching off World War III. Based on what I heard from Martin during dinner, you have your work cut out for you."

"Not *I*. *We*. I have four other committee members to help share the load. And you're one of them."

"Don't remind me."

Rashida sighed heavily. "I don't want to think about Martin, Dennis, committee meetings, or hostile takeovers until next week. You promised to show me a good time tonight. When does the fun begin?"

"Ask and ye shall receive."

Harry pressed the accelerator closer to the floor. After they picked up Rashida's car from the bank's parking lot, they drove to her apartment, where they stripped off their professional personas in favor of their personal ones. Then they headed to Club One.

Rashida heard the thumping dance music before she made it halfway up Jefferson Street.

"If you want to go upstairs for the show," the drag queen at the ticket counter said, "it's ten bucks extra per ticket." A Marlboro Light dangled precariously from one corner of her fuchsia-colored lips.

"Do you want to see the show?" Harry asked. "The next performance isn't for another ninety minutes. I don't know if I'll be here that long."

When Harry made eye contact with an attractive blonde standing just inside the entrance to the main floor, Rashida knew why she had insisted on leaving her Hummer at Rashida's apartment. Based on the silent conversation taking place between her and the blonde, Rashida would be driving home alone.

"It's been a long day," Rashida said. "I plan on making it a short night."

Harry smiled as she and the blonde seemed to come to an unspoken understanding. "You and me both." She forked over the price of the tickets and led Rashida to the main floor.

The thousand square foot dance floor was crowded. A disco ball slowly spun over the heads of couples with a wide variety of age and gender makeups gyrating to the pulsating music. The mirrored walls doubled the number of the room's occupants. Lightness alternated with darkness as multicolored strobes flashed rhythmically.

Though the club's aesthetics had changed over the years, its essence remained the same. Rashida felt the same sense of freedom and acceptance she'd experienced the first time she'd ventured inside.

"Would you like something to drink?" Harry asked, shouting to be heard over the vocal histrionics of the latest dance music diva with solid pipes, a catchy hook, and a talented producer who knew how to showcase both.

"No." Rashida felt the call of the music. "I want to dance."

Harry extended her arm toward the dance floor. "Lead on."

Rashida joined the steadily growing crowd. She danced with an abandon she hadn't allowed herself since she and Diana began to come apart at the seams. Harry danced with her, but Rashida didn't feel a sense of connection with her. She couldn't find the effortless rhythm she fell into whenever she danced with someone she was attracted to. The rhythm Harry found as soon as the blonde cut in on them. Rashida stayed until the music slowed, then bought a bottle of water from the bar and headed to the floor below.

A buffet table laden with canapés was nestled against one wall. For patrons who wanted hot food, waiters filled orders from the bustling in-house restaurant known as the Bay Street Café. Music videos played silently on a series of flat-screen TVs. Video poker and gaming machines chimed as eager players tried their luck. Players of another sort crowded around the three pool tables on the far side of the room. Clusters of people sat on armchairs and loveseats, embroiled in quiet or spirited conversations.

The music upstairs was so loud Rashida had barely been able to hear herself think. Downstairs, her ears rang in the comparative quiet. She sat on a bar stool next to a graffiti-covered column and watched the pool players show their stuff.

At the first table, two sets of seniors were squaring off. Based on their body language, the women were kicking the men's asses. At the middle table, two women who looked barely out of their teens were doing more making out than ball striking. At the third table, a pair of men whose crew cuts identified them as Army Rangers from nearby Fort Hunter were going at it. Their necks were nearly as wide as the trunk of a two hundred-year-old tree, their biceps the size of canned hams. The poor pool balls didn't stand a chance.

Rashida was about to sing a silent praise to the lifting of the ban on gays in the military when she saw Destiny bantering with one of the Rangers. Her breath caught. Destiny looked more relaxed, more unguarded than she had ever seen her. Like she was no longer playing a role she had been assigned and was finally allowed to be herself. Her confidence, which had to have taken a dent after she lost her job eight months ago, had been restored. She appeared to have arrived alone, but Rashida didn't think she'd leave that way. Her energy was magnetic. Women of all sizes, shapes, and colors drifted into and out of her orbit. She paid each equal attention, giving hope to all while encouraging none.

When Destiny looked up and caught her eye, Rashida wanted to join the pilgrimage. She wanted to run the other way. She remained rooted in her seat and waited for Destiny to walk over to her and try yet again to persuade her to choose her desires over her principles. Destiny raised her glass toward her but didn't make a move in her direction. When the Rangers' game ended, she picked up a pool cue and began to play the winner.

Destiny was keeping her distance. She had finally taken the hint. She had finally done what Rashida had asked her to do. So why did Rashida feel disappointed instead of elated?

"There you are." Rashida turned to find Harry standing behind her with her arm draped across the blonde's shoulder. "I came to let you know Cameron and I are leaving. I didn't want you wondering where I was."

"Do you need a ride back to your car?"

"Not tonight. There's a room at the Bohemian with my name on it. The hotel's only a few blocks from here. I can walk that far. I'll pick up my car in the morning."

Rashida climbed off her bar stool. "I'll walk out with you."

"Leaving so soon?" Cameron asked. "You haven't met anyone yet."

"I wasn't looking."

"That's the best time to find someone," Cameron said perkily. "When you aren't looking."

Rashida glanced over her shoulder as Destiny lined up a shot. "So I've noticed."

Chapter Nine

Saturday, March 11
12:17 p.m.
Savannah, GA

Rashida's doorbell rang while she was cleaning her kitchen counters, a task she usually performed whenever she sought to clear her muddled thoughts. Today, she felt like a dog chasing its tail. She had a goal within sight but it remained tantalizingly out of reach. Martin's unexpected counter to her business proposition had something to do with her discomfort, but seeing Destiny afterward was the main reason she felt off kilter.

Destiny's standoffishness at Club One had felt like a rejection. A turning away. Avoiding seeing each other outside of work was something that needed to be done, but why had she spent all morning wishing she could undo it? She couldn't figure out if it was only sex she was longing for or a deeper connection. Could she have a relationship with Destiny? Did she even want one?

She hadn't expected one night of mindless passion to affect her so greatly. She had told herself—told Destiny—their night together couldn't be repeated. Little by little, however, Destiny kept chipping away at her resolve like a lumberjack swinging at a mighty oak. Like that tree, Rashida felt herself beginning to fall. She wanted another night. And another. And another. She wanted to spend time with Destiny. She wanted to get to know her. Hear more about her past; learn what, if anything, she had planned for the future.

"Does she even have a plan?" she asked out loud. She wasted no time answering her own question. "If she did, she'd have a better fallback than sleeping in the spare bedroom of a friend's house. She'd have a place of her own." She pulled off her latex gloves and dropped them in the trash. "Why do I even care? Worrying about employees' living arrangements isn't in my job description."

But Destiny was different. There was something about her—a hint of vulnerability that showed through her obvious toughness—that intrigued her. When Destiny had talked about her father throwing her out of the house when he discovered she was gay, she had seemed to shrink inside herself. As if she had briefly reverted into the frightened teenager she had once been. When she talked about moving on with her life, Rashida could see the strong woman she had become. But at what price? Rashida wanted to comfort the girl and soothe the woman. Unfortunately, both were out of reach.

The doorbell rang again, more insistently this time.

"Just a second."

She put her cleaning supplies away and quickly washed and dried her hands. She crossed into the living room and opened her apartment door without looking through the peephole, fully expecting to see Harry on the other side. The last time she had checked, Harry's car was still sitting in the same parking space she'd left it in last night. Checkout time in most of the downtown hotels had come and gone. Harry should be arriving any minute now. By Rashida's calculations, she was already overdue.

"How was your walk of shame?"

"I wouldn't know. I've never taken one." Destiny stood in the doorway with a bag of takeout food in her hand. When she held up the bag, Rashida caught a whiff of Asian food. "Peace offering?"

"I didn't know we were at war."

"With you, I'm never certain. Have you had lunch yet?"

"No." Rashida held the doorknob with one hand and the doorjamb with the other to dissuade Destiny from inviting herself in. "Now that I'm no longer on call, I was about to head out and grab something."

"Then I guess I'm right on time." Destiny pushed through Rashida's makeshift barrier and stepped inside.

Rashida closed the door and took a quick look in the mirror to see if she looked presentable, then silently chastised herself for worrying about her appearance. "You're not working today?"

"I told Charles there was something I needed to do. He agreed to give me the afternoon off."

"What did you need to do?"

Rashida half-expected her to say, "You."

"I'm here for my lesson." Destiny pulled a set of chopsticks out of her back pocket. "Jackie said you were a wiz with these. Can you teach me how to use them?"

"I'm not much of a teacher."

"I beg to differ." Destiny moved closer. "You certainly taught me a thing or two Tuesday night."

Rashida folded her arms in front of her chest to establish distance without giving ground. "I thought we agreed this situation was untenable."

"Un what?"

Rashida was pretty sure Destiny was only feigning ignorance. "If you've come here to attempt to seduce me, you can turn around and—"

"I came here to bring you lunch. The kitchen's that way, right?"

Rashida dropped her arms. "How did you know?"

"You gave me the grand tour on Tuesday, remember?"

Rashida remembered unlocking the front door and leading Destiny to the bedroom while they tore off each other's clothes. Everything that happened after they got naked was a blur.

"Right."

In the kitchen, Destiny put the bag of food on the counter and pulled out a series of plastic and Styrofoam containers. "It took some digging, but I finally found the name of your favorite restaurant. When I went there this morning, I asked them to prepare your favorite dishes. Does this look right?" She indicated the spread in front of her. Soup, salad, sushi, almond chicken, and steamed rice.

"It looks perfect."

"Care to join me? You might as well because I'm not going anywhere until all this is gone." Destiny pried the lid off a container of soup and began to help herself to the contents. "I could probably eat it all myself, but it might be more fun if you helped. Could I have a beer?"

"It's a bit early, don't you think?"

"It's five o'clock somewhere," Destiny said with a shrug.

Rashida shook her head, unable to determine if Destiny was charming, insufferable, or both. Then she grabbed a beer out of the refrigerator and set the bottle in front of her.

"Did you have a good time last night?" Destiny asked after she took a long swallow. "You left before I had a chance to say hi or to tell you how hot you looked in that outfit you were wearing."

Rashida blushed at the compliment but tried to downplay how good it made her feel. "You were busy meeting the members of your fan club. How many members are you up to?"

Destiny flashed a disarming smile. "I've lost count. Grab yourself some soup and meet me in the dining room."

Rashida felt more like the guest than the host. "You don't make it easy to say no, do you?" she asked after she took a seat.

"Why say no when yes works so much better?"

Destiny crumbled a fortune cookie and fished the tiny slip of paper inside out of the pieces.

"Aren't you supposed to save that for after the meal?"

"I like pushing my luck." She unfolded the paper and began to read. "*The world may be your oyster, but that doesn't mean you'll get its pearl.* What does yours say?"

"*Do not mistake temptation for opportunity.*"

"Both our fortunes leave something to be desired." Destiny tossed the slips of paper aside. "I think we should choose our own fate."

Rashida wondered if their fates were intertwined or were destined to remain parallel. "When you were a kid, what did you want to be when you grew up?"

"A track star," Destiny said without hesitation. "A sprinter like Florence Griffith-Joyner, without the hair extensions and one-legged outfits but with the gold medals, world records, and millions in product endorsements."

"Why didn't you pursue your dreams?"

"The story of my life. I thought I knew better than the coaches did and got myself kicked off the team."

"And now? Now what do you want to be?"

Destiny seemed momentarily taken by surprise. The laughter went out of her eyes and she grew suddenly serious as if she thought she was being subjected to a test and didn't want to give the wrong answer. "I want to run my own business one day."

"Really? What kind?"

"A unisex salon. The kind where fathers take their sons for their first haircuts and women come in to try out the latest natural styles. I want it to be like the French Roast. A local place, not a chain. A place you can go and hang out all day and be made to feel welcome. There are a couple of empty storefronts on Broughton Street that would be perfect. If I had the money to buy the equipment and pay the rent, that is."

Rashida could tell Destiny had given the idea serious thought. She seemed to have the drive to put her plan in motion. All she needed was the ways and the means. Rashida had both.

"If you get a business plan together, you could apply for a small business loan. I know several lenders who might be interested in backing a venture like yours. When you're ready, I could give one of them a call. They're always looking for creative and profitable ways to comply with the Community Reinvestment Act, a federal regulation that encourages banks to make loans to borrowers in all segments of their communities, especially the ones who live in low- or moderate-income neighborhoods."

Destiny rubbed her chin with the heel of her hand. "A business plan, huh? I'm not much of a writer. I wouldn't know where to begin."

"I'll help you, if you like."

"Really?"

Destiny's eyes glittered with so much excitement Rashida couldn't help but smile.

"I'd be happy to."

Destiny seemed so grateful to hear the words Rashida wondered when was the last time someone had offered her a helping rather than hurtful hand.

"That's not all I want to do. If I didn't have to worry about making ends meet, I'd love to open a homeless shelter for teenagers so a young girl or boy who's in my old situation could have a place to lay their head at night without worrying about someone trying to chop it off."

The bubbling enthusiasm Destiny had displayed only moments before gave way to sadness. She glanced at Rashida as if embarrassed by her show of emotion.

"I don't know why I said anything. They're just pipe dreams." She pushed the empty soup container away from her. "My parents always said I'd never amount to much and they were right."

"What makes you say that?"

Destiny spread her arms helplessly. "I'm thirty-four years old and what do I have to show for it?"

"More than you're giving yourself credit for. You have a job, you have a place to stay, and you have people in your life who care about you. What more could you ask for?" Rashida watched Destiny's eyes fill with tears. "The people who tried to hold you back aren't in your life now. Don't worry about proving them wrong. Concentrate on proving yourself right. Your ideas aren't pipe dreams. They're goals. You can achieve them if you try."

Destiny was quiet for a long moment. When she finally spoke, her voice was filled with amazement. "No one has ever believed in me like you do. People who have known me a lot longer than you—"

"Don't recognize the potential I see in you."

"You think I have potential?" Her obvious disbelief made the word sound like a foreign concept. "How do you know I won't prove you wrong?"

"I don't. But it's like you said Sunday afternoon. I can't be in control of every situation. Where you're concerned, the last thing I feel is in control."

"And that scares you?"

Rashida laughed nervously. "It scares the shit out of me."

Destiny pushed her chair away from the table. "I don't mean to make you uncomfortable. Perhaps I should go."

She rose to leave, but Rashida grabbed her hand before she could.

"No. Stay."

"Are you sure?" Destiny looked at her, her eyes filled with expectation. "Does this mean—"

"I don't know what it means. Let's just enjoy today and worry about tomorrow when it comes."

"Can you do that?" Returning to her seat, Destiny smiled as if she already knew the answer.

"I don't know, but you make me want to try." Rashida enjoyed the feel of Destiny's hand in hers. "Harry taught me something last night."

"Harry Collins, the cougar from work? What did she teach you?"

Rashida placed her hands inside the V of Destiny's T-shirt and slowly slid them up the sides of her neck. "She taught me to take advantage of every opportunity when it presents itself because I might not be guaranteed another. I don't want to miss out on being with you because you don't match my preconceived idea of what I'm looking for in a partner. It doesn't matter how much money you have or what kind of car you drive. You're a good person with a good heart. That's all that matters."

"Harry taught you well." Destiny leaned forward, bringing her mouth close enough to kiss. "What are you going to teach me?"

Rashida brushed her fingers over Destiny's mouth. She waited for her lips to part in anticipation before she pulled away. "How to use chopsticks."

Destiny's lips slowly curled into a smile. "Has anyone ever told you you're a tease?"

"No."

"Then let me be the first."

Rashida headed to the kitchen. Destiny followed. Rashida pulled the salads out of the refrigerator and poured ginger dressing on top, spilling some on her finger in the process. She reached for a dish towel, but Destiny grabbed her hand.

"Allow me."

Destiny slid Rashida's finger into her mouth and licked it clean. Her tongue teased Rashida's fingertip long after the dressing disappeared.

Rashida kissed her before she could convince herself not to. As the kiss deepened, she asked herself the same question Emily Colton had posed to Harry so long ago. *What took you so long?*

"Whoa. Time out." Destiny came up for air. "If you keep that up, we won't make it to the main course."

"Good point." Rashida sneaked one last kiss. "Are you ready for your lesson?"

Destiny reached for the cutlery drawer. "I'll grab a fork just in case. I'll take a bib, too, if you've got one."

Rashida resumed her seat. "You'll be fine."

"I think you have more confidence in my abilities than I do."

"You forget. I've seen your abilities firsthand. I'm a bit of an expert on the subject. Now I'm going to share some of my expertise with you."

Rashida ripped open the paper wrapper on a pack of chopsticks and broke the bamboo utensils apart. Destiny mirrored her actions—after tucking her napkin inside her shirt like she was about to crack into an especially juicy lobster claw.

"To use chopsticks, all you need are your ring finger, middle finger, index finger, and thumb. Your thumb, index finger, middle finger, and the chopstick on top do all the work. The chopstick on the bottom remains still and your ring finger is just a prop."

She draped the chopsticks across the base of her right thumb, resting the bottom chopstick against the tip of her ring finger. She gripped the top chopstick with her thumb, index, and middle fingers. Then she grabbed some of her salad and brought it to her mouth.

"With me so far?"

Destiny struggled to place the chopsticks in the proper position. Each time she tried to pick up a piece of lettuce, it fell back into the bowl. "I'm a few steps behind, but don't wait for me. I'll catch up."

"Here. Let me help." Rashida put her hand over Destiny's and guided her fingers into the correct position. "Like this."

Together, they snared some of the salad and slowly lifted it out of the bowl. Destiny tracked the movement with her eyes. "I'm going to drop it," she said when the clump of lettuce precariously clutched between her chopsticks began to wobble.

Rashida loosened her grip, letting Destiny take control. "No, you aren't."

The lettuce slipped another inch or two. Destiny drew it into her mouth a fraction of a second before it fell free. "I did it."

Rashida smiled at the look of triumph—of accomplishment—on Destiny's face. "Yes, you did."

Destiny reached out and gently caressed Rashida's cheek. "Are we really going to do this?"

"Yes, we are."

"How?"

Rashida leaned into the pressure of Destiny's hand. "We'll figure it out."

Destiny abruptly stood and pulled Rashida to her feet. "Come with me."

"Where?"

"You'll see."

Destiny pulled her across the room and stood in front of the CD tower next to the small entertainment center. She ran her finger down the row of plastic cases. Rashida was a fan of classic and modern soul. Her CD collection was primarily composed of artists who fit into those genres.

"Look at you. Patti LaBelle, Luther Vandross, Alicia Keys, Teddy Pendergrass, Maxwell, Barry White. You've got all the good baby-making music." Destiny chose a CD and slid the disc into the player. "May I have this dance?" she asked as Sade's slightly raspy voice began to waft out of the speakers like a curling tendril of cigarette smoke.

Rashida stepped into Destiny's arms and followed her lead as they slowly moved to the sounds of the sultry sax and seductive bass. Destiny's hands slid down her back and came to rest on the curve of her hips.

"I'm not surprised you like this kind of music," Destiny said. "You're the kind of woman who likes to be romanced. Not necessarily wined and dined but swept off her feet." She skimmed the knuckles of one hand against the line of Rashida's jaw. "I want to treat you like the queen you are. Will you let me do that?"

The doorbell rang before Rashida could answer. "Hold that thought."

"I came to pick up my car," Harry said after Rashida opened the door. "I wanted to tell you how my night went." Her smile faltered when she saw Destiny. "Am I interrupting something?"

"We were having lunch."

"If, by lunch, you mean afternoon delight." Harry's sharp eyes took in the entire scene. "Romantic music. A table set for two. Are you two together?"

Rashida opened her mouth to reply, but nothing came out. She couldn't decide which would be the worse outcome, telling the truth or being caught in a lie.

"Destiny and I were just…" Rashida trailed off. She hadn't expected the first test to come so soon. She was failing miserably. "We were just—"

"I was telling Miss Ivey about an idea I had." Destiny turned off the CD player. "I brought some food by hoping I could bribe her into helping me draft a business plan."

"Well, aren't you the little entrepreneur. I'll let you two get back to your meeting. Sorry to interrupt." Harry fixed Rashida with a knowing smile. "See you Monday."

"That was awkward," Rashida said when they were alone again.

Destiny looked troubled. "I don't know if we can trust her."

"We don't have any choice."

Rashida kissed Destiny's furrowed brow, a gesture meant to soothe her own fears as well. She was taking a chance greater than any she had ever taken before. She hoped the reward would be worth the risk.

Chapter Ten

Wednesday, March 15
9:30 p.m.
Savannah, Georgia

A knot of tension resided in Rashida's gut. Not even Destiny's passionate ministrations had been enough to untangle it.

"Stop thinking so much," Destiny whispered, giving her a gentle shake. "You're as stiff as a board." She ran her hands over the taut muscles in Rashida's neck, shoulders, and lower back. "You've undone all the hard work I just put in getting you to relax. Now I have to start all over again."

Destiny rolled her onto her back. Rashida hissed as Destiny's tongue slowly slid over her bare skin, scorching a path from her neck to her mound.

"Fuck."

Her eyes shuttered when Destiny's mouth closed around her clit. Destiny's merciless tongue teased the hard knot, first with long, slow strokes then quick flicks that sent Rashida's hands searching for something—anything—to hold on to. Destiny stroked faster, keeping pace with her rapid breathing.

Rashida felt the pressure begin to build. A tidal wave of energy strained to find release. Destiny's hands skimmed over her stomach, dragging her closer to the edge. Then Destiny's tongue was inside her, filling her depths while her thumb massaged her clit.

Rashida gripped the back of Destiny's head with both hands as she ground her pulsing center against Destiny's mouth. Then the dam burst. Arching her back, she growled in satisfaction.

"There. That's better." Destiny drew Rashida into her arms. "Once you leave the office, your focus is supposed to shift from work to me. What were you thinking about? Because I know it wasn't us."

"Can you keep a secret?" She slid the sole of her foot against Destiny's leg.

Destiny kissed the back of her shoulder. "I've done a pretty good job so far, haven't I?"

They had been practically inseparable since Saturday, parting only for work. If they happened to be in the same branch on a given day, they kept their exchanges strictly professional. Away from the office, their interactions were anything but. Destiny came over every night around seven. They'd have dinner, rehash the events of the day, and spend the rest of the night making love. Destiny would leave before dawn to go home and get ready for work. Then the cycle would begin again.

Rashida often wondered what she would say to her bosses if they discovered her illicit relationship, but she'd cross that bridge—or burn it—when the time came.

She turned on the bedside lamp and leaned against the headboard. The sheet slid off her shoulders and pooled in her lap.

"Surely you don't expect me to care about a lame-ass business meeting when you're tempting me with such a distracting view."

Rashida covered her bare breasts with the sheet and slid under the covers. "Harry and I had a conference call with a former business associate. He has a team of investors in place. They're in position to quietly amass enough stock to become the bank's majority shareholder."

"I thought Harry's mother was the majority shareholder."

"She is. For the moment. That could soon change."

"What does all this maneuvering have to do with you?"

"The investment team wants to push Dennis out and install me in his place."

"That's good news, isn't it?"

"I haven't decided yet."

"Did you give your 'business associate' an answer?"

"I said I'd think about it. I can't decide if he's bluffing or if he's serious. If he's bluffing, I can't let him draw me into a game of chicken. His quarrel is with Dennis, not with me. I don't have a dog in the fight. I want to get to the top, but I want to do it the right way. Something about this feels wrong to me. Dennis has made a few decisions I disagree with, but on the whole, he's been an effective leader. Our deposit numbers could be better, but stock prices are holding steady and profits are on the upswing. Why would anyone want to push him out now?"

"These days, you don't have to have a reason for wanting somebody gone. You simply cut them loose, usually without the nice golden parachute Dennis will probably receive to help slow his fall."

"No matter what he's offered as severance, he doesn't deserve to be blindsided. No one does. I feel like I'm stuck between a rock and a hard place. If I warn Dennis, I could jeopardize the deal I'm supposed to be working on. If I say nothing and he catches wind of Martin's plan anyway, he may think I'm gunning for his job. Harry probably gave her parents the heads-up as soon as we ended the call this afternoon. I should have done the same with Dennis. Instead, I'm sitting here twiddling my thumbs."

Destiny pulled Rashida down on top of her. "Don't be so hard on yourself. From what I've seen, you don't do anything without thinking it over first. You'll make the right decision. I know you will." She traced the line of Rashida's jaw with her fingers. "No matter what you decide in this instance, you'll make a great CEO one day."

Rashida lifted her head to look Destiny in the eye. "How do you know?"

"Because your heart's in the right place."

Rashida placed a hand on Destiny's chest, reestablishing the connection she'd felt from the moment they'd laid eyes on each other. "This is crazy." She rolled off Destiny and lay on her side.

"How can I feel so drawn to you when I barely know anything about you?"

Destiny slipped her leg between Rashida's and wrapped an arm around her waist. "What don't you know?"

"What's your favorite color? How old were you the first time you kissed a girl? Do you have any brothers or sisters? Where were you stationed when you were in the military? And, most importantly, where have you been all my life?"

Destiny laughed and began to answer her questions. "Red. Nine. No. Too many places to count. And it doesn't matter where I've been because I'm here now." She rolled one of Rashida's nipples between her fingers. "Anything else?"

"One more thing. Do you have any idea how good that feels?"

"I can imagine."

"You don't have to imagine." Rashida wrested control. She flipped Destiny on her back. "Let me show you. Come for me."

Destiny had proven to be eager to give pleasure, reluctant to receive it. Rashida wasn't surprised when she said, "I don't need to."

"Are you sure?" Rashida reached between their bodies and cupped Destiny's center. Her fingers came away coated in the evidence of Destiny's arousal. "You're so wet I ought to put up flood warnings."

She pinched Destiny's engorged clit between her fingers, eliciting a moan. She slowly unspooled a smile.

"Are you sure you don't need to come?"

She was braced on her left elbow. Destiny nestled her face in the crook of her arm.

"Okay," Destiny said, panting. "Prove me wrong."

Rashida intended to do just that.

"Do you want fast or slow?" she asked as her fingers parted Destiny's slick folds.

Destiny looked at her with eyes filled with desperation. "I want you."

Rashida slowly entered her. She watched the muscles in Destiny's flat belly contract as she inched ever deeper.

CHAPTER ELEVEN

Thursday, March 16
10:39 a.m.
Richmond Hill, Georgia

Rashida seemed to have a sixth sense when it came to predicting when she was about to receive bad news. The sound of her desk phone ringing set her nerves on edge. She reached for the handset with a sense of dread. The feeling was confirmed as soon as Jackie said, "We've got a problem. A big one."

"What now?" Rashida checked the caller ID. Jackie was calling from her cell phone, not a land line. "Where are you?"

"Right now, I'm standing in the middle of City Market."

The area was home to bars, restaurants, art galleries, and souvenir shops. Everything tourists could ask for in a two-block radius. Rashida doubted Jackie was on the hunt for a jar of peach barbecue sauce or the perfect painting.

"Something's wrong with the elevator at HQ," Jackie said. "Smoke is spewing out of it and the whole branch smells like burning oil. We've evacuated the building and called the fire department. Two customers passed out, and Megan is looking a little wobbly. I think Seaton is planning to send her home. If he isn't, he should. She's green around the gills and can barely stand up."

"Is—" *Destiny all right?* Rashida cleared her throat. "Is everyone else okay?"

"I think so. The EMTs are checking them out now."

"What about you?"

"My tongue tastes like I've been French kissing a used oil filter. Other than that, I'm just dandy."

Rashida opened her Internet browser to see if the incident had made the local news. Nothing yet. She tapped out a quick instant message to Dan Parker. *I need you. Now.*

"Is the elevator on fire?" she asked.

"I don't think so," Jackie said. "I didn't see any flames, but Destiny hustled everyone outside relatively quickly. She spotted the problem first and made sure we all hauled ass. Even if there isn't a fire, the smell of burning oil is too powerful to dissipate anytime soon. I'm well clear of the scene and I can still smell it. The odor inside the building must be overpowering. We'll need to get our cleaning crew onsite as soon as the fire officials give us the all clear so they can steam clean the carpets and scrub every surface."

"It's a good thing the branch is going to be closed tomorrow."

In past years, the downtown branch opened for business until the parade started, closed when the festivities began, and reopened as soon as the last float made its way past Chippewa Square. The crowds had grown younger and more unruly over the years, however, forcing the branch's doors to remain closed all day. Employees were given the option of taking a day off without pay or volunteering to work at another location. Most chose to join the citywide party.

"If the smell is as bad as you describe, there's no way we'll be able to reopen the branch today," Rashida said.

"You needed me?"

Dan stuck his head in her office. He had been sorting through boxes of promotional items all morning. Bits of cardboard and Styrofoam packing peanuts clung to his short black hair. Add in his rumpled clothes, and he looked far from camera ready. That needed to change ASAP.

"One second, Jackie." Rashida pressed the Hold button. "Dan, grab the spare shirt and tie you keep in your office. We have a shit storm downtown and you're about to get some face time."

"Let me get changed. Then you can tell me what I'm in for."

She unmuted the phone. "Okay, Jackie, I'm back. Have Seaton coordinate with the other branch managers and send his employees to the other offices as needed so they can get their eight hours in. I need you to call our cleaning crew. Tell them to take as long as they need to get this sorted out. They have the rest of today, all day tomorrow, and the entire weekend to play with. Whatever it takes, I want the smell gone by the time we open the doors on Monday."

"I thought you might say that. Seaton has already printed a sign to affix to the front door."

"What does it say?"

"*This location closed until further notice.*"

"I don't like the wording on that. The verbiage makes it sound like federal regulators have swooped in and slapped us with a cease and desist order. I'll ask Dan to come up with something that won't scare the shit out of our customers or give our competitors reason to think we're vulnerable. He'll be heading downtown soon to field any and all media inquiries. Ted's off today and tomorrow so I'll have to take the lead on this one. As soon as I free myself up here, I'll come down and inspect the damage, get an update from emergency personnel, and call a team meeting to decide next steps. How many members of the executive team were in the office today?"

"Try none. They all started celebrating St. Patrick's a day early."

"Great. I have Dennis's mobile number programmed in my cell. I'll call him as soon as I get off the phone with you. He can update the directors as needed. I'll send a company-wide e-mail letting everyone know there's a situation downtown, we're monitoring it, and will pass on more information as it becomes available. I almost forgot about IT. I need to get one of the tech geeks onsite, too, so they can see if any of the network wiring is fried. Have I forgotten anything else?"

"No, I think you've covered all the bases. Have I mentioned I love you when you're in crisis mode?"

"No, but thanks." Rashida enjoyed the last laugh she thought she'd have for several hours if not days. "I'll see you as soon as I can."

She hung up her desk phone and immediately picked up her cell. She needed to call Destiny to make sure she was unharmed.

The line rang once, twice, three times.

"Pick up. Pick up. Pick up," Rashida chanted like a mantra as she chewed on a manicured nail.

"Hey, babe." Destiny's voice sounded strangely devoid of feeling. Was she in shock?

"Are you okay?"

"I'm fine," Destiny said, but she didn't sound very convincing. "I'm helping the cops with crowd control."

"How bad is it down there?"

"It's…bad." Destiny's voice broke as emotion finally crept into it.

Rashida held a hand over her heart, which ached with concern for the woman who had quickly come to mean so much to her. "I hear it could have been much worse if not for you. Thank you for acting so quickly."

"Don't thank me yet. Megan's in pretty bad shape and several others don't look so good, either."

Rashida closed her eyes as she tried to imagine the scene. "I'll be there as soon as I can. Stay safe. I love you."

"I…" Destiny hesitated. It was probably hard for her to be circumspect with so many people around, but the hesitation was only brief. "I love you, too."

After Destiny ended the call, Rashida took a moment to compose herself. How close had she come to losing someone she had just been fortunate enough to find?

After she got her emotions in check, she drafted a company-wide e-mail and read it twice. Dan returned to her office shortly after she hit Send. He had kept his khakis but traded his polo shirt for a dress shirt, tie, and blazer. He had also combed the debris out of his hair. He looked like a presidential candidate playing the Everyman role on the campaign trail.

"Don't worry about calling Dennis," he said after she'd shared all the information she had. "You need to concentrate on getting the branch back up and running. I'll reach out to him and the rest of the executive management team while I'm driving downtown. Before I leave, I'll create some signage that makes it clear the bank is still open despite the branch's closure. Something along the lines of 'The downtown branch of Low Country Savings Bank is closed temporarily due to a mechanical failure, but customers wishing to conduct business can visit any of our other locations. We apologize for the inconvenience. Thank you for your patience.'"

"Sounds good."

"Great. I'll list the customer service phone number in case anyone has any questions."

"I'll let the customer support team know they might experience an uptick in incoming calls. Make sure Seaton sends one of his employees here to provide the members of the call center with extra support."

Dan made a notation on the leather-bound Day Planner spread across his lap. "I can do that."

"I copied you on the e-mail I just sent. In case you haven't read it yet, we'll have an update call at nine tonight. Each member of the management team is invited to dial in to the conference line and hear the latest news."

"Got it. I'll see you down there?"

"Give me ten minutes and I'll be right behind you."

She answered a few of the questions she had received in response to her e-mail then shut her computer down. She was inputting the codes to forward any calls to her desk phone to her cell when Harry knocked on her door, a large manila envelope in her hand.

"This came for you via interoffice mail. Someone put it in my box by mistake. It looked important so I didn't want to sit on it."

She tossed the envelope on Rashida's desk. The front of it read, *Hand-Deliver to Rashida Ivey*.

"The interns have been mixing up the mail a lot lately," Rashida said. "This morning, I had four envelopes in my inbox and none of them were for me. Thanks for bringing me this. Whatever it is."

She slipped the envelope into her bag without opening it. Whatever was inside could wait. She headed for the door.

"Do you have a minute?" Harry asked, blocking her path.

"Barely. I have to put out a fire downtown. Literally."

"Yeah, I saw your e-mail. I'm still trying to figure out what happened." Harry put her hands on her hips and stared at the floor as if the answers to her questions could be found on the tops of her dark gray stilettos. "The whole thing makes no sense. The elevator downtown is only a few years old. My father owns the company that provides the annual maintenance. This incident could be embarrassing if it blows back on him."

"Depending on what the fire inspector says, I might be giving your father's maintenance team a call."

Rashida made sure to keep her voice neutral not judgmental. She didn't want to alienate Harry when they'd only recently become close.

"I can see you're in a hurry," Harry said. "One quick thing before you go. I've been thinking about Martin's offer."

Rashida grimaced. She and Harry hadn't had a chance to talk since their conference call with Martin the day before. She wanted to get Harry's take on Martin's proposal, but she didn't have the time to get into it now. She needed to get on the road. The discussion surrounding the subject Harry broached would be anything but quick.

"I want you to know I've got your back." Harry gripped her arm. Rashida could see the sincerity in her eyes. Feel it in her voice. "If I'm forced to choose sides, I'm on your team. My parents have guided the bank this far, but you're the right person to take it the rest of the way. When they had a chance to join forces with a regional bank and stretch our footprint from Florida to North Carolina, they chose to listen to Dennis instead of me and spurned the offer. The deal could have made everyone millions. You and I see eye-to-eye. With you at the helm, forget regional. We could go national. Maybe even worldwide."

Rashida was flabbergasted. Harry was essentially handing her the keys to the family car and trusting her not to drive it over a cliff. "I don't know what to say."

Harry grinned. "Don't say anything. Go keep our headquarters from blowing up. We'll talk later." She turned to leave, but Rashida called her back.

"Harry?" Rashida lowered her voice. "I know deposit compliance like the back of my hand, but I'm not nearly as well-versed on the lending side of things as you are. If we're going make a move, I'll need your help."

"Don't worry. I'll teach you everything you need to know."

Rashida tried not to get mixed up in other people's family drama, but her curiosity got the best of her. "What did your mother say when you told her about the investors?"

"I haven't told her yet. Should make for some interesting conversation around the dinner table at the next family get-together, don't you think?" Harry's grin grew wider, giving her a distinctly shark-like appearance. "Speaking of get-togethers, Jared and I are having a few friends over for a St. Pat's party tomorrow night. Join us. And feel free to bring a friend. Preferably an attractive one. We might be getting into some seventies-style key-swapping before the end of the night."

"Thanks for the offer, but I don't know if I'll be able to make it. I may still be babysitting the cleaning crew. I'm sure we'll post a guard outside the building all night tonight, preferably a police officer in uniform, but I want to make sure nothing hinky happens inside. I feel an all-nighter coming on. Maybe two or three."

"If you need help monitoring the goings-on at the branch, give me a call. My babysitting skills are a bit rusty, but I'm willing to pull them out of mothballs for the greater good. I'm busy tonight, though. Cameron and I are having dinner at The Pink House." Harry's one-night stand had lasted several days longer than Rashida had expected. "How does tomorrow morning sound?"

"It sounds perfect." Rashida stuck out her hand. "Thanks, Harry. For everything."

Harry gave her hand a firm shake. "Don't mention it. See you tomorrow night?"

"Fingers crossed. After the week I've had, the thought of sitting on your boat dock watching the sun set holds great appeal." Having a sexual partner chosen at random from a bowl of car keys, however, did not.

Harry clapped her on the back. "I'll be sure to save you a chair."

Rashida drove downtown, parked her car in the bank's lot, and made her way on foot through a maze of emergency vehicles parked haphazardly in front of Low Country Savings' headquarters. A powerful chemical smell assaulted her nose when she drew near. She held her hand over her face to filter the intense aroma.

A cadre of firefighters wearing respirators and reflective suits streamed in and out of the bank's open doors. Curious onlookers gathered behind bright yellow police tape listened attentively as Dan gave an on-camera interview with one of the local TV stations.

"There was no structural damage to the building," Rashida heard him say. "Both it and customers' deposits are safe. We were forced to evacuate because of a malfunctioning elevator. The motor ran all night, heating the oil inside to temperatures in excess of five hundred degrees. Two customers and at least one employee were sickened by the fumes. The customers have already been treated and released; the employee is still being evaluated. If not for the actions of another bank employee, today's outcome could have been much worse. As soon as the oil cools, it will be removed and safely disposed of. The branch will be professionally cleaned and open for business on Monday morning."

"And all those businesses needing money for the St. Patrick's Day weekend?" the reporter asked.

"They will be free to visit any of our other convenient locations."

Another thing for Rashida to worry about. If the vault doors were closed and the time lock set to remain secure until Monday morning, they wouldn't be able to access the money inside. Where would they find the extra cash to replenish the other branches' overtaxed supply? By Friday, the coffers downtown would be bulging, the others bare. If the bank was forced to buy money from another institution, they'd run the risk of buying bad PR as well. Hopefully, some of their commercial customers would be making cash deposits to offset the increase in withdrawals. Otherwise, they were screwed.

Rashida scanned the growing crowd but didn't see any of the branch's employees. Her eyes finally settled on a triage area that had been set up on Jefferson Street. The employees, Destiny included, were crowded around the back of an ambulance. Megan Connelly, the head teller, lay on a stretcher. An oxygen mask covered her ashen face. Two burly EMTs lifted the stretcher into the back of the ambulance and closed the door.

Rashida joined the crowd. "What's going on?"

"Megan had an asthma attack," Seaton said. "The paramedics gave her a breathing treatment, but it didn't work. Her airway's still clogged. They're going to take her to the hospital for further evaluation. Her husband said he'd meet us there. I want to go with her to make sure she's all right, but the branch is my responsibility, too."

He ran his hands through his sandy blond hair, suddenly looking much older than his twenty-three years.

"I'll look out for the branch," Rashida said. "Go take care of your employee."

"Are you sure?"

"I'm positive. Go."

"Thanks, Miss Ivey."

Most of the other employees soon left to head to the branch on Mall Boulevard, where empty office spaces waited their arrival. One headed to the Operations Center in Richmond Hill to help man the phone lines. After Dan moved on to his next round of interviews, only Destiny and Jackie remained.

"You two look none the worse for wear," Rashida said gratefully.

Jackie blew out a weary breath. "Looks can be deceiving."

"I feel like I've been fighting oil fires in the Gulf," Destiny said. "I probably smell like it, too."

Rashida was just glad to see she was still in one piece. She gave her arm a quick squeeze. "Do you need a break?"

Jackie answered for her. "We can sleep when we're dead. Until then, duty calls."

"What happened?" Rashida asked as they crossed the blocked-off street.

"I'll defer to Destiny on that one."

"God, that feels good," Destiny said. "*You* feel good."

Rashida bent and kissed Destiny's tumescent lips. Destiny kissed her hungrily. As if she'd been holding back for some reason and only now felt comfortable enough to let go. The kiss felt like a revelation. An introduction.

"Who are you?" Rashida asked as Destiny spasmed against her fingers.

Destiny continued to move against her, stoking smoldering embers into flame. "I am the woman who loves you."

After her last relationship ended, Rashida had thought she would never hear the words again, let alone say them. "I love you, too."

"I was doing my job when I felt the temperature in the lobby begin to rise." Destiny's voice was calm. She seemed completely in her element. She wasn't made for this job. She was born for it. "At first I thought the A/C unit was on the fritz. Then I smelled the oil heating up and saw smoke billowing out of the elevator. I pulled the fire alarm and began an orderly evacuation of the building. I only wish I'd acted faster. If I had, Megan wouldn't be on her way to the hospital, and none of the customers would have been affected."

"You acted as quickly as you could," Rashida said. "You couldn't have anticipated the situation would deteriorate so rapidly. If you could predict the future, I'd ask you to buy me a lottery ticket." She ducked under the caution tape and showed her business card to the police officer guarding the bank's front door. "The three of us are bank employees. We need to speak with someone about what happened here today."

"Inspector Kirby," Jackie added. "Is he still on the scene?"

"He's inside. You can go in if you like, but you might need one of these." The officer handed each of them a paper face mask.

Rashida stretched the attached rubber band behind her head, positioned the mask over her face, and followed Jackie inside. The thin paper shield did little to filter the noxious odor permeating the bank's lobby. The smell worsened the closer they got to the elevator, the doors of which were propped open. Wisps of bluish-gray smoke curled toward the ceiling, which already sported a telltale stain.

"Have you called the cleaning crew?" Rashida asked.

Jackie nodded. "They're standing by waiting for the scene to be released."

She flagged down a fiftyish man with thinning salt-and-pepper hair. His position and last name were printed in large block letters on the back of his windbreaker. He held a walkie-talkie in one hand, a note-filled clipboard in the other. Jackie provided introductions.

"Bert Kirby, Rashida Ivey. Rashida is in charge of the bank's retail operations."

Bert tucked the clipboard under his left arm and stuck out his hand. "A pleasure, ma'am. I'll get right to it. The building's safe. There's no risk of fire. The residual smoke you see in the elevator is from the oil, which is starting to cool but is still too hot to handle. By tomorrow morning, it should be safe to remove. Do you have someone to do that for you?"

"We've outsourced maintenance on the elevator to a local company." Rashida purposely avoided mentioning the company's name so she could keep Harry's father out of the news as long as possible. "I'll arrange to have members of their team remove the oil and repair the motor."

"I've already talked to them," Jackie said. "Harry called and lit a fire under them, pardon the pun. They've offered to come in tomorrow and make the repairs for free."

"When did she do that?"

"While you were on your way here. She asked me not to say anything, but I thought it deserved a mention."

I guess she meant it when she said she had my back.

"Ladies, it sounds like you've got everything under control," Bert said. "As soon as we're done, I'll take my men and get out of your hair."

After the fire department personnel vacated the scene, the members of the cleaning crew took their places. Karl Gibson, the owner of Top Flite Cleaning Services, walked through the lobby before inspecting the upper and lower floors. When he returned to the lobby, he ran a finger through the oily film coating the walls and wiped the thick sludge on his worn jeans.

"Getting rid of this is going to take some elbow grease. I can scrub the walls, floors, and counters tonight. I can also put down some deodorizer to soak up some of the smell in the carpets, but this place isn't going to smell minty fresh until you get rid of that oil."

"How long do you think it will take?"

Karl took another look around. "Five, six hours tonight. Another seven or eight after the oil's gone."

Rashida thought for a moment. "It's almost one thirty. I want you and your team to grab a late lunch and meet me back here in an hour. I'll stay with you while you do the first round of cleaning. If you finish by nine, I can mention your efforts during tonight's update call. Someone will be here tomorrow to repair the elevator and remove and replace the oil in the motor. I have no idea how long that will take, so let's plan on having your team come in on Saturday to do the deep cleaning on the furniture and carpets. I'll drop by on Sunday to see if there's anything we need to follow up on in order to be ready to open for business on Monday."

"I can do a walk-through before church or after."

"Let's wait until after. If there's anything that needs to be done, I'll want you to get on it right away."

"Yes, ma'am. I'm going to wrap my mitts around a burger and some fries. I'll see you in an hour."

Outside, Rashida removed her mask and took a deep breath of fresh air. Her head was already beginning to hurt from the fumes. By tonight, she'd probably have a full-blown migraine. She rubbed her temples to ease the pain.

"Are you okay?" Destiny asked with a frown.

Rashida patted her arm when all she wanted to do was give her a hug. "I should be asking you that question."

"It takes more than a little bit of smoke to bring me down."

Despite her strong stance, Destiny seemed ready to fall apart. Her stormy eyes betrayed her swirling emotions. Rashida felt handcuffed. She couldn't comfort Destiny the way she wanted without causing undue suspicion, but she couldn't bear to see her in so much turmoil.

This work day couldn't end fast enough. She couldn't wait until she and Destiny were alone and could stop pretending they were nothing more than co-workers. Today she had come close to losing someone for whom she had begun to care deeply. The thought frightened her more than the fear of discovery.

"Who are you going to get to sit with the maintenance crew tomorrow?" Jackie asked. "I have to march in the parade, most of the branch employees are scheduled to be off, and you're supposed to shadow the new teller in the Springfield branch to make sure she doesn't feel overwhelmed on her first day in the field."

"Harry said she might be able to. If she backs out, hopefully, someone else will step up during the conference call tonight to take her place. If not, I'll have the head teller play mother hen instead of me and I'll stay with the maintenance guys."

"Do you want me to arrange security for tonight?"

"I'll stay with her," Destiny said.

"You should go home," Rashida said. "You've had a trying day."

"So have you. I don't see you going anywhere."

Destiny's voice was filled with challenge, but her eyes radiated only concern. Rashida backed down. Besides, Destiny's plan worked to her benefit as well. She didn't plan on letting her out of her sight any time soon.

"Then it's settled. Destiny and I will take first shift. I'll come back on Saturday and Sunday and I'll ask for volunteers for Friday during tonight's update call. Not that I expect to have any takers," she added under her breath.

"Maybe someone will surprise you," Destiny said.

"Maybe," Jackie said, "but I'm not holding my breath. I'm late for a meeting. Do you want me to pick you up something to eat before I go?"

"Olin from IT will be here any second. By the time he makes sure the network is secure, Karl and his team should be back. I'll eat later."

"That's what you always say. Take care of her, Destiny. I can't trust her to do the job herself."

"You can count on me, Mrs. Williams."

"How are you?" Rashida asked after Jackie left.

Destiny looked exhausted. Her face was filled with strain. Her usually pristine uniform was covered in soot and reeked of burned oil.

"Are you okay? Be honest. Do you need to go to the hospital to get checked out?"

"No, I'm fine. Worry about the ones who need your concern more than I do." Destiny must have heard the edge that crept into her voice because she turned immediately apologetic. "I'm sorry," she said with a heavy sigh. "This is new for me."

Rashida smiled at the realization she wasn't the only one who was having to make adjustments in order to be in this relationship.

"I'm not used to having people care about me."

Rashida drew her into her arms and kissed her cheek, not caring who might be watching. "Get used to it."

Karl and his team returned promptly at two thirty. They worked nonstop until a quarter to nine, when they finally put away their brushes, mops, and assorted cleaning supplies. Though the smell in the basement floor had returned to normal, the odor in the lobby and upper floor had only marginally improved. The acrid scent of burned oil overrode that of artificial lemon. The combination made Rashida's headache worse.

"Ready to go?" Destiny kept a wary eye on the front door. The vault was secure, but the perimeter alarm had not yet been set. If someone forced his way inside, the alarm company wouldn't be alerted unless Destiny or Rashida manually depressed one of the many silent alarm buttons located in the teller windows and under the branch manager's and the accounts representatives' desks.

"I'll dial into the conference call on my way home and switch to a land line when I get there."

"I'll pick up dinner. What would you like?"

"Something I can eat while I'm sitting in a bubble bath with you."

"I'll see what I can do."

The husky tone of Destiny's voice made Rashida forget all about her headache.

She set the alarm and headed to her car. She waited for everyone to get dialed in, then began the conference call by asking Seaton to provide an update on Megan's condition.

"I'm happy to report she finally began responding to medication around six. Ian took her home. When I talked to him a few minutes ago, he said she had a big dinner and is resting comfortably. She's going to be okay."

"That's good to hear."

Rashida didn't want to risk losing her cell phone signal in the elevator so she sat in her car outside her apartment building for the duration of the call. She updated everyone on the state of the branch and was pleasantly surprised to hear Harry follow through on her offer to sit with the maintenance crew while they repaired the elevator on Friday.

"If they get started by seven, I should be free to leave by early afternoon. I'll miss part of the parade, but I'll have plenty of time to partake in the rest of the weekend's festivities. Besides, it's my father's company. I feel partially responsible. The least I can do is make sure his screw-up gets fixed."

"Thanks for your determination to see this through," Rashida said. "Good job, everyone. I'll send an e-mail to each member of the recovery team summarizing what we discussed tonight. I'll send a separate one to all employees letting them know we're still on track to reopen on Monday."

"I think I speak for everyone when I say you've done enough for one day," Dan said. "I'll handle the communications. Why don't you call it a night?"

"With pleasure."

Rashida ended the call and wearily crossed the parking lot. Destiny was waiting for her outside her door, a box of pizza and a six-pack of beer in her hands.

"Hungry?"

"Starving. I haven't eaten since breakfast."

She unlocked the door and turned on the lights. Destiny followed her inside.

Destiny placed the pizza and beer on the coffee table. "How did the update call go?"

"Better than expected. Megan's doctors say she's going to be fine and Harry offered to supervise the repair team, which frees me up to tackle the regularly-scheduled items on my agenda."

"Do you have to be quite so dedicated?" Destiny held Rashida's face in her hands, finally breaking the grip that work had held on her for most of the day. "Why don't you sleep late tomorrow? Or, better yet, why don't you take the day off? You deserve it after all the hours you put in today."

"You won't get an argument from me."

"So you'll do it?"

Rashida rested her hands on Destiny's wrists. "I wish I could, but I have to go in. We're stretched too thin. No one else is available."

Destiny ducked her head to force Rashida to look her in the eye. "I have several more hours to convince you to change your mind."

Rashida smiled wearily. "I can't wait for you to try."

Desperately needing to decompress, she left her bags in the foyer, tossed her keys on the counter, and headed to the bathroom.

A fabric shower curtain covered with screen-printed cherry blossoms circled the old-fashioned clawfoot bathtub. Rashida drew the curtain aside, turned on the water, and spun the taps. Hot water rushed out of the faucet. She poured in a capful of coconut-scented bubble bath and waited for the tub to fill.

She began to undress. Her clothes smelled like burned oil. She was tempted to toss the outfit into the trash instead of the dry-cleaning pile. She weighed the price of a cleaning bill against the cost of a new suit and opted to go with the lower amount.

Destiny joined her in the bathroom and handed her a beer. "You look like you needed a drink."

"What I need is to get you naked."

Destiny's tie was loosely knotted around her neck. Rashida pulled it off and unbuttoned her shirt. Then she unbuckled her belt.

"Are you trying to take advantage of me, Miss Ivey?" Destiny asked when her pants hit the floor.

"In every possible way."

Rashida cupped Destiny's ass in her hands and drew her closer. Their breasts met and compressed. Rashida felt a rush of warmth on her thighs. If she had her way, the river would soon turn into a raging tide. Destiny, however, had other ideas.

"Eat this." Destiny shoved a slice of pizza in her mouth. "Jackie asked me to take care of you, remember?"

Rashida swallowed a bite of pepperoni pizza and held up the remaining slice. "I didn't think this is what you had in mind when you agreed to do so."

"It isn't. That comes later. Here's a preview."

Destiny kissed her long and hard.

"If that's a preview, I can't wait to see the entire show."

Destiny climbed into the tub first. Rashida climbed in second and nestled between Destiny's spread legs. Destiny's breasts pressed against her back. Her stomach nestled against the curve of her ass.

Destiny set her bottle of beer next to the pizza box on the floor. She slid her hands down Rashida's body. Over her shoulders. Down her sides. Her arms circled Rashida's waist. She kissed the nape of her neck, her teeth nipping at the soft skin.

"I love you," she whispered as Rashida's head lolled on her shoulder. Her palms slid down Rashida's slick skin. Her fingers grazed the neatly trimmed triangle of hair at the apex of Rashida's thighs. Then they found the pool of wetness that had gathered between her legs.

Rashida's body tensed, anticipating the first touch. Destiny obliged her, one hand sliding over her turgid clit, the other teasing a firm nipple. Rashida moved against Destiny's hands as her fingers gripped the tops of Destiny's thighs. She arched her back, lost in sensation.

Destiny reached lower. Slipped one finger inside. Rashida groaned in approval. Destiny spread her legs, bracing for the impact of the coming storm. She held Rashida as she rose higher and higher. Whispering her name, Rashida crested. The muscles lining her smooth walls gripped Destiny's fingers, drawing them deeper inside. But she wasn't done. She came again and again until she finally—eventually—stilled Destiny's hand.

"Your turn," she whispered hoarsely.

She grabbed a bar of lemongrass soap and lathered a washcloth. She twirled a finger in the air, signaling for Destiny to turn and face the wall. She slowly rubbed the washcloth over Destiny's skin. She started just under her hairline, moved down her neck, then across her shoulders. Destiny shuddered when Rashida squeezed the washcloth, sending a stream of soapy water trickling down her back.

Rashida soaped the cloth again, then reached around to rub it over Destiny's breasts, covering one then the other with warm, silky lather. Destiny gasped when the rough cotton cloth brushed against her sensitive nipples. Rashida squeezed the excess water from the cloth and set it aside. Rubbing the soap between her palms, she lathered her hands. Then she slowly massaged Destiny's shoulders, arms, and back. Destiny's tense muscles immediately turned to jelly.

"Turn around," Rashida said. "I want to watch you come."

Destiny faced her.

Rashida slowly slid her hand down Destiny's leg and pulled it toward her, hooking the back of Destiny's knee around her waist. She slipped her hand between their bodies. Her fingers moved across Destiny's clit as soft as a whisper. As gentle as a stolen kiss. She slowly increased the pressure until Destiny bit her shoulder to keep from crying out.

"Tell me what you want and it's yours," Rashida said.

"All I want is you. Nothing else. You're all I need."

Rashida's fingers continued to dance against Destiny's clit. Up the hood, down to the bundle of nerves at the tip.

"Tell me when."

"Now. Now, baby, now."

Rashida thrust three fingers inside.

Destiny threw her head back, howling in release. The sound echoed off the porcelain-tiled walls.

Home, Rashida thought as she and Destiny sat wordlessly holding each other in the roiling water. *Being with her is like coming home.*

When she had invited Destiny into her bed, she hadn't expected to invite her into her heart as well. But there was no denying Destiny had set up residence there. Her feet were on the coffee table, her clothes were in the closet, her favorite food in the refrigerator. Destiny's heart was her home.

Chapter Twelve

Friday, March 17
7:15 a.m.
Savannah, Georgia

Rashida tucked her polo shirt into her jeans. She felt Destiny's eyes on her even before she turned and saw Destiny watching her dress. Destiny lay on her back, the rumpled sheets bunched around her hips. The bright morning sun streaming through the window made the contrast between the blanched cotton and Destiny's brown skin more pronounced. Destiny's eyes were heavy-lidded with sleep. A lazy smile lit up her face.

Rashida turned back to the mirror and slid the posts of her earrings through the holes in her lobes. "What are you staring at?" she asked with a smile of her own.

"You."

Rashida squealed when Destiny grabbed her belt loop, pulled her onto the bed, and covered her face with kisses. "Stop," she said, laughing as she endured the ferocious onslaught. "I'm going to be late for work."

"Are you sure you can't play hooky just this once? You don't need to shadow the new hire. Let the head teller do it. I've got the day off. Let's spend it together. We can watch the parade and have some green beer in a crowded bar. Or, if you want, we don't even have to leave this bed."

Thursday was the first time they had spent the entire night together. Today was the first time Rashida had greeted the sunrise with Destiny's arms wrapped around her. She was reluctant to leave the comfort of their embrace.

"Like I said last night, I wish I could, but I can't."

She hadn't had St. Patrick's Day off in years, always conscripted to cover the fort while everyone else went out to play. She longed to watch the parade through Destiny's eyes. To walk the crowded streets with her and take in the nonstop action. But she couldn't. Someone had to keep the bank running. Unfortunately, the task fell to her. She extricated herself from Destiny's grasp and continued to prepare for work.

"Do you mind if I hang out here until the parade starts?" Destiny asked.

"Make yourself at home. I'll show you where I keep the spare key in case you want to let yourself in before I get back."

Rashida liked the idea of having Destiny to come home to. To wake up with. She hoped the phenomena would become common occurrences.

Destiny yawned, stretched, and tossed the covers aside. "Is there coffee?"

"There's a K cup in the Keurig with your name on it."

Destiny pulled on a T-shirt and padded to the kitchen. Rashida joined her there a few minutes later.

"What are you going to do today? Besides watch the parade and drink green beer?"

"After yesterday, that's about all I can manage." Destiny pushed a series of buttons on the single-serving coffee maker and took a sip of the steaming brew that filled her cup. "If you could live anywhere but here, where would you choose?"

"What do you mean?" Rashida struggled to understand the reasoning behind the non sequitur.

"Last week, Jackie was teasing you about going on *House Hunters International*. She said you'd gladly move to another country if you could decide which one you want to live in."

"Oh, that's just a pipe dream. A pleasant fantasy to while away the hours."

Rashida powered up the blender. Just as quickly, Destiny crossed the room and switched it off.

"Remember what you told me? Your idea isn't a pipe dream. It's a goal you can achieve if you try. If you could make your fantasy—your *goal*—come true, where would you end up?"

Though taken aback by the intensity of Destiny's curiosity, Rashida didn't have to take long to come up with an answer to her question.

"I'd go to Malaysia."

"Why?"

"The country is a study in contrasts. Old-fashioned fishing villages line the coasts, while the cities, Kuala Lumpur especially, are as modern as they come. Fabulous meals can be found in five-star Asian fusion restaurants or in hawker stalls lining the streets." Rashida leaned against the counter, growing comfortable with her subject. "Then there are the Petronas Towers. They're the tallest twin buildings in the world. Eighty-eight floors of reinforced concrete with a glass and steel façade. A skybridge between the forty-first and forty-second floors connects the towers and is the highest two-story bridge in the world. It would be so cool to hang out there on New Year's Eve and watch the fireworks marking the end of one era and the beginning of another."

"It sounds like you've done your homework."

Rashida blushed at her passion for a country she had toured on TV and in the movies but had never visited in person.

"What's stopping you from going?"

"I don't speak a word of Malay. That's reason enough."

"So learn."

Destiny looked so serious Rashida laughed to relieve her sudden nervousness. "Are you trying to get rid of me?"

"No." Destiny held Rashida's face in her hands and drew her thumbs across her cheeks. "I want you to be happy."

"I am happy. Right here. With you."

"Then stay with me." Destiny wrapped her arms around Rashida's waist. "Let's do all the things couples do. Let's walk the streets holding hands, people watch on River Street, or go to your favorite bar and watch ships sail down the river all afternoon. Don't go to work today. Pick up the phone and call in sick. I promise to make it worth your while." She nuzzled the side of Rashida's neck, her lips settling into the hollow behind her ear. "Stay with me."

Rashida found it hard to resist such an impassioned plea. Hard, but not impossible. With a groan, she gently pushed Destiny away. "If it was any day but today, I would. But I can't. I'm sorry, but I have to go to work." She finished blending her smoothie and poured the vitamin-packed beverage into a travel mug. Then she gave Destiny a quick kiss. "Enjoy your day. Tell me all about it tonight, okay? And don't leave out a single detail."

Destiny followed her to the living room. "I won't." She ran her hands through her sleep-tousled hair and dropped them to her sides.

Rashida paused with one hand on the doorknob. Destiny looked so sad she wanted to do something to relieve the hurt. "Next year, I'll take the day off, we'll do the parade, the green beer, and anything else you want."

Destiny perked up slightly. "You promise?"

"I'm in this for the long haul, Destiny. We'll have more St. Patrick's Days. I promise."

Destiny finally managed a smile. "I'm going to hold you to that."

"I hope you do." Rashida blew her a kiss. "See you tonight."

In the parking lot, Rashida unlocked her car and placed her bags inside. Before she slammed the trunk, the manila envelope one of the interns had placed in Harry's inbox by mistake caught her eye. In the excitement of the previous day, the mishandled mail had been the least of her worries.

She pulled the envelope out of her computer bag and sat in the front seat. She slipped her car key under the envelope's flap and used the key's jagged edge as a rudimentary letter opener. When she reached inside the envelope, her fingers came into contact with what felt like glossy photo paper.

"What the—"

She pulled the photos out of the envelope and immediately dropped them as if she'd been burned. Half a dozen eight-by-tens fell into her lap. The pictures were grainy, taken with what must have been a telephoto lens, but the images were clear enough to make out the faces of the subjects. She and Destiny were the subjects, but they hadn't posed for the photographer. The photos had been taken without their knowledge. Taken while they made love in the front seat of her car.

Rashida's mind reeled with questions she couldn't answer. Who had taken the photos? Who had sent them? What did the sender want in return?

She covered the images of her topless body with her hands as if to protect herself from additional exposure.

A folded note was taped to the back of one photo. The words typed on the plain white sheet of paper sent a spike of pain through Rashida's heart.

Is this any way for a reputable businesswoman to behave? Obviously, you can take the girl out of the 'hood, but you can't take the 'hood out of the girl.

She had devoted half her life to establishing a solid professional reputation. Countless years of exemplary behavior, solid decision-making, and unquestioned ethics had resulted in her being named an officer of one of the most respected banks in Savannah and had positioned her to climb even higher up the corporate ladder. Was all her hard work about to be undone by one indiscretion?

A honking horn nearly caused her fraying nerves to snap.

"Jesus."

She jumped in her seat, one hand trembling over her racing heart. She looked out her windshield. Trent Lacy, one of the SCAD students who lived in her building, had stopped his car directly in front of hers. She shoved the photos back in the envelope and lowered her driver's side window.

"Good morning, Trent," she said, trying to keep the tremor out of her voice.

"Morning. You've been sitting there for a few minutes. Is everything all right? You're not having car trouble, are you? I can give you a jump if you need one."

"No, everything's fine." She stuffed the envelope and its contents into her glove compartment, where she hoped both would be safe from prying eyes. Then she pressed the ignition button to prove to Trent nothing was wrong with her engine. "I'm just having a little trouble getting going this morning."

"I know the feeling. I'm going to head over to the French Roast before the police close more streets for the parade. Will I see you there?"

"Yeah, probably," she said absently.

She felt like she was standing on top of a mountain and the ground was crumbling beneath her. She needed to talk to someone. She needed to share her burden. She couldn't go to Destiny. Not with this. Destiny would undoubtedly blame herself. Yes, Destiny had pursued her, but she had allowed herself to be caught. Having sex in her car had been Destiny's idea, but she'd been a willing participant. More than willing.

They both were to blame for their current predicament, but she was in a better position to take the hit. If the photos cost her her job, she'd have to deal with the embarrassment of her fall from grace and the recriminations of her friends and family, but she'd be able to support herself with money from her savings until she repaired the damage to her reputation. Destiny didn't have that luxury.

She weighed her options. If she ended the relationship now, she could still have all the things she wanted in her career but not the one thing—the one person—she wanted in her life.

For years, she had tried to find an even balance between her professional and personal lives. For years, work had always tipped the scales. No more.

In their short time together, Destiny had introduced her to so many new experiences. Opened her eyes to so many things. She wasn't ready for the lessons to end.

Having Destiny and her career would be the best of both worlds. If she could have only one, the choice was clear. She chose Destiny.

"Are you sure you're okay?" Trent asked.

"Never better." Rashida broke into a grin. "It's a great day for a parade, don't you think?"

She drove downtown and maneuvered through the maze of barricaded streets. Some thoroughfares would be closed for only a few hours; others would be blocked all weekend to accommodate the heavier than normal foot traffic. Early arrivals had already staked out prime viewing areas to watch the parade. Lawn and stadium chairs lined the streets.

Rashida nabbed a parking spot on Congress Street and hustled inside the French Roast.

"You're working today?" Charles asked after she grabbed a number from the dispenser.

"Not by choice and not for long. After I drop off some provisions for a few working stiffs who aren't as lucky as I am, I'm going to call it a day."

"It's about time you took some time for yourself. What can I get for you?"

"A to-go box of French roast and an assortment of pastries."

Charles cocked his head. "Do you have an army to feed?"

"Close. A team of hungry maintenance workers."

"That's even worse."

The elevator repair team should already be in place and, provided the oil in the motor had cooled to a manageable temperature, hard at work. She'd drop off the coffee and sweets and check the team's progress before she returned home. She'd make herself available by cell in case of emergencies, but she planned on spending this day with her feet up and a green beer in her hand.

"Thanks for steering Destiny my way," Charles said as he helped the baristas fill her order. "She was a good hire."

"For us, too."

"She's hard-working, conscientious. The customers love her."

"So do I."

She might not know the name of the street Destiny grew up on or whether her first pet was a goldfish or a dog, but she knew her heart. As for the rest, they had the rest of their lives to fill in the blanks. Today was the perfect day to start.

Charles boxed up the pastries. "Make sure she sticks around, okay?"

"I plan on it." She handed him her debit card and signed for her purchases after he swiped the card through the terminal next to the cash register. "Have a good weekend."

She deposited the coffee and pastries in the backseat of her car and drove to the bank. Three vehicles were parked in the lot. Harry's Hummer, a battered green pickup truck, and an unmarked white panel van.

Rashida balanced the box of Danishes, crullers, doughnuts, and croissants on top of the box of coffee and carefully made her way to the bank's front door. The shades were drawn, but she could hear the muffled sound of metal pounding against metal coming from inside. The repairs were obviously underway.

She fished her keys out of her pocket and unlocked the door. Out of habit, she reached for the panel just inside the door to input her security code, but the solid green light on the display signaled the perimeter alarm and motion detectors had already been disabled.

Duh. Harry has a code, too. She probably forced the repairmen to show up at five a.m. so she can be out of here before the parade starts.

She inhaled deeply, testing the air. The aroma of burned oil was still present, joined by what smelled like melted metal. She glanced at the elevator. The doors were propped open just as she'd left them last night, but the car and the shaft above it were empty. The new smell—the acrid smell of melted steel—was coming from across the room. It was coming from the vault.

Harry's voice, anxious and somewhat tense, echoed across the lobby. "Come on, guys. Get the lead out. We don't have all day. I've got a plane to catch."

Rashida placed the coffee and pastries on the New Accounts desk and stepped into the lobby. Her brain refused to believe what her eyes were seeing. She rocked back on her heels when she saw the large circular hole that had been cut into the front of the vault. Harry, her back to her, was standing in front of the jagged opening. Inside the vault, two androgynous figures wearing coveralls, latex gloves, and Halloween masks were sifting through customers' safe deposit boxes while another stuffed cash from the money vault into oversized duffel bags. The vault held nearly seven hundred fifty thousand dollars in small and large bills. The haul from the safe deposit boxes was even more valuable. More cash, jewelry, and three gold bars worth half a million dollars each.

Robbery procedures were clear-cut. Remain calm, give the robber what he demanded, write a summary of the incident while the details were fresh in your mind, and talk to no one until the police arrived. Under no circumstances were you supposed to confront the robber or try to be a hero. But normal procedures were useless in this situation. Normal procedures didn't address the betrayal Rashida felt at the hands of a co-worker. One she had come to consider a friend.

She had time to back out of the building without being seen, but she chose to move forward instead. The bank was her livelihood. The employees were her family. Harry was violating both. If she wanted to embarrass her parents or exact some twisted form of revenge, she needed to do it another way.

Rashida looked at the security cameras. The lights were on, but the lenses had been spray painted black, rendering the camera footage useless.

Harry had thought of everything. She had opportunity to commit the crime and ample time to get away. If Rashida hadn't dropped by unannounced, she wouldn't have discovered the theft until Saturday, by which time Harry and her henchmen would probably be splitting their take in some exotic country that didn't have an extradition treaty with the United States.

Split four ways, the stolen loot wouldn't be enough to live off of for more than a few years, but Rashida had a hunch that if she checked Harry's accounts, she'd find they had been drained, the funds wired to a bank in Switzerland, the Cayman Islands, or some other tax haven.

Cursing under her breath, Rashida pressed the silent alarm under the New Accounts desk and prayed the police would arrive relatively quickly. Their usual response time was less than ten minutes. With most of the streets blocked off, it could take much longer than normal for help to arrive. Since none of the robbers appeared to be armed, it was a chance she was willing to take. She was the only obstacle standing between Harry and a clean getaway.

"Harry?"

"It's about time you got here," Harry said without turning to face her. "Did you send Little Miss Perfect on her merry way? She can't get enough of you, it seems. If I were less secure, I'd think the feeling was mutual. Fortunately, one thing I'm not is insecure."

Finally, Harry turned. The broad grin on her face disappeared as soon as she saw Rashida.

"What the fuck are you doing here?" she asked, striding across the lobby. "You're supposed to be halfway to Springfield by now." She snapped her fingers, wordlessly directing the three people in the vault to continue what they were doing.

Rashida frowned. "I didn't share my schedule with you." Entries in the calendar application tied to her e-mail were copied to members of the retail, operations, and customer support teams. Harry wasn't included in any of those work groups. "Who told you I was going to Springfield today?"

Harry's smile returned. The panicked look on her face disappeared. She jerked her chin toward the front door, which swung open and closed with a soft click. "She did."

Rashida turned and saw Destiny standing behind her.

Destiny was dressed in her security guard uniform, the one that had spent the night airing out on Rashida's patio. A gun Rashida didn't realize Destiny had been recertified to carry rested in a holster clipped to her wide leather belt.

Rashida backed away. Her heart sank as she shook her head in disbelief. "Please tell me you're not in on this. Please tell me everything we had wasn't a lie."

Destiny unholstered the gun while Harry pinned Rashida's arms to her sides. "I asked you not to go to work today. You should have listened to me."

CHAPTER THIRTEEN

Friday, March 3
8:10 a.m.
Savannah, Georgia

Destiny Jackson stared at a photo of a fine sister in her mid-thirties as she rehearsed her lines.

Hi, are you ready for a date with Destiny?

She rolled her eyes at the cornball lines Harry Collins had asked her to memorize. She had picked up the sexy redhead in a bar in South Beach on Valentine's Day and given her everything she had begged for in bed. Though she had been the dominant one between the sheets, Harry was definitely calling the shots now. In more ways than one. Harry had what Destiny wanted but had never been able to possess: money, power, respect, and the most valuable asset of all, leverage.

Destiny looked at the photo again. The woman in the picture—the beautiful ebony goddess with warm brown eyes and a welcoming smile—looked like she was too much on the ball to be fooled by cheesy pick-up lines delivered by someone hired to play a part. Sincerity was the way to this woman's heart. Destiny needed to mean everything she said. Or at least sound like she did.

Being careful not to attract attention, she slipped the photo into the inside pocket of her blazer and took a sip of her rapidly cooling coffee. She had been in place for nearly half an hour, giving herself plenty of time to survey the landscape before her target arrived. She had been in town for a little over two weeks, content to hang back and get the lay of the land. Now it was time to put the plan into effect.

How, she wondered, had she allowed herself to be dragged into this? Easy. Harry, whom she had correctly assumed to be both filthy rich and an absolute wildcat in the sack, had thrown a wad of bills her way and promised her there was more—much more—where that came from. For better or worse, the farfetched scheme Harry had concocted after a pitcher of morning-after mimosas was now underway. Destiny didn't know who was crazier, Harry for coming up with the idea or her for agreeing, however reluctantly, to go through with it.

She looked around the French Roast, the coffee shop she had been haunting for the past ten days. According to Harry, the French Roast and Rocks on the Roof were their unsuspecting victim's favorite hangouts in town. Destiny had shadowed her to both in an effort to get a feel for her patterns. Unfortunately, she didn't seem to have any. Her time of arrival and the duration of her stay at the coffee shop varied wildly depending on where she was scheduled to work that day. Her one trip to the bar had lasted less than an hour, most of which she had spent staring dreamily at the view.

Harry had discovered she was working in Savannah today, which meant she'd probably arrive at the French Roast between eight fifteen and eight thirty, giving her plenty of time to get her caffeine fix before the branch opened at nine.

The number of people in line began to swell as the next wave of the morning rush swept in. The owner, a Harvey Feinstein lookalike in tight black jeans and a bedazzled Paris is for Lovers T-shirt, greeted everyone by name.

The prices were steep, but Destiny liked the feel of the place. The atmosphere was laid-back, the baristas friendly and efficient. All the employees seemed to enjoy their jobs, unlike some coffee pushers she had come across. The delusional actor/model/waiter types who were convinced their big break was just around the corner and refused to consider the idea that fate had already passed them by. She didn't want to know which category she fit into.

She read the classifieds in the newspaper she had bought as a prop. Some of the entries brought a smile to her face. “Lordy, Lordy, look who’s forty,” the caption of one ad read underneath a blurry childhood picture of the presumed birthday boy astride a knock-kneed Shetland pony.

Savannah, a small town masquerading as a metropolis, was a far cry from her native Miami. Despite the historic Art Deco hotels dotting the brightly colored landscape, South Beach was all about the new. New money, new experiences, and new arrivals anxious to spend lots of one in order to gain the other. Savannah, in contrast, was all about the old. The city reveled in its past so much Destiny was surprised the date on the newspaper in her hands hadn’t been rolled back two hundred years.

Charles Demery circled his shop, refilling customers’ cups with the contents of the carafe of black coffee in his hand. “Top you off, Destiny?”

“No, thanks. I’m good.” She could use another jolt of caffeine to put herself in the right frame of mind but, considering she would be wearing the liquid in her coffee cup in another few minutes, she decided to go without. She was already risking a slap in the face. She didn’t want to add third degree burns to the mix.

She went over her lines again, tweaking them to make them sound more realistic.

“Hi, I’m Destiny Jackson.”

Destiny. The name didn’t fit. She had gotten used to hearing it but couldn’t get used to saying it. The name still felt strange in her mouth. For at least two more weeks, though, she’d have to get used to the sensation.

She checked her watch. What was this chick’s name again? Rashida something. Ivey. That was it. *Poison. Like the plant.* Destiny smiled at Harry’s description of the woman she was going to such great lengths to humiliate. High school yearbook photos uploaded to the Internet could get the job done faster and a whole lot cheaper. Choosing not to go viral, Harry had opted for the slower route. The one that would have the more long-lasting effects. If her plan was successful, it could ruin Rashida’s career as well as her life. Theirs, too, if they weren’t careful.

What had Rashida done to piss off Harry so thoroughly? Shot down one of her passes or scuttled a business deal? Neither offense seemed egregious enough to warrant such an over-the-top reaction.

Once she got the scheme straight in her mind, Harry had taken her to a salon for a makeover, bought her a wardrobe to suit the new persona she created, paid her way to Savannah, and set her up in a house on 37th Street.

According to her cover story, Destiny was supposed to be staying with an old Army buddy and his wife, but she had the place to herself. Someone else's name was on the lease, but the place was hers. She'd never had a place of her own. The first time she'd walked from the living room to the kitchen without having to step over a passed-out relative or a deadbeat roommate along the way, she'd celebrated like she'd won the lottery. In a way, she had. She stood to make more money over the next fourteen days than she'd earned in her entire life. All she had to do was ruin someone else's.

Did she expect to see any of the riches Harry promised her when all was said and done? Not really. If the plan went south, money would be the furthest thing from her mind. She'd be lucky to avoid jail time if the shit hit the fan. But being here was worth the risk. Pretending to be someone else in Savannah was better than being herself in Miami.

Running cons, playing games, living off the largesse of rich women desperate for a walk on the wild side, trying to convince herself she was the one doing the hustling instead of being hustled. For four weeks, she didn't have to be that person. She could be Destiny Jackson, straight-laced former soldier, not DaShawn Jenkins, grifter extraordinaire.

She shifted uncomfortably in her seat. She hadn't played the role of lovelorn suitor in so long she thought she might need help remembering how. When Rashida Ivey walked in, she knew she wouldn't need any help at all.

Rashida's picture didn't do her justice. The photo Harry had provided had probably come out of a business magazine. In the picture, Rashida's conservative suit made her look like a cookie cutter corporate exec. Bland, boring, and utterly flavorless. In person, she was anything but. She looked sweet with a hint of spice. Like honey infused with a dash of cayenne. Destiny couldn't wait to get a taste.

She sipped her coffee and waited for Rashida to make her way through the line. Rashida checked her watch every few minutes as if she were running late. Harry had said she was something of a workaholic. Destiny wondered how long she'd give the line to thin before she gave up and went somewhere else. When she seemed ready to bolt, Destiny made her move.

She slid out of her seat and walked slowly through the crowded shop. She picked up speed when Rashida began to turn around, initiating a collision. Her coffee, warm enough to feel vaguely uncomfortable but thankfully no longer hot enough to burn, quickly soaked her white cotton shirt. She cringed inwardly when a few drops landed on her new suede shoes, ruining the nap.

Rashida's mouth, framed by full lips painted an enticing shade of red, rounded into an O of surprise. She had been beautiful from across the room. Up close, she was breathtaking. Destiny could imagine getting it on with her with some sweet, romantic music playing in the background. The pleasant thought reminded her of the unpleasant chore she had been hired to perform.

The bank Rashida worked for had some archaic rule about employees not being allowed to date each other. If they got caught breaking the rule, it meant immediate termination. Destiny was supposed to wrap Rashida around her finger, join the staff, and smile for the camera when Rashida got caught with her hand in the cookie jar. While Rashida busied herself trying to find a way to cover her ass, Harry would rob the bank blind. Destiny and her crew could split the take from the safe; Harry wanted the gold bars some customer had been stupid enough to store in his safe deposit box, along with the satisfaction of embarrassing both her parents and the woman she considered the bane of her existence. Destiny and Harry would skip town afterward, leaving Rashida as the face of the biggest scandal to hit Savannah in years.

Sex, money, power. The scheme had it all. When it was revealed, local gossips' tongues would be wagging for months.

Destiny was supposed to leave Rashida with a broken heart and a shattered reputation. Looking into Rashida's trusting eyes, she wanted to see them filled with desire instead of pain.

"Something told me I shouldn't have worn this shirt today."

The line came easily. Because it was something DaShawn would have said, not Destiny.

Rashida took the blame for the accident. Apologizing profusely, she dabbed at the growing stain on Destiny's shirt with a handful of flimsy napkins. The muscles in Destiny's stomach contracted involuntarily when she felt Rashida's fingers pressing against her. She had been touched by more women than she could count in ways—and places—much more intimate than this, but none of those feverish gropes had excited her as much as Rashida's casual touch. She leaned into the pressure.

Blinking as if snapping out of a trance, Rashida apologized again and backed away. She offered Destiny a detergent pen to combat the stain, but it was like giving her a teaspoon to bail water out of the *Titanic*.

Rashida tried to give her money to have her shirt cleaned, but Destiny refused, pretending to take the high road. "Not necessary, but thanks for the offer. It was nice running into you. Literally." She turned to leave, guessing Rashida would follow. She guessed right.

She smiled inwardly when Rashida laid a hand on her arm. Her touch was soothing. Destiny had planned to play it cool the first time out. Make contact, make a memorable impression, and slowly turn on the charm over the next few days. By Wednesday, she hoped to have Rashida on all fours screaming her name as she arched her back in ecstasy.

Rashida's hand on her arm made the plan go fuzzy around the edges. She wanted more of those gentle caresses. When Rashida offered to buy her a cup of coffee, she eagerly agreed to the proposal.

She grabbed a booth by the window. Rashida headed to the counter to place their order. While she was gone, Destiny tried to get back into character. Rashida made it so easy—too easy—to be herself. Not who she was. Who she wanted to be. A woman who had her act together instead of one who was an eternal fuckup.

When she was younger, she had been arrested more times than she could remember. One bust had resulted in a stint in military-style boot camp instead of another lengthy stretch in juvenile hall. The experience had given her the straight-backed posture and *yes, ma'am/no, ma'am* demeanor most people took one look at and assumed was the result of time spent in the armed forces. She didn't feel the need to correct the false assumption. Until now.

Rashida approached the table. Destiny stood to greet her. She wanted to start over. She wanted to introduce herself by her real name. Woo her and win her as DaShawn, not Destiny. Whoever that was. She had been pretending to be someone else for so long she had almost forgotten how to be herself. Besides a checkered past, what did DaShawn have to offer? Nothing that someone like Rashida Ivey could appreciate. That's where Destiny came in.

She made small talk with Rashida, trying to draw information out of her while sharing pieces of her made-up past. After Charles raved about Rashida's recent promotion at the bank, Destiny glanced at the table, subtly drawing Rashida's eyes to the want ads that rested between their coffee cups. Rashida took the bait.

"What kind of jobs are you seeking?" she asked.

"Anything." Tapping into past failures, Destiny tried to seem both embarrassed and a little bit desperate. She swept the newspaper off the table before Rashida could reach for it and see any of the entries she had circled at random. Not only was she unqualified to fill most of the jobs listed, she couldn't even pronounce some of them. What the hell was a gastroenterologist anyway?

"Do you have any idea why your parents decided to name you Destiny?"

Rashida's question elicited an honest response. "My friends call me DJ." Destiny wanted to kick herself for her slip of the tongue. Even more so when Rashida said she preferred the persona to the person.

"That's nice, but Destiny suits you."

Destiny took a sip of coffee to swallow the hurt. "Why?"

"Because you feel like something that's meant to be."

So did she.

Going against her plan to take it slow, Destiny asked Rashida out. Real or imagined, she felt a connection between them. She was something of an expert at reading women and knew Rashida felt it, too. Except Rashida turned her down. Politely but firmly. Rashida claimed she had plans for the better part of the next two days, valuable time Destiny had planned to put to good use.

Destiny scrambled to find a way to regain the upper hand. Then Jackie Williams gave it to her. The married mother of two was Rashida's employee and best friend. She sat next to Rashida and addressed her with a familiarity Destiny decided to use to her advantage.

"I see." She looked at Rashida and Jackie as if she'd intruded on a lovers' *tête-à-tête*, wished them a good day, then got up and walked out. Rashida's eyes followed her to the door.

On the street, Destiny pulled out a cell phone she'd picked up at a gas station near I-95. The cheap phone, known as a burner, was popular with drug dealers because its disposable nature made it difficult for the feds to track with wiretaps. She had three such phones, all with different numbers. Once she hit Savannah, she kept contact with Harry to a minimum. If the authorities subpoenaed Harry's phone records, which they inevitably would, Destiny didn't want her calls to stick out from the others.

It was too early for Harry to be at work so Destiny called her on her cell. Harry answered on the first ring. "What do you have for me?" Both she and her voice sounded distant.

"I'm in."

"Excellent news. When are you going to see her again?"

"Sunday afternoon at the earliest. She's heading out of town tomorrow and she's spending part of Sunday getting gussied up at the spa. I'm guessing she'll finish around lunch and head to Rocks on the Roof for a drink. When she arrives, I'll already be there waiting for her."

"That's Sunday. How are you going to keep yourself occupied in the meantime?"

"What do you mean?" Destiny asked, even though she could tell by the sudden thaw in Harry's voice exactly what she had in mind.

"I need to take the edge off. When can I see you?"

Normally, Destiny would have jumped at the chance to spend thirty-six hours having several rounds of athletic sex with a partner as enthusiastic as Harry, but that was before she'd laid eyes on Rashida Ivey.

"I think it would be best if we stayed away from each other until we reach the end game. You and I don't run in the same social circles. If we slip up and someone sees us together, it could jeopardize everything you've been working for."

"Even though I know you're right, that doesn't make what you're saying easy to hear."

"I've seen your little black book. Something tells me you won't be lacking for company."

"That might have been true once. The only company I want this weekend is yours."

The idea didn't hold nearly as much appeal for Destiny as it had a few weeks earlier, but she couldn't afford to alienate Harry before the big payoff. When she could finally be free of the only life she had known since she was in her teens.

"After St. Patrick's Day, you'll have my undivided attention for as long as you want it. Where are you taking me again?"

"I haven't decided yet." Destiny could hear the smile in Harry's voice. "Someplace where English is a second language and clothing is optional."

"Mmm. I like the sound of that." Destiny walked toward City Market, where drivers were preparing their horse-drawn carriages for the coming work day.

"Did you sweet talk her into giving you a job? We don't have any openings at the moment. She'd have to create one for you, which I don't see happening, no matter how good you are in bed."

Destiny winced at the suggestion she was nothing more than a combination of skilled parts—dancing tongue, probing fingers, and agile torso. "No worries. I can create my own opportunity."

"How?"

"Let me worry about that part. The less you know, the better." Destiny stopped to scratch one of the horses between its ears. While the huge animal nickered and stamped its hoof in appreciation, Destiny watched Low Country Savings' elderly security guard make his way to the bank's entrance. She mouthed her thanks to the horse's handler and continued on her way. "I need an advance."

"How much?" Harry asked.

"Five thousand. No, make it ten."

"What do you have in mind?"

"Like I said, the less you know, the better. Give me a few hours to pull everything together and you'll see for yourself. When can you get me the money?"

"You'll have it by noon. When will I see a return on my investment?"

"You'll have results by this afternoon. I've got to go. I have a hostile takeover to plan."

Harry laughed. "I thought that was my line."

"I hope you don't mind if I borrow it for a while."

"As long as you pay me back."

If Harry had her way, Destiny might be paying for the rest of her life. "I will. With interest."

Harry laughed again. "How do you manage to make everything sound so damn sexy?"

"Practice."

Destiny's smooth façade had slipped several times during her brief encounter with Rashida. Continued exposure could cause her false front to drop for good. She didn't think she had ever wanted anything more. But how was she supposed to build something real on a stack of lies?

You're good at fooling women, not falling for them. Stick to what you do best.

She pulled out another burner and placed a second call. Pit Bull, one of her running mates from back in the day, had been in Savannah for the past ten years. He was the best stickup man she had ever worked with. She hoped his skills hadn't eroded in the time they'd spent apart.

"Wassup? This is Pit."

"Pit. Hey, homey, it's DJ."

"Hey, girl. Long time no talk to. Every time you call, I know it means money in my pocket. What's on your mind this time?"

"I hope you don't have anything planned for this afternoon. I've got a job for you."

"What kind of job?"

"I need you to take someone out."

"Who?"

"The security guard at Low Country Savings Bank."

"That shouldn't take much. The cat must be a hundred years old. Do you want me to get rid of him permanently?"

"No, just knock him out of commission for a while. I'll take care of the rest."

"Do you want me to hit the bank while I'm at it?"

"Not that one. Hit one of the banks on the square if you have to, but not Low Country." When the time came to empty the safe, Destiny wanted the employees to be caught by surprise.

"How much are we talking?" Pit asked.

"How does five thousand sound?"

"Seventy-five hundred would sound better. I'll have to pay one of my boys to hook up with me after I ditch the getaway car. He ain't gonna do it for free, and I don't want his end coming out of my cut."

"You've got a deal."

Destiny ended the call and took the battery out of the phone. After she wiped off her fingerprints, she dumped the battery in one trash container and the phone in another.

Even after Pit's expected mark-up, she would still clear over two grand today. More than enough to skip town in a hurry if the need arose. It never hurt to be too careful. Harry Collins talked a good game, but Destiny trusted her about as far as she could throw her. She needed some insurance. If the heat got turned up too high, she needed to make sure she didn't get burned.

Chapter Fourteen

Sunday, March 5
4:20 p.m.
Savannah, Georgia

As she stood on the patio of Rocks on the Roof, Destiny read the latest edition of the Savannah *Morning News* over someone's shoulder. Pit Bull's attempted robbery of the Bank of America branch on Johnson Square was still front page news. The police didn't have any leads but were pursuing the case from all possible angles, cop talk for they didn't have a fucking clue who they were looking for. Pit and his partner in crime, seventy-five hundred dollars richer and lucky not to be behind bars, had wisely picked up stakes and skipped town.

Destiny scanned the article for news about Frank Redmond. The security guard had put up more of a fight than she had expected. In fact, he had almost ruined her carefully laid plan. If he had held on to Pit's leg for thirty more seconds, Pit would be cooling his heels in jail instead of beating feet for parts unknown, and she'd be trying to explain to Harry what had gone wrong.

She sipped her beer. She'd been nursing the same one for almost three hours. If Rashida didn't show up soon, she might have to call it a day. A few minutes later, her patience was finally rewarded. Jackie claimed a table about twenty feet away. Drinks in hand, Rashida soon joined her. Destiny ducked behind a potted palm and watched them interact.

Jackie was Rashida's opposite in almost every way. Where Rashida was tall and thin, Jackie was short and plump. Rashida spoke with a quiet self-assurance that invited the listener to lean in close. Jackie's booming voice kept her audience at a distance. Rashida attracted attention by appearing to deflect it. Jackie's flashy clothes and oversized personality screamed, "Hey, look at me!"

If she didn't know Rashida and Jackie were nothing more than friends, Destiny would have sworn they were lovers. They finished each other's sentences and used the same conversational shortcuts favored by longtime partners. If they were as close professionally as they seemed to be personally, they made a formidable team. Destiny would have to take on not one but both. If she managed to convince Rashida to break the rules, could she in turn persuade Jackie to look the other way? She wasn't so sure. Her considerable charms would most likely be lost on Jackie.

She ordered another beer and bided her time. She had only twelve days left before the dangerous game she had been roped in to play reached its final stages, but she couldn't afford to rush.

Jackie left shortly after she and Rashida arrived, clearing the way for Destiny and Rashida to spend some time alone. Destiny licked her lips at the prospect but didn't head toward Rashida's table right away. She stayed put to gauge Rashida's interest. Had she laid enough groundwork during their first meeting to prompt Rashida to pursue her or did she need to be the aggressor?

She watched a large cargo ship slowly chug past and feigned disinterest in the conversations taking place all around her. Rashida briefly conferred with the waitress before joining her by the railing.

"Come here often?"

Destiny turned quickly as if she'd been taken by surprise when she'd been surreptitiously ogling Rashida in her jeans and gay pride sweatshirt for several minutes. It took guts to be openly gay in some parts of the Deep South. Rashida didn't seem to have a problem being who she was wherever she might be.

"Are you meeting your friend here?" Destiny wanted to make her first serious play to win Rashida's affections while simultaneously pleading her case to take Frank Redmond's job, but she had to be sure Jackie wouldn't be around to run interference.

Rashida confirmed Jackie was out of the picture and invited Destiny to join her at her table. Destiny hemmed and hawed for a few minutes before "allowing" Rashida to twist her arm.

After they divvied up a selection of finger food, Destiny listened attentively while Rashida opened up to her about her close relationship with her grandmother and her distant one with the rest of her family.

"What about you?" Rashida asked. "Are you and your family close?"

Instead of resorting to a canned answer about an idyllic family life she had never experienced firsthand, Destiny countered with the truth.

"I've been on my own since I was seventeen. My father saw me on a date with my girlfriend at the time. When I got home, he had changed the locks on the doors and my clothes were scattered all over the lawn. Both he and my mother made it clear I was no longer welcome in their home or their lives. I haven't seen them since."

"What did you do?"

"I stayed at a friend's house for a while. When I stopped feeling sorry for myself, I picked myself up, got a job, and never looked back."

Destiny didn't have to pretend to be vulnerable. When Rashida covered her hand with her own, the emotions she felt were real. Too real. She hadn't delved into her past in years. Reliving it often proved as painful the second time around as it had the first. She welcomed the change in subject when Rashida asked her about her job experience.

She listed a fabricated work history that made her seem like the perfect candidate to replace Frank Redmond then waited for Rashida to make the pieces fit. After Rashida questioned her about where she was staying and her nonexistent roommates, she finally put two and two together. She didn't offer Destiny the job but asked if she was interested and directed her to follow up with the bank's human resources department.

Destiny felt a newfound sense of admiration. Rashida was professional and level-headed, aware of the power she possessed but unwilling to use it for her own gain. Getting her to crack was proving to be more of a challenge than she had expected. A challenge she was willing to take on. Not for Harry's benefit but her own.

"If you're up for an adventure, I'd like to show you something."

She took Rashida to Echo Square, the little-known destination on River Street that harbored a spooky natural phenomenon more confusing than frightening. She offered Rashida her arm after she, too, failed to unravel the mystery behind the unmarked echo chamber. They walked the length of River Street, stopping to play tourist in several souvenir shops and an open-air flea market.

"What's next?" Rashida asked, excitement glittering in her eyes. Savannah was her hometown, but she looked like she was seeing the city for the first time.

Destiny was experiencing something for the first time, too. The feeling she was exactly where she was supposed to be with exactly the person she was supposed to be with. She felt a sense of completion she'd heretofore only read about in novels or seen in sappy romantic comedies. She wanted to see Rashida smile. Make her laugh. Share untold adventures with her. She wanted every day to be like today.

"Can we sit and talk? Or have I interrogated you enough for one day?"

"Far from it."

Rashida sat on a bench facing the water. Destiny sat next to her and draped her arm across the back of the seat. "This has been fun," she said. "I'm glad I ran into you today."

"So am I."

"Do you think we could do it again sometime?"

For the first time since Destiny had met her, Rashida looked hesitant. "I should tell you something. I went to Atlanta yesterday to close the book on a relationship and I'm not ready to start another one yet."

This must be the ex-girlfriend Harry had told her about. The real estate agent who had moved on to greener pastures. Despite her prior knowledge, Destiny made sure to ask the appropriate questions. "What was her name?"

"Diana. Diana Vasquez."

"I think I've heard of her." She hadn't, but she wanted to know if Rashida had any hard feelings for her former lover.

"I'm not surprised. She's one of the most successful real estate agents in the Southeast."

Destiny took note of the measure of pride she heard in Rashida's voice. Though she and Diana were no longer together, Rashida seemed to have nothing but the utmost respect for her.

Rashida looked out at the water but quickly turned back. Destiny loved how she always looked her in the eye no matter how difficult the subject at hand. With her, there was no wondering where you stood. Her expressive face let you know. Despite her assertion she wasn't ready to embark on another relationship, her eyes said otherwise. All Destiny had to do was close the deal.

"How long were you and Diana together?"

"Six years."

"What happened?"

"We loved each other, but we weren't in love with each other, if that makes sense."

"It makes perfect sense. Six years is a long time. It takes guts to admit a relationship that has lasted that long isn't working out."

"It doesn't take bravery. It takes honesty."

"You act as if those things are mutually exclusive. Take it from me. They aren't."

Because if I had an ounce of bravery, I'd be honest with you right now.

"Considering what you've been through, you've exhibited a great deal more bravery than I have. I agreed to end a relationship that was failing. You've had to make your way in the world with no support system. *That* takes guts."

"Thank you, but I hope you don't think I was fishing for a compliment."

"I don't. And you're welcome." Rashida sat up straight as if she were putting the problems of the past behind her. "You've heard my sob story. Tell me about your last relationship."

Yet again, Destiny found it impossible to lie. "I don't think I've ever really had one."

"No?"

"I find it hard to open up to people, which tends to keep things on a surface level."

"By choice?"

"By necessity. In my line of work, I don't get too close to anyone. All the relationships I have are professional, not personal."

"You sound like me." Rashida nodded knowingly. "You've been hurt before and you don't want to be hurt again. I can't blame you for being unwilling to trust your heart to someone." She placed her hand on Destiny's thigh. "But I hope you meet someone who'll make you want to change your mind."

Destiny looked into Rashida's eyes, which had captivated her from the very first day. "I think I already have."

CHAPTER FIFTEEN

Tuesday, March 7
2:30 p.m.
Savannah, Georgia

Jackie peered at the results of Destiny's online skills test. Destiny tried and failed to sneak a peek at her score. She thought she'd done well on the hour-long exam, but she could use the confirmation. The interview seemed like it would never end. In addition to taking the test, she had been asked to run through several potential scenarios and participate in role-play. She had been asked to explain how she would react if someone attempted to rob the bank, if an irate customer got out of hand, or if something happened to the building itself. Jackie's questions were intelligent and incisive, forcing Destiny to stay on her toes to keep from giving herself away.

Jackie and someone from the human resources department had conducted the interview. Rashida was noticeably absent.

Had Rashida cited a conflict of interest and let someone else decide whether to hire her? Or was she saving her input for behind the scenes? She was a wilier opponent than Harry had given her credit for. And the sexiest mark Destiny had ever set her sights on.

This con was different from any other she had ever played. It was about more than showing someone a good time and fleecing her out of a few dollars. This time, the stakes were much higher.

Destiny chided herself for going soft. She'd never cared about any of the other marks she'd fooled. Why should this one be any different? Because those other marks didn't make her want to give up the fast life for the straight and narrow. Because those other marks weren't Rashida Ivey.

"That should do it," Jackie said. "Thank you for meeting with me today."

"What happens next?"

"HR has already called to verify your references and your work history. Everyone you've listed speaks highly of you."

The companies Destiny said she'd worked for were real. The contact names and phone numbers listed on her résumé, however, were not. When HR checked her references and work history, the calls had been routed to members of her team. People who had been paid to make her sound like the best worker the companies had ever employed, even though she had never set foot in their doors.

Her military record was just as easy to fake. When Techno established a false identity, the results were always airtight. She was worth every penny of Harry's money Destiny had sent her way.

"After I interview one additional candidate, I'll take all the applicants' qualifications into consideration and make my decision," Jackie said. "I'll be in touch."

Destiny reached across the conference table to shake hands. "Thank you for the opportunity, Mrs. Williams. I hope I hear from you soon."

"You will. Let me walk you out."

Destiny followed Jackie to the door. The job felt like hers to win or lose. Additional candidate or not, she thought she had just won it. All she had to do was wait for the phone to ring. As she walked down the street, she felt a perverse sense of accomplishment. If Rashida had no say in the final outcome and she got the job anyway, that meant she'd earned it on merit, making it the first job she'd ever won without having someone on the inside to grease the skids.

She headed for the French Roast. Charles Demery, touched by her cover story of being unemployed for eight months, had given her a part-time job in his coffee shop. Thirty hours a week on nights and weekends. Today was her second day. The pay wasn't much, but at least she'd be able to keep tabs on Rashida without turning into a stalker. If she didn't get the gig at the bank, the coffee shop could be their only source of contact.

She changed into her uniform and clocked in. The work at the French Roast was honest. Clean. A refreshing change from a job that felt increasingly dirty.

"What do you need me to do?" she asked, adjusting the fit of her black beret. Charles had asked the rest of the employees to break her in slowly. Though they had showed her how to operate most of the machines, she wasn't yet trusted to use them. You pressed a button, pulled a couple of levers, and coffee came out. How hard could it be?

"I forgot to pull a name for last week's drawing for a free gift card," the day manager said. She indicated the jar of business cards sitting next to the cash register. "Pull one of those and give the winner a call. After that, ask Brad to give you a crack at the panini machine."

"Got it."

Destiny pulled a card out of the oversized jar. The official winner of the drawing was Larry Sands, a bouncer at one of the more rough-and-tumble bars on Bay Street. Destiny picked up the phone. Instead of dialing the number on the business card in her hand, she punched in the one Rashida had given her after they got to know each other better on Sunday afternoon. When she had sprinkled facts about her own life on top of the lies she'd made up about Destiny's.

"Sorry, Larry," she said as the phone began to ring. "Better luck next time."

"Rashida Ivey."

Rashida's greeting matched the photo Destiny carried in her wallet. She sounded like a network news anchor. Her tone was polished and professional. Her voice was accent-free and imbued with the right amount of gravitas to earn her listener's trust.

Destiny tried to draw her into a personal conversation, but Rashida wasn't having any of it. Destiny could feel her waiting for her to get to the point.

"You won the gift certificate."

"Oh. That's fantastic."

Rashida's reaction was decidedly unenthusiastic, leaving Destiny wondering what had gone wrong since the last time they had spoken. When they'd said good-bye on Sunday, she thought she had Rashida right where she wanted her. Now she seemed to be pulling away. Or was she playing hard to get? Destiny tried not to overplay her hand. She offered to mail the gift certificate, then casually mentioned the coffee shop was open until ten if Rashida wanted to pick it up one night on her way home.

"I'll pick it up tonight."

"Really?"

Destiny couldn't contain her excitement. When she hung up the phone, she knew two things for sure: she was going to sleep with Rashida Ivey tonight, and she was going to enjoy every minute of it.

❖

Tuesday, March 7
7:05 p.m.
Savannah, Georgia

Rashida caught Destiny's eye when she entered the coffee shop but didn't stop to talk. She grabbed a booth in the back and pulled out the tools of her trade—pen, paper, a laptop, and a pile of reports. She looked up from time to time to glance at the singer performing on stage but, for the most part, she remained focused on work. Destiny gave her fifteen minutes or so before she headed over to take her temperature. She asked point-blank if she'd done something to scare her off. Rashida did something completely unexpected but, given what Destiny had seen from her, not surprising. She told her about the rule designed to keep them apart and apologized for not cluing her in prior to her interview that afternoon.

Destiny took a moment to get her bearings. Rashida had given her the opening she needed. She leaned forward, closing the distance between them while turning up the pressure.

"Let me see if I understand what you're saying. If I take the job, I'd earn a steady paycheck for the first time in months, I'd have insurance and benefits, but I'd never get to kiss you or know what you look like when you come."

She watched Rashida's eyes darken. Sure, she offered token resistance by saying Destiny was jumping the gun assuming they'd ever be more than friends, but Destiny could tell just by looking at her she was making the same assumptions.

Like a shark on the hunt, Destiny smelled blood in the water. She told Rashida what she knew she wanted to hear.

"I want the job, but I want you, too."

Rashida continued to talk a good game, but Destiny could feel her defenses start to crumble. She tried to force her to make a stand. To force her into making a mistake.

"Would you rather I take the job or would you rather see where this leads?"

Rashida's ringing cell phone kept her from responding to a question she obviously didn't want to answer. "This call's for you."

Destiny knew without asking the caller was Jackie looking for her.

"Are you sure you want me to take this?"

She wanted to hear Rashida say yes or no, but Rashida refused to be backed into a corner. She placed the decision where it belonged—in her hands. "Whether you accept her offer is up to you."

Destiny took the cell phone from her and listened to Jackie make her pitch.

"I'm calling today to formally offer you the position of security guard at Low Country Savings Bank," Jackie said. "I'm pleased to say you were the overwhelming favorite out of all the candidates and the unanimous choice of the selection committee. The job is yours if you want it."

The salary wasn't eye-popping but definitely caught Destiny's attention. She could do the job in her sleep. The funny thing was, it sounded like something she'd actually enjoy doing. Too bad she wouldn't be around long enough to collect her first paycheck.

"When would you like me to start?"

Destiny searched Rashida's face, but her neutral expression didn't betray her thoughts. Her troubled eyes, however, hinted at inner turmoil.

"This is an immediate opening, so I'll need you to start right away," Jackie said. "St. Patrick's Day is coming up, and I want to get you trained as soon as possible. Is tomorrow too soon?"

"Tell me when and where."

"Meet me downtown at nine a.m. After you sign the employee contract and complete the necessary paperwork, I'll give you a tour of the building and get you set up with a checking account so we can direct deposit your payroll every two weeks. Welcome aboard."

"Thank you. I look forward to it." When Destiny returned the phone, Rashida didn't offer her congratulations. Those didn't come until Destiny walked her to her car after the shop closed for the night. And they seemed to come at a cost.

"In a few hours, we'll officially be co-workers." Rashida flinched as if the words caused her physical pain.

The reminder of her rapidly closing window of opportunity caused Destiny to lose patience. Tired of waiting for Rashida to give in to the desire she was certain she felt, she gave her a gentle push. She pressed the length of her body against Rashida's and leaned against the side of her car. She slid her hand up the nape of Rashida's neck and cupped the back of her head. Rashida trembled in her arms but didn't push her away.

Destiny melded their lips together, kissing the luscious mouth that had been fueling her fantasies for days. She'd meant the kiss to be quick, leaving Rashida wanting more. But once she started, she couldn't stop.

Rashida's breasts pressed against her chest. Destiny could feel her firm nipples rubbing against hers. Rashida parted her lips, inviting Destiny to explore her mouth. She met Destiny's probing tongue with her own.

Destiny felt a jolt of excitement. Women often elicited physical responses from her when she was working, but not like this. This unexpected reaction hadn't come from her body but her heart. She needed to pull back before she got in too deep. Before she began to mistake something imagined for something real.

"I'm sorry," she said, apologizing for her aggression, "but I couldn't go another minute without feeling your lips pressed against mine."

She traced a finger across those lips, wanting to hear them whisper her name.

"Get in the car."

Rashida's voice was feral, bearing no trace of its usual measured tones. The desire flowing from her was so palpable Destiny wanted to take her here and now. To take her as DaShawn. Unfortunately, that wasn't part of the plan. She climbed in the car. Jo was waiting for her.

When she'd clocked out, she had texted Jo Slater, another member of her crew, to get set up in the Victorian District. She couldn't avoid what was coming even if she wanted to. The dominoes had already been set in motion. In ten days, the final one would fall.

"Pull over," she said when they neared the designated spot.

They were only a few minutes away from Rashida's apartment, and she was reluctant to stop. Destiny convinced her to do it anyway. She spotted Jo standing in the shadows, camera at the ready. She subtly positioned their bodies so Jo could have a clear angle for the shots she needed.

She told herself to forget about the camera and relax and enjoy the experience, but she couldn't. She was much too aware of the fact that she was working. That what she was doing was part of an act. An act she no longer wanted to be a part of.

When it was over, when Rashida spent herself against her fingers, she didn't feel the emptiness she normally felt after such encounters. She derived no pleasure either. Overwhelming guilt filled the void.

How was she supposed to bring Rashida down when she wanted to see her succeed?

She was in it up to her neck. In too deep to back out now. She didn't know if she'd be able to turn an increasingly hopeless situation to her advantage, but she had to take the chance.

Chapter Sixteen

Wednesday, March 8
8:50 a.m.
Savannah, Georgia

After Destiny walked into the lobby of Low Country Savings, she paused to take in the vintage fixtures and rococo architecture. Yesterday she'd been too nervous prior to her interview to see anything but what lay directly in front of her feet. Now she freely absorbed the sights and sounds of the busy bank. Tellers waited on customers, corporate lenders worked their smartphones, customer service representatives scurried to and fro, and the phones rang nonstop.

These people lived a life to which she had always aspired. A life of power and privilege. A life the employees and their customers took for granted but had always been just out of her reach. Until now. The life she had always wanted was right there for the taking. All she had to do was wrap her fingers around it. And keep her heart out of the equation.

She approached the pretty blonde seated behind the New Accounts desk. The blonde's nameplate read Winter Humphries. Destiny idly wondered if Winter had sisters at home named Spring, Summer, and Autumn.

"May I help you?" Winter asked.

"I'm here to see Mrs. Williams."

Destiny pulled at the collar of the cheap polyester suit she'd picked up at a second-hand store. She would have preferred to wear some of the designer labels hanging in her closet, but those clothes didn't fit the character she was playing. As the old saying went, the devil was in the details. The key to assuming an identity other than your own was looking the part. To a casual or interested observer, she'd look like exactly who she claimed to be—a down-on-her-luck blue-collar worker eager to make a good impression on her first day on the job. She had slipped a little on Sunday when she had worn a pair of her best jeans, but today she was back in character. Like it or not.

"Is Mrs. Williams expecting you?"

"We have an appointment at nine."

"One moment. I'll see if she's ready for you." Winter reached for her phone. "Destiny, isn't it?"

Destiny shifted her portfolio with the cheap plastic cover from one hand to the other. "You remembered."

"You're hard to forget," Winter said with a wink.

Destiny had hoped to blend in rather than stand out. So much for that plan.

"Mrs. Williams, I have Destiny Jackson here to see you." Winter listened for a few seconds before replacing the phone in its cradle. "She'll be right up. Have a seat in the waiting area if you like."

"I'd rather stand, thanks. If I'm going to be on my feet all day, I'd better get used to it now."

"You got the job?"

"Yes, I did."

"Yay." Winter clapped her hands like a delighted child.

The diamond ring on the third finger of Winter's left hand was so bright Destiny squinted from the glare. The rock had to be worth at least five Gs. How many hours of legitimate work would she have to put in to buy someone a ring like that? A year? Two? She could earn the scratch in a fraction of time on the street, but she doubted the resulting purchase would provide the same sense of satisfaction.

She had been living the fast life since she was seventeen, when her parents had forced her to find her own way. Lately, though, she had started to question the direction she had chosen. She was tired of staying one step ahead of, or more often, behind the law. She had never been tempted to walk the straight and narrow, but meeting Rashida Ivey made her want to put her life of crime behind her.

No matter how this job turned out, this was her last con. Not for a while. Not until the money ran out and she needed an infusion of cash. Forever. After this, she was done.

"Welcome to the family," Winter said. "You're going to love it here. It's a lot of hard work, but a lot of fun, too."

"I can't wait to get started."

"That's exactly what I want to hear."

Destiny turned to find Jackie Williams standing behind her. Jackie's smile revealed a slight gap between her front teeth that made her look like Esther Rolle, the late actress who had played everyone's favorite ghetto mama on *Good Times*. Destiny couldn't look at Jackie without thinking, "There goes Florida Evans." If she wasn't careful, she might bust out a Jimmie Walker-style "Dy-no-mite!" in the middle of their conversation.

"We have a great deal to go over today," Jackie said. "If you'll come with me, we can get started."

Destiny followed her downstairs to the same conference room where they had conducted her interview. The room, with its long cherry wood table surrounded by twelve leather-bound chairs, wasn't nearly as intimidating the second time around as it had been the first.

They spent a good two hours completing more forms than Destiny could count. Insurance forms, benefits forms, assorted policies, and the infamous employee contract.

"By signing this," Jackie said, "you attest you will not have intimate relations with any of your co-workers. If you violate the contract, you and your fellow employee will be subject to immediate termination."

Jackie seemed to hesitate before she slid the contract across the table. As she signed the form, Destiny wondered if Rashida had told her about what popped off between them last night. She doubted it. Rashida didn't seem like the type to put her business in the streets.

"And last but not least, the Internet policy. By signing this, you attest you will limit your online activity to professional use only. Any websites you access must be for a valid, business-related purpose. In other words, don't watch porn on company time."

"People actually do that?" Destiny asked when what she meant to say was, "Who had balls big enough to think he could get away with something that stupid?"

Jackie cocked one artfully plucked eyebrow. "You'd be surprised." She lowered her voice to a conspiratorial whisper. "You didn't hear this from me, but one of our former corporate lenders had all sorts of free porn sites saved in his favorites. And one of the branch managers saved naked pictures of his wife on his desktop. The IT guys used to race each other to his office whenever he had a problem with his computer."

"Are the pictures still there?"

"No. Both he and the file are long gone. I saw to the removal personally. If you haven't guessed, this place is as dysfunctional as any other. But you've already signed your life away, so it's too late to back out now. Do you have any questions about any of the forms?"

"No, they seem pretty straightforward."

"Good." Jackie sorted the pile of papers into a neat stack and reached for another set. "The FBI recently released its latest batch of crime statistics."

Destiny sifted through a sheaf of graphs, pie charts, and spreadsheets.

"As you can tell from the charts, there were over a thousand bank robberies last year and ninety percent were in commercial banks like ours," Jackie said. "A little more than half of the robberies took place at the teller window after the thief presented a demand note or made an oral request for cash. The culprits were overwhelmingly male. Women accounted for less than ten percent of the robberies. Weapons were used or threatened in over half of the crimes."

"I'm not currently certified to carry a gun. Would you like me to get recertified?"

"I'll leave that up to you. We've been fortunate at Low Country Savings so far. We've never been robbed, knock wood. It isn't a requirement that you own a gun, and your predecessor never carried, but if you'd feel safer armed, by all means, make it happen."

Destiny didn't think she'd need a weapon. If everything went according to plan, she and her crew would get in and get out without having to worry about hostages or witnesses.

She read the stats for herself. Most of the robberies had taken place on Fridays between nine and eleven a.m. or between three and six p.m. Branch offices in commercial districts were the most common targets, due in large part to easy access to and escape from the scenes of the crime. By targeting Low Country Savings' headquarters, she and Harry were bucking all the trends. She hoped one trend, at least, would continue to hold true. According to the report, robbers got away with their loot nearly ninety percent of the time. Additionally, law enforcement reported a full or partial recovery rate of a scant twenty-three percent. The odds were definitely in her favor.

"It's almost eleven." Jackie rose from her chair. Destiny followed suit. "I'll take you on a tour of the building and we can grab some lunch. After we eat, we'll get you outfitted for a uniform. Sound good?"

"It sounds wonderful. Thank you again for giving me this opportunity."

"Don't thank me. You earned your chance." Jackie headed to the elevator. "I almost forgot," she said, pressing the Up button. "I need you to make an appointment with human resources to get your fingerprints taken."

Destiny's heart fell to her feet. Despite the cool, climate-controlled temperatures, she felt beads of sweat form around the edges of her hairline. "Why do you need my fingerprints?"

"It's standard procedure for all employees. We perform an initial background check during the interview process and a more thorough one after someone has been hired."

Destiny's mind raced as she and Jackie rode the elevator to the main floor. If someone in HR ran her fingerprints, she'd be exposed as soon as the results came in. This was one test even Techno couldn't rig. She was good, but she wasn't that good.

Destiny needed to stall. If she could conveniently forget to call HR or schedule the appointment for a couple weeks from now, she might be okay. She could do what she needed to do and get the fuck out of Dodge before anyone was the wiser. Oh, who was she kidding? As thorough as she seemed to be, Jackie would probably insist she get the task done before the end of the day and she'd be out on her ear and on her way to jail by nightfall.

This is why I don't work with amateurs.

Harry had conveniently failed to mention the secondary background check. If she didn't find a way around it, they'd both be screwed. Because Destiny would be damned if she'd be the only one going down for this fuckup.

The elevator doors opened. Harry, Rashida, and some flashily dressed guy Destiny had never seen before were waiting to come inside. Jackie introduced her to Rashida, Harry, and Mr. Best Dressed. Everyone responded with the right amount of professional courtesy. Almost. Daniel, the guy in the expensive suit, tried to get under her skin about replacing the beloved old codger Pit Bull had tangled with. Destiny didn't let him walk all over her, but she didn't make a big deal out of it, either. The rules here were the same as they were in jail. Keep your head down, keep your nose clean, and don't make any enemies on the first day.

She smiled in Rashida's direction, but her smile wasn't returned. The slight hurt much more than she expected it to.

Their encounter in Rashida's car had gone even better than she had anticipated. She hadn't been nearly as excited as Rashida, but that wasn't anything unusual. She never completely got into the act when she was working. Except with Rashida, it hadn't felt like work. In Rashida's apartment, Rashida had come close to accomplishing what no other mark ever had—making her lose control. She hoped the lapse was a one-time thing. If not, she was in even more trouble than she thought. She couldn't afford to develop feelings for someone in her sights. That would make her just as much of a sucker as the woman being conned.

She and Jackie invited Rashida to lunch, but Rashida said she was about to head into a meeting. Harry had mentioned something about trying to broker a deal with a mortgage company in South Carolina. Since it didn't directly affect her plans, Destiny had only been half paying attention.

"Change of plans," Jackie said after Rashida and her cohorts disappeared inside the elevator. "I'll show you around the building after we have lunch. Give me five minutes to grab my purse, visit the ladies' room, and put these forms in the interoffice mail."

"Okay, I'll meet you out front." Destiny used the respite to make a phone call. "Can you talk?" she asked when Harry picked up.

"I think you know full well I can't. Make it quick. My meeting's about to start."

"I need to see you tonight."

Destiny heard the background noise diminish as Harry undoubtedly moved away from the rest of the group to avoid being overheard. "I thought you didn't want to risk our being seen together."

"I changed my mind. We need to talk. Can you meet me tonight at seven?"

"I'll be there with bells on. Panties, I hope, are optional."

Destiny hung up when she saw Jackie approach. She intentionally peppered her new boss with so many questions during lunch and afterwards that the subject of having her fingerprints taken didn't arise. Shortly after five, she bade Jackie good-bye and headed to a pawn shop on Broughton Street, where she dropped two hundred dollars on a secondhand video camera not much bigger than a deck of playing cards.

In the house on 37th Street, she made a brief recording and tested the camera's playback before she searched for a place to hide her new purchase. Harry would probably try to move their meeting from the living room to the bedroom, but Destiny was determined to keep her mind on business, not the boudoir. Harry's half-assed scheme was starting to circle the drain. Destiny intended to try to talk her into pulling the plug, but if Harry insisted on pushing forward, she needed an insurance policy to wrap herself in. She needed to negate Harry's advantage and level the playing field.

She hid the camera in plain sight, tucking it between a pile of books stacked on top of the TV. Her eyes were immediately drawn to the small recording device and its all-seeing lens, but she doubted Harry would be able to detect its presence because she wouldn't be looking for it. She placed a piece of duct tape over the red power indicator to add additional camouflage.

Harry rang the bell at seven fifteen. Destiny pressed *Record* on the camera before she headed to the door. Harry hustled inside as if she had someone on her tail. "I knew there was a reason I don't come to this neighborhood," she said with an overly dramatic shudder.

"Can I get you something to drink?"

"Yes, you may." Harry corrected Destiny's grammatical error with the fervor of an especially tough English teacher. "I'll have a glass of wine if you have it, beer if you don't."

"Is chardonnay okay?"

"You know what I like."

Harry trailed a finger down Destiny's arm. Destiny's skin crawled at her touch. The more time she spent around Harry, the less she liked her. Or did Harry simply pale in comparison to Rashida? Harry was cold and calculating, Rashida warm and openhearted. For Destiny, the choice was clear. She pointed to the couch.

"Take a load off. I'll be right back."

In the kitchen, she poured two glasses of wine and tried to organize her plan of attack. First and foremost, she needed to keep her cool. If she played this right, she'd have the upper hand instead of being pinned under Harry's thumb. What would happen if Harry discovered the camera? Nothing. Harry couldn't go to the police without implicating herself. She wouldn't last a day in jail. Destiny could pull a long stretch without breathing hard, but she'd seen the inside of enough cells to last a lifetime and didn't plan on seeing any more.

She had made up her mind. She was going to play it straight from now on. She never thought she'd be one of those clock punchers who lived paycheck to paycheck, but she was tired of looking over her shoulder to see who might be trying to stab her in the back. The life she used to lead was over. All she had left to do was tackle the impossible task of getting Harry to see things her way.

She carried the glasses of wine to the living room and handed one to Harry, who took a sip and gave her a small nod of approval. She dutifully took a seat after Harry patted the spot next to her on the couch.

"I like what you've done with the place," Harry said. "It's a far cry from the dump I repossessed a few months ago."

Destiny looked around at the flea market finds and import store purchases she had amassed over the previous two weeks. The collection produced a funky but eclectic vibe she was proud to call her own.

"How's the view from the bedroom?" Harry placed her hand on Destiny's knee and slowly slid it up her leg. "Have you missed me as much as I've missed you? Based on the pictures you sent, I'd say no. Nice job, by the way. I had no idea Rashida was so photogenic." She moved closer. "I'd like to re-create the scenes from the pictures. Without the camera, of course."

Keeping her eyes from straying to the video camera a few feet away, Destiny grabbed Harry's hand before it could dive bomb toward her crotch. "That isn't why I invited you here."

"Too bad. What did you want to talk about?"

"Jackie Williams wants to take my fingerprints."

"Why?" Harry looked genuinely stunned, a sure sign she hadn't anticipated the unexpected complication.

"She says it's standard procedure for all Low Country Savings employees."

"Since when?" Harry tried to play off her obvious unease. "I guess I should pay closer attention during employee meetings."

"This is no joking matter, Harry. This shit is serious."

"You don't see me laughing, do you? I'll take care of Jackie. You stay focused on Rashida." Scowling, Harry patted the air with her hand as if she was trying to tell Destiny to keep her cool when she was the one who had obviously lost hers. "Someone as skilled as you are shouldn't have too much trouble in that regard."

Destiny tried to combat the jealousy she thought she heard in Harry's voice. "I was doing my job. The one *you* hired me to do."

Harry smirked. "I'm so glad you enjoy your work."

Destiny didn't know how much footage the tiny digital camera could hold. She needed to get to the point before the storage disk ran out of memory. "I've been having second thoughts. Your plan is a good one, but I don't think it's such a good idea to hit the bank. The heat's on right now. We need to lay low for a while or call the whole thing off."

"We'll never have a better opportunity than the one we're being afforded. St. Patrick's Day offers the perfect cover. The branch will be closed so we'll have the place to ourselves. We can blend in with the crowd during our getaway. As for witnesses, forget it. Everyone will be too drunk to remember their own names, let alone be competent enough to provide accurate descriptions of five people they've never seen before. The security company will call after I disable the alarms, but I'll come up with an excuse to keep them from sending the police to check on the building. No one will discover the money's missing until Monday morning, which will give us a three-day head start. By the time someone realizes what we've done, I'll be long gone."

"You mean *we*, don't you? *We'll* be long gone."

"Of course." Harry's smile looked as artificial as her hair color. "You didn't think I'd leave you behind, did you?"

Destiny wouldn't put it past her. "You're betraying your own parents. Why should I be any different?"

Harry's eyes flashed. "You accept me for who I am. They don't. Which is why I don't understand their eagerness to anoint Rashida Ivey as the chosen one. How could they pass over their own flesh and blood for someone outside the family? They barely talk to me, but they can't stop raving about her. We both like pussy. What makes her so much better in their eyes?"

"She doesn't hide who she is. You do."

"I know who I am, but it's no one's business who I like to fuck besides me and the person I'm fucking." Harry looked at her hard.

"All this talk about changing the plan has me concerned. You're not getting cold feet, are you? I can count on you, can't I?"

The steeliness in Harry's voice made Destiny's blood run cold. For the first time, she saw the person behind the mask. The sight shook her to her core. She held up her hands in mock surrender.

"I'm on your side, remember? I'm just trying to make sure nothing goes wrong."

"If you continue to do exactly what I tell you to do, everything will be fine. If you don't, I'll be forced to do some things I don't want to do."

"Such as?"

"Let's see if I remember this correctly." Harry tapped a finger against her lips as if she was trying to jog her memory. "As a condition of your early release from prison on your most recent charge, you were supposed to serve six months of parole. During that time, you were not allowed to leave the state of Florida or associate with known criminals. Traveling to Savannah and reaching out to the members of your old team constitutes not one but two parole violations. Enough to send you back to jail for quite some time. If you give me reason to question your dedication to me or the plans we've made, I'll be forced to give your parole officer a call and let him know where he can locate you. Then I'll find someone else to take your place. On this team and in my bed. Do we understand each other?"

"Perfectly."

With or without her, Low Country Savings was going to be robbed on Friday. With her, Rashida might have a chance of coming out relatively unscathed. Without her, anything might happen.

Looks like I might have to put off retirement for a few more days.

Harry patted her cheek as if she were scratching a puppy between the ears. "As much as I'd love to stay, I'm afraid I have to leave you. Jared and I are having some people over."

Destiny flashed back to the night she'd met Jared. When she and one of the studs she knew zeroed in on him and Harry in a club in South Beach. She and Ahmad had followed them back to their hotel. Judging from the sounds drifting from the adjoining room, Ahmad had shown Jared the time of his life. She was still unclear on his role in the break-in—if he had one—but she wasn't in position to ask questions. She walked Harry to the door.

"If this goes wrong, don't forget all this was your idea."

Harry smiled. "When it goes right, don't forget you'll have me to thank."

Destiny watched Harry walk to her car. After the Hummer pulled away from the curb, she retrieved the camera from its hiding place and pressed *Play*. Both the images and sound were crystal clear. She had a perfect recording of Harry conspiring to commit a felony. But was it enough? Harry was so determined to punish her parents and embarrass Rashida, Destiny doubted anything could stop her from trying. Not even the evidence on the tape.

Defeated, Destiny stashed the camera in the small fireproof safe she'd hidden in the back of her closet. She kept the key to the safe on a chain she wore around her neck. The safe held the ticket to her future.

She counted the growing stack of bills. She'd tucked away almost fifteen grand. Not enough to live on, but more than enough to begin life anew. She could disappear and start fresh. But she couldn't leave. Not like this.

Sitting on the floor of a house she didn't own, pining for a life she couldn't have, she felt trapped between a woman she was starting to fear and one she was starting to care for. Greed had gotten her into this mess, but only one thing could get her out of it. Love.

She put the money away, pulled her cell phone out of her pocket, and called Rashida. Not because it was part of the con but because she wanted to hear her voice. Talking with her—being with her—was the only part of this whole thing that felt real, even though it was anything but.

Destiny leaned her head against the closet door. She imagined Rashida in her business suit and heels, poring over reports or planning a hostile takeover like Donald Trump with better hair. Destiny liked seeing a sister so strong and in charge. She didn't want to see her taken down. She wanted to see how far she could go. And she wanted to take the journey with her.

"Rashida Ivey."

Destiny felt herself break into a goofy grin like a lovesick schoolgirl. "You don't have to sound so professional. Work is over for the day."

"How may I help you?"

Rashida was determined to play by the rules. Destiny wished she could make her see the rules didn't matter. With Rashida's book smarts and her street smarts, they could be so good together if given a chance. She had to make her see that—if only for a few days.

"Brr. Is it chilly in here or is it just me?"

"I'm sorry," Rashida said with a tired sigh. "Long day at the office. How was your first day?"

Destiny smiled at the appreciable thaw. "I signed so many forms I think I have writer's cramp. If you're not busy, maybe you could rub out the kinks."

"That's an appetizing idea, but it and others like it are off the table." Rashida's voice grew frosty again. "We're co-workers now."

"Which means?" She knew perfectly well what it meant, but she wanted to hear Rashida say it.

"What happened between us was a...one-time thing." Rashida fell just short of calling it a mistake.

"What if I said once wasn't enough?"

"I'd be flattered, but I wouldn't change my mind."

"You will."

"You sound pretty sure of yourself."

"There are only a few things I'm sure of. One of them is one night of feeling you underneath me is not enough."

She heard Rashida's breath catch. Was she replaying their night together, scenes that ran through her own head in an endless loop?

"Contract or no contract, I want to be with you, Rashida, and I know you feel the same way. You've already said as much. Now tell me. When can I see you again?"

"No, Destiny. Stop." Rashida's voice was firm as she drew a line in the sand. A line she refused to cross no matter how hard

Destiny pushed. “Yes, I wish things could be different. I’d be lying if I said I didn’t. I accepted your decision to take the job. I need you to accept mine.”

“Which one? Your decision to sleep with me or your decision to ignore how I made you feel? Our connection wasn’t just physical, was it? That night meant something to you. If it didn’t, you wouldn’t find it so hard to be in the same room with me.”

Rashida’s silence gave Destiny hope her argument had proved convincing.

“Destiny, I can’t keep doing this with you. I *won’t* keep doing this with you. If there’s nothing else I can help you with, I will see you at work. And, please, don’t call me again. Good night.”

Rashida hung up before Destiny could protest. Rashida’s reasons for saying no were clear-cut. Destiny’s reasons for wanting her to say yes were not quite as transparent.

Rashida made her want things she had never dared dream. She wanted a life far different from her own. She wanted a life free of deception. She wanted a life with Rashida. She wanted to see her smile and make her laugh. She wanted to protect her from harm and kiss away the hurt if she found it anyway. She wanted to hear her say, “I love you,” and feel free to say it in return.

She knew she couldn’t have any of those things. Once Rashida discovered who she really was and what she had been hired to do, she’d never forgive her, let alone love her.

Still, her foolish heart dared dream. Would Rashida’s heart, once exposed to the truth, dare to listen?

Chapter Seventeen

Friday, March 10
8:45 p.m.
Savannah, GA

Club One tonight at nine. Our mutual friend will be there. Get her back on board.

Destiny listened to Harry's voice mail message with a mixture of excitement and trepidation. She had been trying to get Rashida back on board for three days to no avail. Harry's carefully laid plans were in increasing jeopardy. Fuck the plans. Destiny wanted Rashida in her life, plain and simple. Each time Rashida rebuffed one of her advances, the rejection bruised her ego and dented her heart. A busted ego she could take. A tender heart was something new.

She had never cared what people thought of her before. Why was she starting to care now? Take yesterday, for example. She had seen Tony perform his attempted sleight of hand with the money from the vault but hadn't thought he'd be dumb enough to think he could actually get away with it. When she had concocted the story that directed Rashida where to look, she had tried to convince herself she was protecting her investment. Trying to stop someone from taking money out of her pocket. But the appreciative look and sincere thanks Rashida had given her after the attempted crime was solved were even better than the payoff she stood to receive next week. The praise had made her feel like part of a team. Like she and

Rashida were on the same side. Like her assumed identity had taken on a life of its own. Like she had proven herself worthy of respect.

"You proved you could be trusted," she said, addressing her image in the bathroom mirror. "How will she react when you show you can't?"

During their celebratory dinner at a barbecue restaurant, Rashida had revealed facets of her personality Destiny had been previously unaware of. Her passion for Asian food seemed to denote a love affair with the culture itself, not just a fondness for the cuisine. Destiny could picture Rashida equally at home on the streets of Beijing or Tokyo as she was on the thoroughfares of Savannah. She could imagine her looking just as good rocking a sleeveless Mandarin collar dress as she did one of her power suits. Destiny wanted to peel her out of both. Lay her down and make love to her with no ulterior motives in mind. To come together as one and remain that way for as long as Rashida would have her.

She was finding it increasingly difficult to divorce herself from her feelings. To think of Rashida as a pawn instead of a person. Tonight, she needed to put Destiny on the shelf and let DaShawn come out to play.

She took a shower and dressed to go out. Levi's, a form-fitting white Henley, and a pair of battered brown Doc Martens. She tied the outfit together with a wide leather belt she carefully threaded through the loops of her low-slung jeans. When she looked in the mirror again, she felt like quoting one of Will Smith's famous one-liners from *Men in Black.* "I make this look good."

She drove to Jefferson Street, paid for one of the few remaining spots in the parking lot, and walked toward the nightclub with a blue awning above the entrance. She paid the entry fee and popped for a ticket to the drag show. Even if Rashida didn't plan on staying for the entertainment, she certainly did. Tonight wasn't about chasing Rashida. It was about letting her go.

She bought a beer from the bar and made a slow circuit of the main floor. The music was loud, throbbing with an insistent beat. She bobbed her head to the rhythm. Several women attracted her attention. She made eye contact with them but didn't try to strike up a conversation. She wasn't on the prowl for company. Between Harry and Rashida, she already had more than she could handle. She headed downstairs before any of her prospective suitors could ask her to dance.

She bypassed the finger foods and turned to the pool tables, all three of which were occupied. She focused on the one that seemed to be attracting the most attention. Two muscle-bound Army Rangers were flexing and flirting over a game of eight ball while three-quarters of the men and a much smaller percentage of the women drooled into their drinks.

The Ranger in the Abercrombie and Fitch T-shirt, leather flip flops, and loose-fitting designer jeans had stripes. His identically dressed companion with the barbed wire tattoo circling his bulging left bicep had solids.

Destiny placed a quarter on a corner of the table, reserving the right to play the winner. The Ranger with the ink on his arm was clearly leading. If he sank three more balls, including the eight, the game was his. Five striped balls littered the felt-topped table.

"Are you sure your stick's big enough to play me?" the tattooed Ranger asked with a dimpled grin.

"I'd put mine up against yours any day." She took a long sip of her beer. "I haven't had any complaints yet."

"You go, girl."

He sank the six ball in a corner pocket and held up his hand for a high five. She slapped her palm against his and leaned against the brightly painted concrete wall. She couldn't remember the last time she'd gone out with no goal in mind except having fun. Tonight almost qualified. Almost. Because as soon as Rashida walked into the room, she could practically hear Harry urging her to get back on task.

Rashida looked slightly out of breath. The way she drank greedily from the bottle of water in her hand, she must have hit the dance floor pretty hard. Her work clothes had been replaced by a bronze silk shirt and a pair of black slacks. Her black stack-heeled ankle boots looked comfortable enough to cut a rug in but sturdy enough to prevent having her toes crushed by other dancers' misplaced feet.

Destiny waited for Rashida to meet her eye. When Rashida finally looked her way, she went against her natural instincts. Instead of walking over to say hello, she gave Rashida a wide berth. She raised her bottle of beer in greeting but stayed put. Rashida looked initially relieved. Then her expression slowly changed to surprise followed by confusion. By the time Harry appeared with her arm draped across the shoulders of a hot blonde, Rashida looked completely out of sorts.

Destiny wanted to back Rashida into a darkened corner and kiss her breathless. She wanted to take her upstairs, lead her to the dance floor, and move with her to the music. She wanted to sweep her into her arms, press her lips against her ear, and whisper an invitation to leave. She somehow willed her feet not to move.

Feigning nonchalance, she turned back to the Rangers. She asked them a few questions about military life but barely listened to the answers. Her attention, if not her gaze, was focused on Rashida.

Harry and the blonde were leaving. Rashida trailed them out of the room. Before she disappeared from view, Rashida turned and looked over her shoulder. Just once and only for a few seconds, but long enough for Destiny to see the regret etched on her face.

I've got her.

Instead of lifting her spirits, the thought left her utterly depressed.

I've got her. Now what do I do with her?

CHAPTER EIGHTEEN

Saturday, March 11
12:15 p.m.
Savannah, GA

Destiny waited until the next morning to press her advantage. After Harry pried herself away from her new conquest long enough to give her the name of Rashida's favorite restaurant, Destiny went there and asked the staff to prepare Rashida's favorite meal—the one she ordered so often everyone in the place referred to it as her usual. The way the cashier went on and on about "Miss Rashida," Destiny half-expected to see the order listed under her name on the menu. Right between the General Tso's chicken and something called the Happy Family.

She left her piece of shit Honda parked in front of the house on 37th Street and took a pedicab to Rashida's apartment. The unusual mode of transportation reminded her of a rickshaw, which felt fitting considering the bag of Chinese and Japanese food in her lap.

The weather was pleasant enough for shorts and a T-shirt. The spring sun warmed her arms and legs. The birds' cheerful songs were in stark contrast to the mournful dirge playing in her heart. She climbed out of the pedicab after the driver lurched to a stop. She was about to be with Rashida again. She had been looking forward to this moment for days. Until the moment finally drew near. Seeing Harry's car in the parking lot reminded her she wasn't in Savannah of her own free will. She was here because she had been hired to do a job. A job that no longer held the same appeal as when she had agreed to take it on.

How could she possibly go through with the plan when she was developing feelings for the woman whose life and reputation she was supposed to ruin? Rashida was supposed to be just another victim. Destiny hadn't expected to like her. Maybe even love her. She hesitated outside Rashida's door. How was she supposed to do what was right when all she knew how to do was wrong?

She slowly raised her arm and rang the bell. While she waited for Rashida to answer, she tried to determine how to perform the scene to follow. Should she go back to playing games or keep it real? The time for playing games was over.

Rashida opened the door as if she expected to see Harry standing on the other side. Her smile faltered slightly when she saw Destiny there instead.

Destiny wondered about the personal history between Rashida and Harry. Was there something in their shared past both women had conveniently forgotten to mention? If so, it could explain the ax Harry was grinding. But what was Rashida's angle? She didn't seem like the type to hold grudges, and she spoke about Harry as if they were just acquaintances, but what if they had once been more than friends? Imagining them as lovers brought Destiny's possessive instincts to the fore. She couldn't stand the idea of anyone touching Rashida, but especially not Harry. Harry had it all. A high-paying job, a big house, and a fancy car. Did she have to have Rashida, too?

Not if I can help it.

Destiny held up the bag of food. "I'm here for my lesson." Displaying more confidence than she felt, she pulled a set of chopsticks out of her back pocket. "Can you teach me how to use these?"

Would Rashida toss her out or let her stay? Her arm bar across the door gave Destiny her answer, so Destiny decided to ask a different question.

"The kitchen's that way, right?"

In the kitchen, she unpacked the bag of food and spread the containers on the counter as if Rashida had welcomed her in instead of giving her the cold shoulder.

"Did you have a good time last night? You left before I had a chance to say hi or to tell you how hot you looked in that outfit you were wearing."

Rashida's answer, although vague, made it clear she wished Destiny had bridged the distance between them instead of maintaining it. "You were busy meeting the members of your fan club."

Rashida drew doodles in the condensation on her can of soda. She was thinking much too hard. Why couldn't she just give in? Destiny led Rashida to the dining room, where they took their seats at the sturdy mahogany table.

"You don't make it easy to say no, do you?" Rashida asked.

"Why say no when yes works so much better?"

Destiny was in her element. Flirting with Rashida was easy. It was everything else that was hard. Lying about her past. Hiding who she really was. She wanted to come clean. But how could she? Rashida was attracted to Destiny not DaShawn. She wanted the character not the actress playing the part.

Destiny looked around the room. The decorations were simple and understated, dominated by a pair of colorful oil paintings that hung side by side on the far wall. In one, an elderly African-American woman shelled butter beans on the front porch of a whitewashed house. In the other, several children cavorted in the spray of an open fire hydrant on a stifling summer day.

"Do you like those?" Rashida asked.

Destiny nodded. She didn't have the words to describe the effect the paintings had on her. They made her feel as though she had found a part of herself she had once considered lost. Rashida made her feel the same way.

"When we were kids, my brother, sister, and I used to spend every summer at my grandmother's house." Rashida rested her chin on the heel of her hand. Her voice was as dreamy as her posture. "Each year, she'd buy a bushel of purple hull peas and make us shell them. She had so many bags of frozen vegetables in her freezer she could barely close the lid. Half the time, my parents didn't have to go to the store for food. All they had to do was make a list and send me to Grandma's house like I was Little Red Riding Hood. I'm surprised my fingers don't have permanent stains from the shells." She looked at her hands, which were perfectly manicured and so smooth they looked like they hadn't seen a hard day of work. "Those paintings take me back to a time that was simple and unhurried. I miss those days."

Destiny wanted to relive them with her.

"Which one speaks to you?"

"That one." Destiny pointed to the painting of the children playing with the fire hydrant. "I was one of those kids. I can still remember the feel of the cold water rushing between my toes as I stood on the sizzling pavement. I can hear the laughter of my friends, the music thumping from cars riding by, and the curses of the cops dispatched to the scene." She took a sip of her beer. "I had forgotten how much fun that used to be."

"Isn't tampering with a fire hydrant a felony?"

"Maybe, but who's counting?"

Destiny's good mood soured at the unexpected reminder of her criminal past.

"What did you want to be when you grew up?"

Destiny told Rashida about her one-time dream of becoming a track star. Then she told her something she had never confided in anyone. "I want to run my own business one day."

Instead of laughing at her dream, Rashida offered ways to make it come true.

"If you get a business plan together, you could apply for a small business loan. I know several lenders who might be interested in backing a venture like yours. When you're ready, I could give one of them a call."

Destiny didn't know how to react to such a generous offer. No one else had ever expressed such confidence in her abilities. Rashida's show of faith prompted a confession, one even closer to her heart.

"I'd love to open a homeless shelter so a young girl or boy who's in my old situation could have a place to lay their head at night without worrying about someone trying to chop it off." She heard herself drift into the language of the streets, the place that had been her home away from home for far too long.

"The people who tried to hold you back aren't in your life now," Rashida said. "Your ideas aren't pipe dreams. They're goals. You can achieve them if you try."

Hearing Rashida say nice things about her made Destiny want to cry. "How do you know I won't prove you wrong?"

Once again, Rashida was unfailingly honest. "I don't."

Destiny had had enough. She couldn't play this game for another minute. "I don't mean to make you uncomfortable. Perhaps I should go."

She tried to leave, but Rashida stopped her before she could. Destiny looked at her, wanting to believe what was happening was genuine.

"I don't want to miss out on being with you because you don't match my preconceived idea of what I'm looking for in a partner," Rashida said. "It doesn't matter how much money you have or what kind of car you drive. You're a good person with a good heart. That's all that matters."

For a second, Destiny allowed herself to imagine Rashida had shared the sentiment with her instead of the person she was pretending to be.

In the kitchen, Rashida pulled the salads out of the refrigerator and poured ginger dressing on top. When she splashed some of the dressing on her finger, Destiny slid the digit into her mouth and licked it clean.

Rashida pulled her hand away. The muscles in her jaw crawled beneath her skin. Her eyes flashed with what looked like anger. Destiny feared she had gone too far. Then Rashida's cloudy expression cleared. She took a step forward and captured Destiny first with her eyes then her lips. Destiny's body responded favorably to the unaccustomed shift in power. She was used to being in control, but Rashida had effortlessly wrested it away. Destiny wasn't sure she wanted it back.

"Whoa. Time out," she said when she came up for air. "If you keep that up, we won't make it to the main course."

"Good point."

They returned to the living room. Rashida tried to show her how to eat with chopsticks, but Destiny couldn't manage the feat.

"Here. Let me help," Rashida said with the patience of someone used to showing others how things were done. She put her hand over Destiny's and guided her fingers into the correct position. "Like this."

"I'm going to drop it," Destiny said when the clump of lettuce precariously clutched between her chopsticks began to slip from her clutches.

Her fear and uncertainty were real, but neither emotion was brought about by her inability to grasp her food between two thin pieces of bamboo. Both were byproducts of the other lesson Rashida was teaching her—how to fall in love.

Rashida loosened her grip, letting Destiny take control. "No, you aren't."

The lettuce slipped even further. Destiny drew it into her mouth a fraction of a second before it fell free. Rashida beamed with pride in Destiny's accomplishment, not her own. If she weren't a banker, she'd make a wonderful teacher. An excellent mother.

For a brief, absurd moment, Destiny pictured the two of them raising a family. Like that could ever happen. You couldn't pay her to change dirty diapers. But why did the idea of cradling a little girl with a smile like hers and eyes like Rashida's sound so good?

Destiny caressed Rashida's cheek. "Are we really going to do this?"

Rashida didn't hesitate. "Yes, we are."

"How?"

Rashida leaned into her. "We'll figure it out."

"Come with me."

"Where?"

"You'll see."

Destiny pulled Rashida into the living room. She chose a CD from the vast music collection and slipped it into the player. Rashida moved into her arms as if she belonged there. Destiny hoped she'd never leave. When the doorbell rang, she felt the real world intrude on her fantasy.

“Am I interrupting something?” Harry walked into the apartment like she owned the place. A small smile crossed her face when she saw Destiny and took in the scene. She turned back to Rashida. “Romantic music. A table set for two. Are you two together?”

“I was telling Miss Ivey about an idea I had.” Destiny reluctantly turned off the music. “I brought some food by hoping I could bribe her into helping me draft a business plan.”

Harry laughed as if Destiny had made some kind of joke

“I don’t know if we can trust her,” Destiny said after Harry left.

Rashida kissed her forehead. “We don’t have any choice.”

“We always have a choice. And I choose you.”

She took Rashida’s hand and led her to the bedroom, where she made love to her with infinite slowness. She wanted to make sure all of Rashida’s needs were met. Every desire fulfilled.

“Any regrets?” she asked when they were done.

Rashida flashed a lazy smile. “You asked me that the first time, too.”

The first time, Rashida had said the only thing she regretted was waiting so long to give in to desire.

Destiny spooned her body around Rashida’s. “Has your answer changed?”

Rashida guided Destiny’s hand to her warm, wet center. “What do you think?”

Destiny drew her fingers across Rashida’s opening, eliciting a moan. “I think I want you.”

“Show me.”

The words were more of a plea than a command. Destiny pulled Rashida tight against her. She wanted to feel her when she let go. She wanted to ride the wave with her, which, until this point, she had not allowed herself to do. Her pride kept getting in the way. She wanted to hear Rashida call out for her. She wanted Rashida to come for her. Each time she didn’t—each time Rashida climaxed with the wrong name dripping from her lips doused the flames of Destiny’s libido. But each time Rashida looked at her, the fire built up again.

Destiny sighed when Rashida shuddered and cried out. Rashida’s body was loose, her limbs slack with pleasure. Destiny kissed the nape of her neck. "Why can't every day be like this?" she wondered out loud.

Rashida turned to face her. "You'd be bored with me in no time."

"Not a chance."

Destiny ran a finger over the planes of Rashida's face, committing every inch to memory. She could feel their time together growing shorter. In a few days, Rashida would most likely be out of her life forever. If she couldn't see Rashida in person, at least she could carry her image in her heart.

"You're incredible."

Rashida's cheeks warmed. She looked away to hide her embarrassment, but Destiny saw through her defenses.

"Hasn't anyone ever told you that?"

"During but not after."

Destiny didn't return Rashida's smile. She wanted to give the moment the seriousness it deserved.

"I've never met anyone like you," Destiny said. "You're the most amazing woman I've ever had in my life. I don't want to lose you."

"What makes you think you will?"

"Past experience. Whenever I get something I've yearned for, I've never been able to enjoy it for long."

Rashida pulled her into her arms. "I don't plan on going anywhere, so I guess you'd better get used to having me around."

Destiny closed her eyes. For one of the few times in her life, she felt safe and secure. How long would the feeling last?

Chapter Nineteen

Tuesday, March 14
11:00 a.m.
Savannah, Georgia

Destiny watched the armored car park in front of the bank for its normal weekly delivery. Two armed guards climbed out of the back of the reinforced vehicle. The driver remained in his seat. The guard holding the shotgun kept a watchful eye on the street while the one with the pistol on his hip unloaded boxes of coins and plastic-wrapped stacks of bills. Curious passersby slowed but didn't stop, no doubt dissuaded by the guards' obvious firepower.

Megan Connelly, the head teller, met the guards at the door and led them toward the vault. Destiny's mouth watered as the money rolled past her. Over half a million dollars in cold, hard cash. Add in the gold and jewels that were supposed to be stashed in the safe deposit boxes and you were looking at a take of over two million. Harry wanted the gold bars, which were worth a million and a half. Destiny and her crew were supposed to split the rest. Harry's share might be larger, but it wouldn't be as easy to fence. Cash was portable and jewels could be sold at any neighborhood pawn shop without attracting too much of the wrong kind of attention.

Destiny followed the money with her eyes. The payday she had been dreaming about for weeks was so close she could touch it. Rashida was even closer. For the first time since she was a teenager,

Destiny wasn't servicing a woman. She was seeing her. The phrase was ironic considering Rashida had no idea that the woman she was seeing wasn't who she appeared to be. That the woman in her life—in her bed—was nothing but an illusion. Perhaps one day soon Destiny would be able to set things right.

"Have you made an appointment with HR yet?"

Jackie's voice in her ear almost made Destiny jump out of her skin. She had a feeling Jackie didn't completely trust her. She had come around a bit after the incident with the missing cash, but Destiny's slowness to comply with the edict to have her fingerprints taken was eating away at the goodwill she had engendered.

"No. I meant to do it yesterday, but the head teller in Springfield ran out of tens and I had to make an emergency trip up there to restock the vault."

Destiny had taken every precaution, but she had felt like a rolling target the entire way. Even though she had been in uniform, would a cop have believed her story if he pulled her over? Her heart had filled her throat each time another driver looked at her sideways. She would have felt safer carrying the nine millimeter she kept stashed next to her bed, but she couldn't afford to get popped on a gun charge. She had to be a Girl Scout for three more days. Then she would be home free.

"Do me a favor," Jackie said. "You have Friday off and this branch is going to be slammed with customers all day Thursday. Tomorrow, I want you to go to the operations center and get your prints done. Let me know when you're planning on leaving, and I'll get Wynn to come in and cover for you."

"Yes, Mrs. Williams."

Destiny didn't try to make an excuse because she knew it wouldn't do any good. Her time had run out. Jackie had obviously reached the limits of her patience. Harry had said she'd take care of Jackie. Once more, she had fallen down on the job. Destiny knew she would have to solve the problem herself. One way or another, she needed to create a distraction big enough to divert Jackie's attention away from her and onto something new. That was in addition to figuring out what to do about Harry. She was running out of time.

Think, DJ. Think.

Planting something in the ventilation system was too risky. There were cameras everywhere, and she couldn't be certain no one would have an allergic reaction to the chemicals she used.

Then it came to her. The elevator was the key.

There were no cameras inside the elevator car, a security lapse Jackie said she planned to fix but had not yet addressed. If Destiny opened the access panel and crossed the right wires, she could bypass the motor's idle function and cause it to run nonstop. Once the motor overheated, the oil inside would burn. The resulting fumes would be odious but not toxic. The building would have to be evacuated as a precaution and, most likely, need to remain closed to be cleaned, which meant her crew would have all the time in the world to crack the vault on Friday and empty it out. She wouldn't even have to be there.

Her plan was perfect. Everyone could get what they wanted without anyone getting hurt. Harry could have the gold, her crew could have the money, and she could have Rashida. Until Rashida discovered she wasn't as innocent as she seemed.

Who was she fooling? Did she really expect to be able to stick around after the heist went down? Did she expect Rashida to stay with her after she told her who she really was? Was it too late to salvage the situation?

I don't know, but I've got to try.

CHAPTER TWENTY

Wednesday, March 15
9:45 p.m.
Savannah, Georgia

Destiny could tell Rashida was distracted. Their time together was limited to a few hours each night. Tonight, Rashida was filling way too many of those hours with talk about work.

While Rashida obsessed over an offer she had received to become the new CEO of Low Country Savings, Destiny wondered how well her own plans were progressing. How long would it take for the elevator motor to overheat? A few minutes, a few hours, or a few days? Techno had said it would take about twelve to fourteen hours for the oil to reach the optimal temperature, but Destiny half-expected Rashida's cell phone to ring any moment with news that the fire alarm had gone off downtown. She needed the smoke to billow during business hours, not after.

When Destiny finally dragged herself out of her own head, Rashida was still going on and on about the job offer she'd received and all the secret meetings she'd been having both at work and after hours. Destiny didn't want to hear about buyouts or corporate maneuvering. She wanted to feel Rashida's body moving against hers before it was too late. In two more days, she might not experience a night like this again.

"Don't be so hard on yourself," she said, trying to stop Rashida from stressing out over something that was probably part of the shell game Harry was running. Destiny thought Rashida had the goods to run the bank, but was the carrot being dangled in front of her real or imaginary? She didn't want to see the look on Rashida's face if the gig turned out to be as phony as Destiny's work history. "No matter what you decide in this instance, you'll make a great CEO one day."

Rashida's eyes searched hers, seeking confirmation for something that was obvious to everyone except her. "How do you know?"

"Because your heart's in the right place."

Rashida placed her hand over Destiny's heart, which had begun to fill with love for the woman whose fate she held in her hands. "This is crazy." Rashida moved away. "How can I feel so close to you when I barely know anything about you?"

Destiny's heart hammered as a conversation she had dreaded began to take shape. "What don't you know?"

Rashida posed a series of questions. Destiny wanted to stay up all night honestly answering them and any others Rashida might have, but she couldn't share herself. Not yet. She needed to hold herself back for a few more days or everything could blow up in her face. Unfortunately, Rashida stubbornly refused to wait.

"Come for me."

Destiny felt herself grow wet, but she couldn't give Rashida what she wanted. She couldn't let Rashida make love to her under false pretenses. If Rashida wanted to be with her in that way after the truth was revealed, fine. Until then, she would continue to take Rashida over the edge but wouldn't follow her over the precipice.

"I don't need to."

"Are you sure?" Rashida parted Destiny's folds with two fingers. Her touch was electric. Destiny stiffened, jolted by the shock. "You're so wet I ought to put up flood warnings."

When Rashida pinched her swollen clit, Destiny nearly popped her cork.

"Are you sure you don't need to come?" Rashida asked with a teasing smile.

Destiny thought she'd die if she didn't. "Okay," she said, giving in. "Prove me wrong."

Rashida's fingers resumed their explorations. "Do you want fast or slow?"

Destiny should have said, "Neither," but need and desire overwhelmed reason. "I want you." She pulled Rashida closer. Their bodies met as Rashida thrust her fingers inside. Destiny's hips matched their rhythm. "God, that feels good. *You* feel good."

Rashida's mouth met hers. Destiny felt like she was being kissed for the first time. She let her façade fall.

"Who are you?" Rashida asked as Destiny's body convulsed in blessed release.

"I am the woman who loves you."

For Destiny, truer words had never been spoken. As a result, the next two days were going to be the hardest of her life.

CHAPTER TWENTY-ONE

Thursday, March 16
10:20 a.m.
Savannah, Georgia

"Come on. Come on," Destiny said under her breath as she held the burner to her ear.

Harry sounded irritated when she finally picked up. "What is it?"

"Are you sure you want to go through with this?" If Harry gave the right answer, she had time to reverse what she'd done to the elevator and no one would ever know what they had planned to do in a day's time. "I don't think we should—"

"So you are getting cold feet."

"Never. I'm just—"

"Developing a conscience. Take my advice. Don't. It isn't a good look for you. Remember what I said the last time we spoke. Friday happens with or without you. Now I'm asking you for the last time. Are you in or out?"

"I'm in," Destiny said through clenched teeth. "In case you were wondering, Friday starts now."

"What?"

Destiny ended the call, cutting off Harry's squawk of surprise. Then she stepped away from the front door. She could feel the temperature on her side of the lobby beginning to rise, but the oil in the elevator motor had not yet begun to burn. She could, however, smell it heating up. Before she caused a scene, she needed someone else to notice the smell, too.

Winter came out of the break room, where some of the corporate lenders had already begun to gather for their daily lunchtime poker game. Winter had a reheated cinnamon roll in one hand and a cup of coffee in the other. The roll was a leftover from the box of pastries one of the tellers had brought in this morning. The coffee was fresh, courtesy of a customer who loved plying his favorite Low Country Savings employee with gifts. If Destiny didn't know better, she'd swear the guy was planning to rob the place by forging an alliance with someone on the inside. Too bad Harry had beaten him to the punch.

Winter wrinkled her nose as she crossed the lobby.

"What is that ungodly smell?"

"The elevator has B.O. today," Destiny said.

"I'm not surprised. The whole building's haunted. Sometimes, when I'm working late, I swear I can hear voices echoing in the lobby. It sounds like someone's throwing a fabulous party and forgot to invite me. And each morning when I come in, the painting behind my desk is crooked, even though I straighten it every night before I go home."

"Uh huh." Destiny nodded as the first wisps of smoke began to drift out of the elevator. The smell immediately grew exponentially worse. "Don't panic, but I think we need to call someone."

Winter's eyes drifted to the elevator. Her face grew pale. "Is that smoke?"

"Yes."

Winter's mug and saucer slipped from her hands and shattered on the floor. The loud noise of the breaking ceramic dinnerware prompted several heads to whip around. Someone saw the smoke and screamed. One customer made a mad dash to the door, the deposit she had planned to make clutched tightly in her hand.

So much for not panicking.

Destiny's nose burned as fumes quickly filled the lobby. She held her arm over her face to act as a makeshift gas mask. A woman waiting in line in front of Megan's teller window slowly crumpled to the floor. A man in another line soon followed.

Winter, her eyes bugging in shock, stood frozen in place. Destiny squeezed her arm to snap her out of fantasy land. "Winter, call nine one one."

"Right." Winter stepped around the spilled coffee, sprinted to her desk, and picked up the phone while Seaton and Megan tended to the fallen customers.

Destiny placed her hands on the elevator doors. The metal was warm to the touch but not burning hot. She pressed the Down button. When the car arrived and the elevator doors slid open, she locked the doors in the open position so no one could access the elevator. Then she pulled the fire alarm. With the elevator disabled, the people on the third floor and on the basement level would have to use the stairs to exit the building.

"I need everyone out of the building now," she said over the sound of the blaring alarm.

The tellers secured their work stations and followed the customers out the door. Seaton, Winter, and Megan stayed behind. Destiny ran down to the basement. After finding it empty, she headed up to the third floor, where staff members continued to work despite the warning bells.

"Out! Everybody out! This is not a drill!" Ignoring their protests, she hustled them downstairs as quickly as she could.

"What's going on?" Jackie asked as she, the corporate lenders, and the executive staff flooded the lobby.

Destiny loosened her tie to get more air. Out of breath, she pointed to the elevator, which was filled with thick, bluish-gray smoke.

"Crap." Jackie kneeled next to one of the stricken customers. "How's he doing?"

Seaton shrugged. "I'm not a paramedic. He's breathing, but he's not conscious. That's all I know."

"Same here," Megan said. Her voice was raspy, her face beet red.

Jackie placed a hand on Megan's shoulder. "Are *you* okay?"

Megan reached for the inhaler she always kept nearby. “I’ll be fine. It’s Miss Edna I’m worried about.” She patted the hand of the elderly woman sprawled on the floor.

Winter hung up the phone. “The paramedics are on their way. The fire department, too. The police department probably won’t be too far behind.”

Destiny’s mouth went dry. Two people were passed out and Megan might make it three. Though none of the sick looked likely to kick, she didn’t know if they would remain that way for long.

“We’ve got to move them,” she said. “They need fresh air.”

She bent to pick up the frail woman Megan was comforting, but Jackie held her back.

“We can’t take the risk,” Jackie said in a fierce whisper. “If they have neck, back, or head trauma, moving them could make their injuries worse, and we could open ourselves up to potential litigation. I know how you feel, but let’s wait until someone who has more medical training than we do gives the okay.” She released Destiny’s arm and began barking orders. “Seaton, print a notice saying this location is going to be closed until further notice. Then lock the vault. We need to make sure the contents are secured when emergency personnel swarm the lobby.”

“What about the teller drawers?”

Jackie looked at the thick plume of smoke polluting the air. “Put the drawers in the vault and set the timer for the full complement. I hope we’ll be able to reopen by Monday, but I won’t know for sure until the smoke has cleared and the cleaning crew can come in and take a look at things. Either way, we’re done for the day. We’ll worry about balancing on Monday.”

Seaton went to his office, tapped a few keys on his computer, and hit Print. He taped a piece of bank-branded letterhead to the front door and headed to the vault. After the teller drawers were locked away, he set the timer and closed the heavy steel door. Then he spun the circular handle to make sure the vault was secure.

Leaving the vault open would have made it easier to empty it out, but Destiny’s crew would have plenty of time to get the job done. She had yet to meet a safe they couldn’t crack or a vault they couldn't break into, no matter how reinforced the steel or sophisticated the alarm system.

The whine of approaching sirens competed with the fire alarm for noise supremacy. Six firefighters burst through the door first, followed by four EMTs. The paramedics examined the customers, placed oxygen masks over their faces, and wheeled them outside. Destiny looked around at what she had wrought. She hadn't meant for the situation to get so out of hand.

"This is wrong." She held her hands to her head. "This is so wrong."

"I need you to evacuate the building, ma'am," one of the firefighters said while his colleagues went to work on the elevator. "Are you the last one?"

"Yes," Destiny said. "The rest of the building is empty. I checked it myself."

"I'll check behind you to be sure. In the meantime—" He extended his arm toward the door.

Destiny reluctantly joined the others outside. The area looked like a M.A.S.H. unit had set up shop. Two ambulances were parked in the middle of the street. By the sound of it, more were on the way. The customers affected by the fumes were being treated by medical personnel. Megan stood between two of her fellow tellers. Her breathing labored, she didn't look like she could stand on her own. When she began to melt into the ground, one of her companions frantically waved for an EMT.

Destiny's shoulders slumped. She had gotten to know these people. Come to care about them. Now they were suffering because of her. "What have I done?"

Megan—dear, sweet Megan—seemed to be suffering the most. All the customers loved her. She greeted everyone by name as if they were bosom buddies. She blessed them with a smile that looked sincere, not forced. Her fellow employees adored her, too. Each day, she regaled them with funny stories about her husband Ian and their crazy menagerie of pets. Though tiny in stature, Megan was the glue that held the branch together. If something happened to her, Destiny would never forgive herself. When Rashida called, the obvious concern in her voice made Destiny feel even worse.

"Are you okay?"

"I'm fine."

"How bad is it down there?"

"It's…bad." Destiny tried not to cry as she took in the chaotic scene around her.

"Stay safe. I love you."

"I—" Destiny said the words Rashida probably wanted to hear instead of the ones she needed to hear. Not "I'm sorry" but "I love you, too."

Her other phone rang almost immediately. Harry calling to chew her out.

"What's going on down there?"

Destiny summoned all the bravado she possessed as she pressed the burner to her ear. "I've got everything under control."

"If this is your idea of control—"

Destiny cut her off. "Harry, I've got this."

"We need to meet."

"No, we don't. The plan hasn't changed that much."

"What am I supposed to—"

"Think, Harry. Your father's company is in charge of keeping the elevator in working order. Use that to our advantage. Step in before someone calls for service. If my crew can replace your father's maintenance team, we're golden."

Harry blew out a deep breath that sounded like a mixture of relief and admiration. "I knew there was more to you than a pretty face and a silver tongue. Welcome back."

Destiny snapped the phone shut and slipped it into her pocket. "Is Megan going to be okay?" she asked the EMTs as they placed Megan on a stretcher.

"We can't do anything else for her in the field. Her airway's too constricted. We need to get her to the ER as soon as possible."

Rashida showed up after the ambulance door slammed shut. "What's going on?"

Seaton, who had just finished placing a call to Megan's husband to tell him what had happened, repeated the story for Rashida's benefit. She offered to keep an eye on the goings-on at the branch so he could follow Megan to the hospital. Winter and two of the tellers volunteered to tag along.

"I'll look out for the branch," Rashida said. "Go take care of your employees."

"Thanks, Miss Ivey." Seaton waved good-bye as he jogged toward the parking lot.

"I hope she's going to be okay."

Rashida sounded genuinely worried, but she quickly turned to the task at hand. As they crossed the street, she asked for an explanation of what had taken place. Jackie, her cell phone plastered to her ear, asked Destiny to do the honors.

Instead of waiting to gather her thoughts, Destiny made the mistake of diving into the retelling while her emotions were still close to the surface. She started out calmly enough, but as soon as she got to Megan, she began to lose it.

"I only wish I'd acted faster," she said, her voice quavering. "If I had, Megan wouldn't be on her way to the hospital and none of the customers would have been affected."

If she had said something when she'd first spotted the smoke, chances were Megan and the others would be okay. Now, for one or all three, the road to recovery might be long and winding. If they recovered at all.

Rashida rubbed her arm to assuage the hurt. The tender gesture made Destiny's heart ache. She should be the one giving comfort instead of receiving it. "You acted as quickly as you could. You couldn't have anticipated the situation would deteriorate so rapidly."

Yes, she could. Not only that. She could have prevented the situation from happening at all. Tampering with the elevator had been her idea. She should have known it wouldn't end well. Everything she touched turned to shit. Today was yet another example.

She, Rashida, and Jackie headed inside the bank to meet with the fire inspector. Destiny couldn't believe the amount of damage that had occurred in a relatively short time. The smell was almost overpowering, permeating every soft surface. The walls and countertops were lightly stained, the inside of the elevator and the walls nearby more heavily so. The cleaning crew would have to be magicians to make this mess disappear.

After the fire department cleared the scene, Karl Gibson, the owner of the cleaning company, inspected all three floors before sharing how long he thought he and his employees would need before the branch could reopen for business.

"Five, six hours tonight. Another seven or eight after the oil's gone."

"I'll stay with you while you do the first round of cleaning," Rashida said. "Someone will be here tomorrow to repair the elevator and remove and replace the oil in the motor. I have no idea how long that will take, so let's plan on having your team come in on Saturday to do the deep cleaning on the furniture and carpets. I'll drop by on Sunday to see if there's anything we need to follow up on in order to be ready to open for business on Monday."

Harry had the window of opportunity she needed. As long as she volunteered to babysit the elevator repair team, nothing could go wrong. If she dressed them in coveralls and work clothes, they wouldn't raise any eyebrows when they waltzed through the front door Friday morning. When the job was done, they could split their take, strip off their costumes, and disappear into the crowd.

"Do you want me to arrange security for tonight?" Jackie asked.

"I'll stay with her." It had been a long day, but if she had to pull an all-nighter, so be it. From now on, she wouldn't leave Rashida's side. Because after Friday, she might never see her again.

"Then it's settled," Rashida said. "Destiny and I will take first shift. I'll come back on Saturday and Sunday, and I'll ask for volunteers for Friday during tonight's update call. Not that I expect to have any takers."

"Maybe someone will surprise you."

Nearly seven long hours later, Harry stepped up to the plate.

"How did the update call go?" Destiny asked after she followed Rashida into her apartment.

"Better than expected. Megan's doctors say she's going to be fine and Harry offered to supervise the repair team, which frees me up to tackle the regularly scheduled items on my agenda."

Destiny wished Rashida would stop pushing herself so hard. "Do you have to be quite so dedicated? Why don't you sleep late tomorrow? Or better yet, why don't you take the day off? You deserve it after all the hours you put in today."

"You won't get an argument from me."

"So you'll do it?" Destiny asked hopefully.

"I wish I could, but I have to go in. We're stretched too thin."

So was she. She looked exhausted. When she headed to the bathroom, Destiny followed her to make sure she didn't pass out on the way. She offered her something to drink, then tried to get her to eat. Neither had eaten since breakfast. Rashida inhaled a slice of pepperoni pizza. Destiny did the same.

Destiny climbed in the tub. She sighed when the warm, scented water instantly began to soothe her aching body. Rashida soon joined her. When Rashida nestled against her, Destiny wanted to wrap her arms around her and keep her safe from harm. Safe from her.

"I love you."

Rashida smiled in response. When Destiny began to touch her, Rashida's smile quickly turned into a grimace. Of pleasure, not pain. Destiny held her as she came. She would have kept holding her if Rashida didn't insist on returning the favor.

"Your turn."

At Rashida's direction, Destiny turned and faced the wall. Rashida slowly lathered her skin. The tiny bubbles coated her neck, shoulders, arms, and back. Then Rashida gently rubbed the washcloth over her breasts, teasing her nipples awake. Rashida massaged her shoulders, kneading the tension out of her taut muscles. Destiny had never felt so content. Or so turned on.

"Turn around," Rashida said. "I want to watch you come."

Destiny turned to face the only woman who had ever captured her heart. The woman whose own heart she knew she would soon break.

"Tell me what you want," Rashida said, "and it's yours."

"All I want is you. You're all I need."

And the one thing she couldn't have.

Chapter Twenty-two

Friday, March 17
7:10 a.m.
Savannah, Georgia

Destiny groaned as she rolled over in bed. Everything hurt. Her feet. Her legs. Her back. But especially her head. She had been thinking way too much, examining the problem at hand from every possible angle. Sticking to the plan was out of the question, but what other option did she have? The easiest solution—the *only* solution—was the one right in front of her. She had to do what Harry wanted. Whether she wanted to or not.

She stretched her aching muscles. She couldn't remember the last time she had been so tired. Was this what it felt like to put in an honest day's work? She had certainly spent an honest night. Last night, she had laid herself bare. Last night, the gentle but insistent probing of Rashida's fingers, lips, and tongue had drawn the truth out of her.

"I love you," she had said more times than she could count. "I love you."

She smiled at the memory, but her smile quickly turned into a scowl when she remembered what was on her agenda for the day. Today was the day Harry's plan would finally come together. Today was the day Destiny could make a fortune but lose someone who meant more to her than money. Today was the day.

She reached for Rashida but came up empty. She opened her eyes, squinting against the glare of the morning sun.

Rashida was dressed and halfway out the door. Standing in front of the floor-length mirror in the bedroom, she carefully applied a coat of lipstick and reached for a pair of earrings. "What are you staring at?"

"You."

Destiny crawled across the bed, grabbed Rashida by the back of her pants, and pulled her down. She pinned Rashida's body with her own and kissed the face she had quickly grown to love. After a few minutes of girlish giggles, Rashida pushed her away. Destiny couldn't hide her disappointment as she watched Rashida prepare to head to work. She didn't want her to go. She didn't want their time to end. She wanted one more day to try to figure things out.

"Are you sure you can't you play hooky just this once? I've got the day off. Let's spend it together. We can watch the parade and have some green beer in a crowded bar. Or, if you want, we don't even have to leave this bed."

"Like I said last night," Rashida said with what seemed to be genuine regret, "I wish I could, but I can't."

Trying not to pout, Destiny dragged herself out of bed and went to the kitchen to make herself a cup of coffee. Across the room, Rashida blended herself a smoothie. Destiny felt like half of a happily married couple going about their usual morning routine. Unfortunately, her image of domestic bliss was nothing more than an illusion. She wished she could make the image real. She wished she could steal away with Rashida. Catch a plane somewhere and never look back.

"If you could live anywhere but here, where would you choose?"

"What do you mean?" Rashida's eyebrows knitted in confusion.

She probably thought the question had come out of nowhere, but Destiny needed to know the answer. Chances were she'd never see Rashida again after today. Even if she did, their relationship, such as it was, would never be the same. She wanted to have one more piece of Rashida to take with her when they went their separate ways.

Destiny repeated her question then listened, fascinated, as Rashida shared her dream of visiting Malaysia. Rashida's words painted vivid images in her mind. She could clearly see the things Rashida spoke about. Wizened fishermen casting their nets on the water. Street vendors sautéing a series of mystery ingredients and serving them up as lunch. Tourists taking in rustic charm one day and basking in elegant sophistication the next.

When Rashida talked about spending New Year's Eve on an enclosed walkway that stretched between two skyscrapers, Destiny could picture herself dancing slow with her under a canopy of stars. Surrounded by people but feeling utterly alone.

"What's stopping you from going?"

Rashida laughed as if the question was the silliest thing she had ever heard. "I don't speak a word of Malay. That's reason enough."

"So learn." Destiny wasn't as willing as Rashida was to let go of her fantasy. To let go of her own. She held Rashida's face in her hands and looked deep into her eyes. "I want you to be happy."

"I am happy. Right here. With you."

"Then stay with me." Destiny held onto Rashida. Held on because she didn't want to let go. "Don't go to work today. Pick up the phone and call in sick. I promise to make it worth your while. Stay with me."

Rashida broke free with apparent reluctance. "If it was any day but today, I would. But I can't. I'm sorry, but I have to go to work."

Destiny felt sick to her stomach as she followed Rashida to the living room. Rashida had no idea what she was in for. What they were both in for. Rashida tried to toss her a bone by offering to take time off next year, but next year would be much too late.

"See you tonight," Rashida said, obviously trying to cheer her up.

"See you."

Even before the door clicked shut, Destiny knew what she had to do. Instead of doing what was easy, she had to do what was right.

She grabbed her uniform and got dressed. Her clothes smelled like oil and she smelled like sex, but she didn't have time to take a shower or find something else to wear. She needed to get downtown as fast as she could.

She ran downstairs, climbed in her car, and headed home. After she grabbed what she needed, she drove to the Savannah Chatham Metro Police Department faster than the law allowed. Frankly, though, a speeding ticket was the least of her concerns.

The desk sergeant took in her disheveled appearance and eyed her with suspicion. "May I help you?" he asked, his hand easing toward his gun.

"My name is DaShawn Jenkins and I need to see Chief Wilson."

"The chief is a busy man. What can I do for you?"

"If you don't want to be shackled to that desk for the rest of your career, you'll get off your ass and take me to the man in charge."

"Give me a reason."

Destiny pulled her video camera out of her pocket. "A bank's being robbed and I have the proof right here. Is that reason enough?"

"Which bank?"

Destiny shook her head. "I'll divulge that information as soon as I'm standing face-to-face with Chief Wilson."

The desk sergeant licked his lips as if he were envisioning the commendation and resulting promotion he could receive for breaking a high-profile case. "Come with me."

Destiny followed him through the crowded police station.

"Wait here," he said before disappearing into Chief Keith Wilson's office.

She stood outside the door while the desk sergeant conferred with the chief and two detectives. She looked at her watch as several precious minutes ticked by. Finally, the desk sergeant opened the door and waved her inside.

Chief Wilson sat behind a desk overflowing with paperwork. One detective leaned against the desk, the other spilled over the sides of a chair positioned in front of it.

Chief Wilson steepled his fingers and leaned forward as if he were trying to earn her trust. That might have worked if his hands hadn't been resting on copies of her mug shots from past arrests.

"Sergeant Anderson says there's something you want to tell me."

"Low Country Savings Bank's main office is being robbed. A team of three is breaking into the vault."

"When?"

"Right now."

"If that's the case, we should have received an alarm call. No one has been dispatched to that location today."

"The alarm's disabled. An employee let them inside. She's the fourth member of the team."

Chief Wilson's eyes widened slightly, but his face remained impassive. "And you know this because?"

"I'm the fifth."

Cashing in her insurance, she played the secret recording she had made of Harry's confession. When the playback ended, she expected Chief Wilson to send every available officer to the bank to thwart the crime. Instead, he allowed the detective leaning against his desk to do the talking.

"Miss Jenkins, you've got a record a mile long." His expression and posture broadcast his skepticism. "Why should we believe this tape is anything more than a hoax? From my perspective, it could be real or it could be part of a scheme to extort money out of Harrison Collins. She's an upstanding member of the community. It makes no sense for her to be involved in the crime discussed on the tape."

"Whether it makes sense or not, she is involved. You saw it for yourselves. Why would I lie?"

The detective reached back, picked up the copy of her file, and rattled off a list of her past charges. "You've lied about everything else. Why should today be any different?"

"Look," she said, sighing in frustration at her inability to escape her past. "We don't have a lot of time. This thing is going down as we speak. My team works fast. They won't be in the building a minute longer than they have to be, which means we need to stop jawing and get moving. If you think I'm lying, fine. But give me a chance to prove I'm not. Put a wire on me and follow me to the bank. My team is expecting me. My presence won't come as a surprise. Yours would. Hang back and let me go inside alone."

"Not a chance," the detective said.

Destiny had expected one or all of them to balk at the suggestion. "If you bull your way inside guns blazing, you'll wind up with a bloodbath on your hands. If you play it my way, everyone makes it out alive and you'll have the FBI asking you for pointers."

They responded to the ego stroking with the expected acquiescence. She could feel their icy demeanors begin to thaw so she turned up the heat.

"You'll be able to hear every word I say. If it turns out I'm not telling anything but the God's honest truth, slap the cuffs on me, toss me in jail, and throw away the key. Just don't sit here and do nothing."

Chief Wilson leaned back in his chair. "What do you want in return for coming forward with this information? Immunity?" He spread his hands to indicate his helplessness. "You need someone in the DA's office to offer you that, not me. I'm a police officer, not a lawyer. It's not my job to worry about sentencing. I put people in jail and let the guys in the expensive suits fight over how long they get to stay there."

She had expected him to take the hard line. She hadn't expected not to give a rat's ass about it. "I don't care about me."

If she went to prison branded as a snitch, she'd have to sleep with one eye open and be prepared to fight at a moment's notice. But every bruise would be worth it if it meant she could clear her name.

Chapter Twenty-three

Friday, March 17
8:15 a.m.
Savannah, GA

Destiny clenched her fists to keep from clawing at the wire. The adhesive tape the police technician had used to affix the recording device to her skin itched like a motherfucker.

The technician adjusted the fit of his headphones. “Say something so I can get a level on the microphone,” he said as he fiddled with the knobs on a bank of monitors in the surveillance van.

Destiny rolled her eyes. They’d already had two sound checks back at the station. “This is bullshit. We’re wasting time.”

“That came through loud and clear.” The technician laughed. “You’ve got a pretty big pair of balls. For your sake, I hope they aren’t just for show.” He signaled to the head of the tactical team readying to surround the building. “Okay, she’s up.”

Destiny hoped Harry hadn’t appointed anyone to act as lookout. Though they weren’t in uniform, the gathered hordes were easy to spot if you knew what you were looking for.

“Here’s the prop you requested.” Joe Shearouse, the detective who had been giving Destiny grief all morning, handed her a nine millimeter and a holster. “The firing pin’s been removed, so for your sake, I hope you don’t get the urge to play hero. In there or out here.”

Destiny cinched the holster to her belt and slid the nine into the suede-lined slot. The gun was heavier than she had expected it to be. Or was she feeling the weight of expectation instead of molded chrome and steel?

Her crew never performed a job armed with anything other than their tools and their wits. Ford was as big as a house. His presence provided all the intimidation they needed, and it didn't come with a felony gun charge attached. But this job was different. If the situation inside the bank went sideways, she could wave the nine around and get everyone under control. The gun would allow her to get the upper hand. She hoped.

"I know what I'm doing."

Shearouse herded her out of the van. "That remains to be seen."

Chief Wilson broke free from a knot of plain clothes policemen dressed like St. Patrick's Day revelers. Some wore T-shirts so profane they would have gotten a citizen arrested.

"Do you remember the code word?" Chief Wilson asked.

"Parade."

Destiny had come up with the code word herself. It seemed like something she could fit into conversation without drawing too much attention. To be honest, it reminded her of the conversation she'd had with Rashida that morning. Was it the last conversation they would ever have?

"As soon as I hear you say, 'parade,' I'll know you and the others are preparing to exit the building. When the doors open, my men will be waiting to take your team down."

"Down, right? Not out."

Chief Wilson looked at her coolly. "I'm not an executioner, Miss Jenkins. I don't want to see anyone get hurt today. My men are trained professionals. They'll take their cues from your friends. What happens today isn't up to my people. It's up to yours."

"No," Destiny said, "it's up to me."

She took a deep breath and crossed the street. Beads of sweat poured down her face as she unlocked the front door and stepped inside. The smell of smoke and scalded oil hung heavy in the air.

She expected to hear Harry urging on her team like a jockey leading her horse down the homestretch of the Kentucky Derby. The voice she heard instead made her blood run cold. The voice she heard was Rashida's.

She pulled the door shut and locked it as quietly as she could. She nearly tripped over her own feet as she stumbled toward the lobby. What was Rashida doing here? She was supposed to be far, far away. She was supposed to be safe.

Rashida had her back to her. Her hands were fisted at her sides. "Who told you I was going to Springfield today?" Her voice shook with confusion, anger, and fear.

Harry flashed a menacing smile. "She did."

Destiny's knees nearly buckled when Rashida turned toward her. She forced herself to face the recrimination she saw in Rashida's eyes.

Rashida backed away, betrayal etched on her face. "Please tell me you're not in on this. Please tell me everything we had wasn't a lie."

Destiny tried to keep her emotions in check as Harry secured Rashida in a bear hug. She ignored her protective instincts, which were urging her to swat Harry like the pesky fly she had become. She couldn't afford to make an enemy out of Harry just yet. She needed her to go on believing they were on the same side. She needed to be convincing, even though she had lost faith in the original mission.

She pulled the gun. As she'd hoped, Rashida's eyes drifted from her face to the barrel of the nine.

"I asked you not to go to work today. You should have listened to me."

"I don't understand." The tears that filled Rashida's eyes revealed she understood all too well. "What's happening, Destiny?"

"That's pretty obvious, isn't it?" Harry asked. "Your girlfriend and I are going to take a long vacation and you'll be left trying to explain why you allowed your clit to do your thinking for you. You're an articulate girl. I'm sure you'll come up with something good, though I doubt it will be good enough to save your job. After the bank absorbs a two and a half million dollar loss, heads will surely roll. Yours will undoubtedly be the first."

Rashida's chin quivered briefly, but she maintained her composure. "Why would you do this to the bank? To your parents? To me? What have I ever done to you?"

"You took my place."

Harry pushed Rashida down with such force the chair she landed in rolled several feet away. Harry placed her hands on the arms of the chair and leaned forward, forcing Rashida to give ground.

Destiny wanted to run to Rashida's defense, but forced herself to stay put.

"This bank has been in my family for years," Harry said. "I'm supposed to run it one day, not you. Yet everyone from my mother to Ted Hollis and even Martin fucking Foster wants to anoint you as the heir to the throne. After today, I doubt you'll be able to get a job as a trash collector in this town, let alone as CEO." She straightened as if she thought she had made her point. The look on her face was triumphant. "Did you enjoy the pictures? You certainly seemed to be enjoying yourself in them, that's for sure. Consider them a gift from me to you."

Destiny watched Rashida's face fall. Her heart fell right along with it. She wanted to turn away, but she couldn't. Her hands shook as she trained the gun in Harry and Rashida's direction.

"You were responsible for the photographs?"

Rashida's question was directed at Destiny not Harry. Destiny's answer, however, was meant for Harry's ears. "Smile for the camera."

The dam finally broke. Rashida's tears fell unabated. "I trusted you," she said, her voice choked. "I loved you."

The words Destiny had been waiting her whole life to hear had come too late. Or had they? She still had a chance to redeem herself. She still had a chance to win Rashida back. After she finished breaking her heart.

She looked in the vault. Both the safe and safe deposit boxes were nearly empty. "How much longer are you going to be?" she asked her team.

"We're almost done," Ford said, stuffing stacks of strapped bills into the last of four identically sized duffel bags lined up on the floor of the vault. He zipped the bags shut and tossed each into the lobby. Then he reached for a fifth bag. He hefted it easily, even though the bag's contents strained against the reinforced material keeping it secure. "Do you want me to carry it for you?"

"No, thanks." Harry took the bag from him and draped the straps over her shoulder. She staggered under the weight of the gold bars inside the duffel.

"Suit yourself," Ford said with a shrug.

He tossed one of the other bags toward Destiny. The duffel landed on the floor and slid across the smooth marble surface. Destiny halted the bag's progress with her foot but didn't make a move to pick it up. She kept her eyes trained on Rashida.

"What do you want to do with her?" Ford asked. "I don't want to leave any witnesses." He looked Rashida up and down in a way that made Destiny fear for her safety.

"I'll take care of her."

"Take care of her how?" Harry glanced at Destiny's gun. "I want her alive. I want her to suffer."

"She already is." Destiny quickly corrected herself. "I mean, she will." Destiny could feel her own heart bleeding. She swallowed around the catch in her throat. "You brought me in to handle the rough stuff, Harry. Let me do my job. You'll be home in time to watch the parade."

Her adrenaline surged as she used the code word. She hoped the police officers gathered outside would have cooler heads than she did at the moment. If not, things could get ugly in a hurry.

"Screw the parade. I've got a plane to catch. *We've* got a plane to catch." Harry gave Destiny a bruising kiss, a gesture more about power and control than affection. A gesture meant more for Rashida's benefit than Destiny's pleasure. "I'll see you at the airport."

Destiny wiped her mouth with the back of her hand. "You still haven't told me where we're going."

Harry remained vague, lending more credence to Destiny's theory that Harry was stringing her along. "You'll find out when we get there." She tapped two fingers against her forehead in a mock salute. "So long, Rashida. It's been a pleasure."

"You'll never get away with this."

"Such a moribund cliché is beneath you, Rashida." Harry patted her duffel bag, reminding everyone of the fortune inside. "Besides, I've already gotten away with it."

She, Ford, and the others headed to the door. Each carried a bag laden with loot. Destiny picked up her own bag, then reached down, grabbed Rashida's elbow, and pulled her to her feet. Rashida tried to jerk away, but Destiny tightened her grip. "Trust me," she said under her breath.

"You'd have better luck trying to walk on water."

"Please, Rashida," Destiny begged in a fierce whisper. "Trust me. Stick close. Don't leave my side, no matter what."

Rashida lost a bit of defiance. Hope flickered in her eyes. Destiny could see how desperately she wanted to believe her. To believe in her. "Tell me what's going on."

"I will in due time." Destiny holstered the gun and led Rashida toward the door. Rashida yelped when Destiny wrapped an arm around her neck. "Shh. It's all right. I swear everything I'm doing is just for show." She patted the gun at her side. "Even this is a prop. Everything's going to be okay as soon as we go out that door. Just keep your head down and do everything I tell you to do. Can you do that?"

After a moment's pause, Rashida slowly nodded.

"Good."

Ford peered through the blinds. "I've never seen so much green in my life. And I'm not talking about money." He looked back with a grin. "Well, maybe that, too."

Through the parted blinds, Destiny could see dozens of people in green-accented outfits milling around. Were they members of the tactical team or were they simply spectators descending on Bay Street for the events to come?

"If you think you're seeing green now, wait until the parade starts."

Destiny had used the code word twice. Surely she had given the police plenty of time to move into position. If not, the shit was about to hit the fan. How was she supposed to stop her crew before they scattered?

Evidently deciding the coast was clear, Ford unlocked the deadbolt and opened the door. "After you." Bowing low, he allowed Harry to exit first.

"Thank you, kind sir."

Harry sidestepped Ford's bulk and crossed the threshold. Ford followed. Destiny tensed, expecting them to be swarmed right away. Nathan and Walsh exited the bank next. Still nothing.

"I love you. Never forget that." Destiny kissed the back of Rashida's neck and gently urged her forward. "Here we go."

Destiny had barely walked out the door when ten police officers formed a semi-circle around the bank's entrance, pulled their guns, and yelled, "Show us your hands! Down on the ground!"

Ford and Walsh looked like they wanted to beat feet, but they wisely dropped their duffels, raised their hands in surrender, and lay facedown on the sidewalk. Cursing under his breath, Nathan followed suit.

Rashida remained standing. "Get down," Destiny whispered.

"But I'm not—"

"Get down." Destiny kneeled on the sidewalk, hands upraised, and slowly lowered herself to the ground. "The cops will sort out the good guys from the bad guys later."

Rashida lay on the sidewalk with her arms stretched in front of her. She turned to face Destiny, lifting her head so they could see eye-to-eye. "Are you working with the police?"

Before Destiny could answer, Ford gave her a malevolent look and launched a gob of spit in her direction. Destiny flinched when the saliva landed inches from her face. "Snitches end up in ditches, DJ," Ford said with a glare.

"Officers, I'm so glad you've come," Harry said. "These… thugs have been holding me against my will." She dropped the bag of gold bars on the ground but remained on her feet. She took a step toward the officers as she tried to plead her case. "Do you remember the incident we had yesterday? Our elevator caught fire and we had to call nine one one. When I came to supervise the repair work, these people forced me inside and—"

"Stop right there!" one of the officers barked. "Down on the ground!"

"Young man, I'm sure you're just doing your job, but do you have any idea who I am? Do you know who my parents are?"

Harry probably paid more in taxes than most of the police personnel surrounding her took home, but neither her money nor her family name could buy her out of this one.

Joe Shearouse dangled a set of handcuffs from the tip of one finger. “I know exactly who you are. Your name’s Harrison Revere Collins, and you’re under arrest for attempted robbery and kidnapping. I’m sure your parents will be proud.” He spun her around, read her her rights, and fastened the handcuffs around her wrists. Harry hissed as the manacles bit into her skin. “Too tight?”

“Yes, they are.”

She lifted her hands as if she expected Shearouse to loosen the cuffs. He took her by the elbow and led her to a nearby squad car.

“You should have thought of that before you decided to commit a felony. Watch your head.” He shoved her in the back of the car and slammed the door.

Harry’s face looked ghostly white through the tinted glass windows. Destiny couldn’t enjoy the sight for long. Four officers cuffed her and her crew and lifted them to their feet while spectators’ cell phones recorded every moment for posterity.

Chief Wilson offered Rashida his hand. She stood and brushed herself off. Her clothes were covered in dirt and grime. One side of her face was pitted from lying on the debris-strewn sidewalk. Her eyes sparkled from adrenaline. Destiny had never seen her look more beautiful.

“Miss Ivey, I’m Chief Keith Wilson. I need you to come down to the station and make a statement. After we hear your side of the story, you should be free to go in a matter of hours. My car’s across the street if you need a ride.”

“I have my own car, thank you, Chief.”

“I’ll gladly bring you back to your vehicle when we’re done.”

Rashida nodded as if she understood the visit she was about to have wasn’t going to be as friendly as Chief Wilson had initially made it out to be.

“What about her?” she asked, indicating Destiny.

“I’m afraid Miss Jenkins will be staying with us a great deal longer than you will.”

Rashida swiped at a pebble imbedded in her cheek. "Jenkins? You mean Jackson, don't you? You must have her mistaken for someone else. Her name's Destiny. Destiny Jackson."

"No, I'm afraid there's no mistake. Her name is DaShawn Jenkins. She's a con artist from Miami. Destiny Jackson is the latest of her many aliases. I'm sorry if you were taken in by her, but if you were, you aren't the first. If her sentence is long enough, however, perhaps you'll be the last."

DaShawn ducked as an officer placed her in the back of a squad car. She told herself not to look at Rashida, but she couldn't resist taking one last glance. She had to see Rashida's face one more time. She was looking her dead in the eye when Rashida said, "I'm sorry, too."

DaShawn watched Rashida walk away. She watched Rashida walk out of her life for good.

Shearouse sat in the front seat of the squad car and turned to look through the steel mesh that separated him from her. Behind them, Rashida was climbing into Chief Wilson's car. "This isn't good-bye," he said. "You'll see her again."

"Really?" DaShawn perked up, thinking Chief Wilson had brokered a deal with the DA's office on her behalf even though he had said it wasn't his job to do so.

"Yeah, you'll see her when she testifies at your trial."

"There isn't going to be a trial."

Shearouse lit a cigarette and blew out a stream of smoke. "Do you know something I don't?"

"Yeah, I'm going to save the tax payers some money and plead guilty. I did the crime, right? Why pretend I didn't?"

"Call me crazy, but I think your lawyer will convince you to change your mind." He stretched his arm across the back of the seat. "It's too bad. You did a good job in there. You kept the hostage calm and made sure no one was harmed. I don't know if it will mean anything to the DA, but it certainly can't hurt." He turned to look at her. "You could have had a future in this business if things had been different."

"What, as a hostage negotiator? I don't think so."

"You're smart, Jenkins. Too smart to keep doing what you're doing. But where you're going, you'll have plenty of time to find something else to do with your life." Shearouse took another deep drag on his cigarette. "You and the hostage seem to have some kind of relationship."

DaShawn knew she probably shouldn't say anything else without a lawyer present, but fuck it. She didn't care what Shearouse thought about her. She had to keep him from getting the wrong idea about Rashida.

"She's an innocent victim. She isn't a part of this. She wasn't even supposed to be here today."

"I'll verify that for myself if you don't mind." He looked at her through a cloud of cigarette smoke. "Whatever you had seems to be over now. Did you honestly think you could have a future with her?"

"No," she admitted, "but it was nice thinking I could."

DaShawn rested the back of her head against the squad car's stained fabric seat. Her hands were cuffed behind her back. Her shoulders and arms ached as they began to lose circulation. She felt like crying. Not from the pain in her body but the ache in her heart. She had fucked up. And she had no one to blame but herself.

"The hostage—"

"Would you please stop calling her that?" DaShawn rubbed her face against her shoulder to dry her tears. "She has a name."

Shearouse flicked his cigarette out the open window. "You should have started by telling her yours."

Chapter Twenty-four

Friday, March 17
11:30 a.m.
Savannah, GA

Rashida was so tired she couldn't think. Outside the bank, Chief Wilson had treated her like a colleague. Once they arrived at the police station, he began to treat her more like a suspect as he tried to determine what role if any she had played in the attempted theft.

Jackie had been dragged off the parade route and subjected to the same treatment. Rashida could hear her voice rising in anger in one of the other interview rooms as she undoubtedly tried to explain how Destiny managed to pass all the background checks Jackie had allegedly subjected her to. Rashida wondered the same thing, but she was too busy trying to save her own ass at the moment to worry about someone else's.

She had been answering questions for hours. She had told her story so many times she could recite it by heart, yet she was no closer to understanding what had happened. Had she been so blinded by her feelings for Destiny it had affected her ability to see the truth? She should have trusted her instincts. She had told herself they were moving too fast. She had told herself she didn't know enough about Destiny to fall for her, but she had tumbled anyway.

Destiny, who had seemed too good to be true, had turned out to be exactly that. She wasn't an out-of-work security guard. She wasn't a former soldier. She wasn't the sensitive woman who had sparked Rashida's interest and found her way into her heart. She was a liar and a thief who had been using her from the day they met. She had been recruited by Harry and paid to feed her lies.

And I swallowed every one of them.

Rashida shook her head disconsolately. She had been fooled by not one woman she thought she could trust but two. Was she really that naïve?

Chief Wilson showed her Destiny's rap sheet. Thumbing through it, Rashida could hardly believe what she was reading. Check fraud, deception, identity theft, breaking and entering. The charges went on and on. The Destiny she knew wasn't capable of such things. The Destiny she knew didn't cross the line between right and wrong. But the Destiny she knew didn't exist. Destiny Jackson wasn't real. She was someone DaShawn Jenkins and Harry Collins had created.

Rashida pushed the file away. The answers she needed weren't inside a manila folder. They were in DaShawn Jenkins's head. And, perhaps, her heart.

Rashida knew little about Destiny, but what she did know she loved. She knew far too much about DaShawn. None of it good.

She wanted to know why DaShawn had done what she did. She wanted to know how DaShawn could seem to care about her yet use her so cruelly. She wanted an explanation. But not from DaShawn's lips. DaShawn was the most skilled liar she had ever met. She wouldn't give her another chance to weave her spell.

She rubbed her eyes, which itched from unshed tears. The answers she sought would have to wait. Today she just wanted to get away from it all. Let someone else deal with the fallout for once. She was done.

"You're free to go," Chief Wilson said after nearly three hours of questioning.

Rashida stepped out of the interview room like a punch-drunk boxer. She stared at her cell phone, but she didn't know who to call.

She was the person everyone reached out to in such situations, not the one who did the reaching. Who could she count on to have her back? Jackie was still being put through the wringer, Dennis and the members of executive management were partying on the sidelines, and Ted had taken his wife and kids out of town for a weekend getaway. Who was left?

"There you are."

Relief flooded through Rashida's body when she saw Daniel striding across the lobby. She could always count on him to be calm even in the midst of a storm. She listened to him detail how he had explained the attempted robbery to the rest of the employees and informed them she was okay. He had also drafted a press release he would issue as soon as he and the police department's public spokesperson conducted a joint press conference scheduled to take place within the hour.

"What do you need me to do?" she asked.

He gave her a much needed hug.

"Go home and get some rest. You've done enough for one day."

"Should I tender my resignation now or later?"

Daniel placed a hand on her shoulder and fixed her with an earnest look. "Your job is safe. So is Jackie's. What happened wasn't your fault. It was Harry's and Destiny's. DaShawn's." He waved his hand. "Whatever her name is. This unfortunate incident has illustrated there are some obvious flaws in our screening and selection process for new employees, but those can be addressed at a later date."

Rashida lifted her shoulders in an awkward shrug. "I have to tell you I'm at a loss. A crime was being planned right under my nose and I didn't see it happening. I'm personally and professionally embarrassed for allowing this to transpire on my watch. Please accept my deepest apologies."

"Rashida, you didn't do—"

She raised her hands to prevent the expected show of sympathy. She didn't want forgiveness. She didn't want understanding. Because she didn't feel worthy of either. She felt empty inside. Like she'd given everything she had to give and then some. She had spent every minute of every day trying to prove her worth. In two short weeks, all the hard work she had put in establishing her personal and professional reputations had been erased. Nearly twenty years gone. Just like that. She didn't have the energy to start over.

"I've told my story to the police and you've already notified the staff," she said with a weary sigh. "I'll write a detailed memo for the board as soon as I get home, but I don't know what else I can add that won't appear in the official police report or be reported on the news. Obviously, I'll make myself available to testify when the case comes to trial."

"There isn't going to be a trial. DaShawn confessed to everything and the rest of her cohorts are tripping over themselves trying to cut deals of their own. Even Harry's spilling her guts. Her parents are on their way to the station with a prominent attorney in tow, but she must not be too confident in his ability to get her off because from what I hear, she's telling everything she knows."

Rashida felt her heart begin to race. She didn't care about Harry's admission of guilt or the others' attempts to make life easier for themselves. Despite everything that had happened, she cared about DaShawn. Still.

"DaShawn confessed?" She felt a silver lining begin to form on the dark clouds hovering over her head. "So she *was* working with the police."

Daniel's skeptical look blunted her burst of happiness.

"She's working to reduce her sentence. I don't think becoming an informant at the last minute is the same as working undercover. It will get her out of prison faster, but it won't make her any less guilty." He led Rashida out of the police station to his waiting BMW. "How did you manage to see through her?" he asked after he deposited her in the passenger's seat and slid behind the walnut-accented steering wheel.

"What do you mean?" she asked, fastening her seat belt.

Daniel drove toward the bank's parking lot, taking Rashida to her car. "You were scheduled to be in Springfield today, not downtown. Did you sense something was wrong?"

Rashida pinched the bridge of her nose between her fingers. She could have lied to make herself look good in Daniel's eyes, but she chose to go with her favorite mainstay, the truth.

"I didn't sense anything. She had me completely fooled."

She remembered how stupid, how gullible, how deluded she had felt when Destiny—*DaShawn*—had revealed herself to be a common criminal. A product of the life Rashida had escaped not the one she had built.

Fool me once, shame on you. Fool me twice, shame on me.

DaShawn had pulled the wool over her eyes once, but Rashida would make sure neither DaShawn nor anyone else would ever get a chance to repeat the feat because she would never allow anyone to get that close to her again.

CHAPTER TWENTY-FIVE

Eighteen Months Later
8:00 a.m.
Alto, Georgia

DaShawn squinted as she walked through the front door of Arrendale State Prison. The sun seemed brighter, the air tasted cleaner on this side of the razor wire-topped fence than they did in the prison yard.

"See you soon," the guard said as he began to pull the reinforced steel door shut.

"Not if I can help it."

The guard snorted laughter. "That's what they all say."

DaShawn flinched when the door closed with a heavy metallic clang. She had been dreaming about this day for well over a year. Now that it had arrived, she didn't know what to do first.

To her left, another now former inmate was running toward the husband and child she'd been separated from for five years. To her right, another ex-con was passing around a forty of malt liquor with a group of friends. The woman hadn't been outside for more than five minutes and she was already getting the party started. At this rate, she'd be making a return appearance in no time flat. DaShawn didn't intend to follow her example.

She wondered which direction she should go, left or right? What did it matter? No one was waiting for her no matter which way she turned.

She tossed her duffel bag over her shoulder. The bag weighed next to nothing. It didn't contain much more than a change of clothes, a dog-eared copy of this year's *Sports Illustrated* swimsuit issue, and a stack of letters stamped Return to Sender.

She had written Rashida once a week for the eighteen months she had been inside. Every week, without fail, she had tried to make Rashida see her side of things. She had apologized for all the things she had done wrong and told Rashida how much she loved her. She had told her she was a changed woman and begged her for the chance to prove it. But each week, the letters had come back unopened. Even the one that contained the business plan she had spent nearly a month trying to draft. The plan for the hair salon she hoped to own and operate as soon as she got her feet under her on the outside.

Alto, a tiny town in north Georgia, had a population of less than a thousand permanent residents. The inmates in Arrendale often exceeded that number. DaShawn couldn't wait for the city and the prison to become nothing more than blips in a rearview mirror. She couldn't wait to get back to Savannah. She couldn't wait to get back to Rashida.

She needed to see Rashida face to face. It was the only way she'd ever get her to listen.

The closest bus station was in Gainesville, nearly twenty miles away. The fare for a ticket would put a substantial dent in her meager stash. The cash she had amassed in Savannah was probably locked in an evidence locker if some crooked cop hadn't pocketed it for himself. She'd left some money behind in Florida, but the IRS had probably seized it while she was behind bars. Until she got a look at her accounts, the only green she could count on was what was in her pockets. She'd made enough money working various jobs around the prison to afford a ticket on the first thing smoking. She just needed to figure out how to get there. The prison van was headed that way, but she'd rather walk than spend another second surrounded by armed guards.

She strode across the parking lot, ready to begin the long trek to Gainesville. She had barely made it to the road when a dented

Mustang pulled up beside her. The Mustang needed some TLC, but it still looked like a sweet ride. She bent to see who was inside. She didn't recognize the driver, but the grinning passenger was one of her former cell mates.

"Going my way?" Patty Stewart asked. She had the face of an angel but the mouth of a sailor. Her quick temper and willingness to use her fists when she lost it were the reasons she'd ended up in Arrendale.

"I'm headed to the bus station. Do you think I could get a ride?"

"Hop in."

After Patty opened the door, DaShawn tossed her duffel bag in the backseat and climbed in the car. She nodded at the stone butch behind the wheel, giving her the respect she deserved.

"Where are you headed?" Patty lowered the volume on the Carrie Underwood song blaring on the radio. "Are you going to try to win back the woman you told me about, the banker you fell for?"

"That's the plan."

"Good luck."

"Thanks. I think I might need it."

❖

The Next Day
8:46 a.m.
Savannah, Georgia

DaShawn heard the gasps after she pushed the door open and stepped into the lobby of Low Country Savings Bank. Winter, Seaton, and the tellers openly gaped at her. They were probably wondering how she had the balls to show her face here again. She was wondering the same thing. The security guard—she couldn't help but think of him as her replacement—eyed her warily as she walked toward Winter's desk.

Winter blanched and looked around as if being seen with her would sully her reputation.

"Relax. I won't stay long," DaShawn whispered to keep from being overheard. "I need to talk to Rashida. Just tell me where she's working today, and I'll get out of your hair."

"I—I can't—"

Winter's eyes looked as panicked as they had the day the elevator almost caught fire. The day three people nearly succumbed to the fumes. Seaton rode to her rescue. "Is there something I can help you with?"

DaShawn repeated her request. She could feel everyone's eyes on her. For one of the few times in her life, she shrank from the attention. "Please, Seaton. I just want to talk to her."

He drew her aside. "It isn't the bank's policy to divulge personal employee information to customers or, in your case, a *non*customer. Your request seems to be of a personal nature. Even if Miss Ivey were still working for the bank, I couldn't tell you in which location."

"What do you mean *if*? She doesn't work for Low Country Savings anymore?"

According to the headlines she had read during her imprisonment, Rashida had been named executive vice president, which meant she had been promoted not fired. How could she go from being one step away from the top to being shown the door? It didn't add up.

Seaton stood firm. "I've said all I plan to say. Unless you intend to open an account or apply for a loan, please allow me to walk you out."

For eighteen months, DaShawn had dreamed of being reunited with Rashida. She had gone to sleep each night dreaming of the day the prison's doors would open and she would be free to return to Rashida's side. She had thought the day had finally arrived. But her dream had quickly turned into a nightmare.

Numb, she trudged down the street not caring where she might end up. She stopped her mindless walking when she heard someone calling her name. She turned to find a familiar face bearing down on her.

"I don't know whether to slap you or thank you," Jackie Williams said.

"One I definitely deserve. The other I'm not so sure about."

"If not for you, I might have lost my best friend. Thank you for looking out for her."

"Even though I was the reason she needed looking after in the first place?"

Ignoring the question, Jackie rested her hands on her ample hips. "I hear you're looking for her."

"Does that surprise you?"

Jackie looked up at her, her eyes guarded. DaShawn could see why Rashida trusted Jackie with all her secrets. All except one. Rashida had told Jackie she and DaShawn had slept together, but she hadn't told her anything about their relationship. Had Jackie forgiven either of them for the omission? Probably not. Jackie didn't look like she was in a forgiving mood.

"What if Rashida doesn't want to be found?"

DaShawn hadn't considered the possibility. She wasn't stupid. She knew Rashida didn't want to talk to her, but did Rashida really intend to avoid her for the rest of their lives? Would she never give her a chance to explain?

"Didn't she return all the letters you wrote?"

"Yes." DaShawn remembered the sinking feeling she got in her gut each time one of the guards shouted her name during mail call and handed her an envelope emblazoned with the words that marked her failure to break through to Rashida. Return to Sender.

"I think it's time you took the hint, don't you?"

A few returned letters weren't enough to make her accept defeat. "Thank you for being the protective best friend, but Rashida's a grown woman. She can take care of herself."

"That's what she's been doing for the past eighteen months. Now here you are trying to waltz back into her life and rip open the wounds she's tried so hard to heal."

"I don't want to hurt her. I just—I want to—"

"You want to what? Kiss it and make it better? Say you're sorry, tell her you've been successfully rehabilitated, and try to convince her to give you a second chance like she's the head of a parole board holding the keys to your pardon? Or did you come here to rub it in? To twist the knife a little more?"

"I have been rehabilitated. I used my time inside to think about all the things I've done wrong in my life. I vowed I would never do them again."

"I'm happy for you, but your revelation came much too late, as far as I'm concerned. Do you have any idea what you put Rashida through? What you put *us* through? Everyone who works for the bank was affected by what you and Harry did, but especially Rashida. I'm glad you realized the error of your ways before the situation got completely out of hand, but I really wish you'd seen the light a lot sooner than you did. Take my advice. The next time a woman tries to convince you to participate in a crazy scheme, just say no."

Jackie turned and began to walk away. With three words, DaShawn stopped her in her tracks.

"I love her."

Jackie slowly turned to face her. "You have a funny way of showing it."

"She loves me, too."

Jackie looked at her but didn't respond. DaShawn felt the tide begin to turn in her favor.

"Rashida knows me," she said. "She knows my heart. All I want is a chance to prove I'm the woman she thought I was all along."

Jackie stiffened. "If you meant as much to each other as you claim, you shouldn't need me to tell you where she is."

Kicking herself for pushing Jackie further than she was willing to go, DaShawn watched her walk away. She would have to find Rashida on her own, but she didn't know where to start.

She turned in a slow circle, taking in the sights and sounds of the historic city that surrounded her. Then she closed her eyes and blocked out every noise except the one she most wanted to hear. She listened for the sound of Rashida's heart.

CHAPTER TWENTY-SIX

Wednesday, December 31
11:20 p.m.
Kuala Lumpur, Malaysia

Rashida walked out of the secure compound. She waited for the automated gates to close behind her before she began the short walk to town. She was wearing sandals, a short black skirt, and a white silk blouse with daring *décolletage*. Was it too much for a first date or just enough? Time would tell.

The warm breeze kissed her exposed skin. The average temperature in Malaysia in December was eighty-seven degrees Fahrenheit. If not for the festive decorations adorning most of the houses and condos in her neighborhood, she'd have no idea it was the middle of winter.

She had been living on the outskirts of Kuala Lumpur for nearly six months. Long enough to stop feeling like a tourist but too short a time to feel like a local.

She greeted Wan Ku with a smile. The kindly caretaker braked to a stop. His bicycle's oversized tires squealed against the rough concrete of the uneven sidewalk. The basket attached to the bike's rusting handlebars was filled with enough fresh produce to feed an army. Then again, he and his wife did have six kids living under their roof and two adult children who were frequent visitors.

"If you're on your way to the park," Wan said in Malay, "save room for me and Amirah."

"I'll do my best. At this point, I'll be lucky to find room for one, let alone three."

Wan laughed amiably and pushed off, the muscles in his wiry legs bunching with effort. "See you there."

Rashida looked back at the expansive turnkey property Diana had helped her find. Diana hadn't handled the sale, obviously, but she'd located a few choice listings and put her in touch with a reputable local realtor. A little over five weeks after Rashida had decided she couldn't take any more pitying looks or unwanted testimonials to her supposed bravery, she had put the stigma of recent events behind her, left Savannah, and moved to Malaysia, hoping for a fresh start.

She hadn't ventured far the first month, preferring to stay in her condo and get her bearings. The caretaker delivered her groceries and saw to her needs. When she grew tired of being waited on hand on foot—when she was sick of feeling sorry for herself—she made her first tentative steps back into civilization.

The cost of living was low enough she could comfortably subsist off her savings for as long as she desired. She spent her days exploring the busy streets and winding alleys of Kuala Lumpur and the surrounding cities. The vendors and shopkeepers soon began to recognize her by sight then by name. She was as comfortable here as she had been at home. More even. Here she didn't have to live up to anyone's expectations or rise above someone's stereotypes. Here she could be herself. Nothing more. Nothing less.

She had never been happier. At least, that's what she told herself. The move to Malaysia felt transitional, not permanent. As if she had reached another stop on her journey through life but not her final destination.

Kuala Lumpur was wonderful, but Savannah was home. She missed cobblestone streets, Southern accents, and sweet tea. She missed wraparound porches, church hats, and family reunions. She missed her family. She missed her friends. She also missed work and the accompanying sense of accomplishment she felt each time she achieved a self-imposed goal or resolved a pressing issue.

She had an offer to return to Savannah to take over for the departing CEO of Georgia's oldest minority-owned bank, but she hadn't decided whether to accept or spurn the proposition. When—*if*—she returned to work, she wanted to do things right. She wanted to strike the proper balance between the personal and the professional, giving her home life the attention it deserved instead of allowing work to take up so much of her time.

But there was one thing she missed more than anything else. Something she hadn't realized she was missing until a note turned up in her mailbox. Romance.

She hadn't been on a date since she'd arrived in Malaysia—hadn't even thought about it—but the note had changed all that.

We've seen each other many times but we've never been formally introduced, the note read. *Meet me at the Petronas Towers on New Year's Eve if you'd like to get to know me as much as I would like to get to know you.*

Rashida wondered who had penned the letter. The vendor at her favorite hawker stall who flirted shamelessly with her while dishing out steaming bowls of prawn noodles, the clerk at the gift shop whose English improved in direct proportion to the amount of overpriced souvenirs customers purchased, or was it someone she hadn't noticed but had noticed her?

The thrill of the unknown washed over her as she entered Kuala Lumpur City Center Park. The twenty hectare area, with its lake, fountain, garden, and jogging path, normally offered a peaceful contrast to the thriving city that surrounded it. Tonight the park was filled with rowdy revelers waiting for the dazzling fireworks display that would mark the arrival of the new year.

Rashida bought a glass of palm wine from the closest bar stand and turned to look up at the skybridge that connected the twin skyscrapers collectively known as the Petronas Towers. She wished she could take in the activities from the skybridge, but visiting hours ended at seven, forcing her to settle for a ground level view.

She checked her watch. The fireworks display was just about half an hour away. Plenty of time to meet her admirer and decide if she wanted to go their separate ways after sharing a friendly drink or head somewhere quieter so they could talk more intimately.

The crowd noise was increasing by the minute. A procession of bands followed each other on the strobe light-strewn stage.

Rashida's ears rang from the din. How was her admirer supposed to find her in the delirious mass of humanity that surrounded them?

She imagined how they would meet. At midnight, the crowd would part and her admirer would appear in the open space. The woman—she was ninety-nine percent sure it was the noodle vendor—would beckon her with a confident, welcoming smile. They would walk toward each other without saying a word while fireworks exploded overhead.

She took a sip of her wine, an aromatic beverage made from the sap of coconut and palm trees, and laughed quietly as the image disappeared.

"Get a grip, Rashida. Scenarios like the one you're imagining are relegated to romance novels, not real life."

Then her fantasy became real. Except the woman who disentangled herself from the crowd and made her way toward her wasn't the noodle vendor. It was Destiny. Not Destiny. DaShawn. God. Why couldn't she keep that straight?

"Hi." DaShawn extended her hand. "We haven't officially met. My name is DaShawn Jenkins. It's a pleasure to finally meet you. There's something I've been meaning to tell you."

Rashida blinked, unable to believe her eyes. Was DaShawn actually standing in front of her? Talking to her? Introducing herself as if they were entering each other's orbit for the first time? She shrank from the apparition, overwhelmed by the presence of a ghost from the past she had tried to leave behind. The fountains in Lake Symphony roared to life, startling her but delighting the onlookers who flocked to the daily shows.

"Did Jackie tell you where to find me?" she asked, struggling to find her voice.

DaShawn smiled. The sexy, slightly shy smile she'd thrown Rashida's way the day they met. Rashida's heart lurched at the familiar sight.

"No, *you* did. Remember the last day we saw each other?"

How could she forget? It was the day the strong foundation she thought she'd built vanished like a sand castle overrun by a tsunami.

"Before you went to work that morning," DaShawn said, "I asked you a question."

Rashida remembered the question. She remembered the intense expression on DaShawn's face when she had asked, "If you could live anywhere in the world, where would you choose?"

"You chose here."

DaShawn spread her arms to indicate the sprawling city Rashida now called home.

Rashida's jaw tightened. How long would DaShawn continue to use her secrets against her? From the moment they had entered each other's lives, DaShawn had been pretending. Pretending to have an interest in her. Pretending she was someone she wasn't. Was she pretending now? Rashida was beyond caring. Wasn't she?

She wanted to run. She wanted to return to the safety and serenity of her house, but her legs wouldn't obey her. She felt as trapped as she had the awful morning she'd realized she was nothing more to DaShawn than a pawn in a heartless game.

In that moment, she had lost everything. Her self-confidence. Her ability to love. Her ability to trust. She'd found the courage to attempt to regain some of what she had misplaced only to have DaShawn show up and snatch it away again.

"Did you get my note?"

Rashida saw red. Did DaShawn actually think she could saunter back into her life and woo her as if the past twenty-one months had never happened?

"Fuck you and your note."

She threw her drink in DaShawn's face and walked away.

"Rashida, wait."

DaShawn grabbed her by the arm, but Rashida broke free. "Don't touch me. You've lost the privilege."

"Sorry."

DaShawn raised her hands in apology. She continued to follow Rashida through the park but made sure to keep her distance. Her permed hair had given way to a short, neatly-trimmed Afro. She was wearing jeans and a T-shirt, reminding Rashida of the look she'd sported the night they'd seen each other in Club One. Had that night offered a glimpse of the real DaShawn, the woman Rashida was now meeting for the first time?

"You probably expect me to say something sappy like I wish I could turn back time. If I said that, I'd be lying. As crazy as it sounds, chances are if I'd rejected Harry's offer, I never would have met you. Meeting you was the best thing that ever happened to me."

Rashida didn't want to hear any more of her lies. She darted toward the garden, trying to lose her persistent tail. DaShawn followed her as if she had anticipated the move.

"I always knew I was a screw-up, but you made me realize I didn't have to continue being one. I can't say I never meant to hurt you because that's what I was hired to do. What I never meant to do was fall in love with you. But I did."

Rashida slowed but didn't stop. DaShawn seemed sincere, but she had learned the hard way that appearances could be deceiving.

"Even though you may not think so now, what we had was real."

"What we had was a lie. If you came to try and convince me otherwise, you wasted your time and your money."

She reached a dead end and turned to retrace her steps, but DaShawn stood in front of her, blocking her path. With nowhere to run, Rashida was forced to stand her ground.

"Being with you is never a waste of time," DaShawn said, her voice as gentle as a first kiss. "If I cared about money, I wouldn't have wasted so much of it on postage mailing all the letters you returned. If I cared about money, I wouldn't have spent almost every dime I have on a one-way plane ticket in the hopes I'd get a chance to stand before you and ask you—*beg* you—for another chance."

"You did that?"

Rashida was so shocked to see DaShawn, she hadn't taken into account the expense it had taken for her to be here. Even the cheapest ticket from Savannah to Kuala Lumpur cost more than four figures. After Uncle Sam and the legal system had their way with DaShawn, her finances must have been left in shambles. Despite that, she had bought a ticket she couldn't afford just to be able to stand here and plead her case with no guarantee Rashida would accept what she had to say.

"I had to see you, no matter what price I had to pay."

Rashida felt herself getting taken in once more. DaShawn was too smooth. Too polished. Too sure of herself. Rashida felt like she was being played for a fool yet again. Unable to keep the pain at bay, she lashed out.

"You've taken everything that ever mattered to me. What more do you want? I don't have anything else to give you." She nearly screamed the words. She wished she could still the tremor in her voice, but her runaway emotions wouldn't let her. "You may have paid your debt to society, but you haven't even begun to pay your debt to me. You betrayed me in more ways than I can count and you're standing here like you expect me to give you a pass for what you did."

"That's not it at all."

"Then what is it?"

DaShawn's confident exterior began to slip. Or was it just another part of her act? Rashida couldn't allow herself to fall for another well-played performance.

"Please say what you came to say and leave me alone. Whether it was real or not, what we had was over as soon as I realized who you really were. We can't get it back, DaShawn. Don't ask me to try."

"But I've got a plan this time. A way to make something of myself. A way to make you proud of me." DaShawn seemed to be grasping at straws. Her dour expression brightened when one apparently entered her reach. "Do me a favor."

"Why in the world would I grant you a favor?"

"Please. Hear me out. Answer one question for me. That's all I'll ask you to do. I know how much I hurt you. I know how much you must hate me. But put aside all your anger and doubts and look into your heart. If your answer to my question is no, I'll walk out of your life forever. But if it's yes, I promise I will never hurt you again. I will never betray you again. I will never give you any reason to doubt me. And most of all, I will never break your trust."

"What's your question?" Rashida asked impatiently. She was ready to get this disastrous evening over with. To say good-bye to DaShawn once and for all so she could finally get on with her life.

"Did you love me? Do you love me?"

DaShawn's question was like a crushing body blow in the final round of a title fight. The figurative impact nearly put Rashida down for the count.

"That's not fair."

"Yes or no?"

Rashida took a deep breath to gather herself. Her feelings for this woman were tangled in a knot so tight she could never hope to unravel it. Anger. Betrayal. And despite it all, lust. She still wanted DaShawn. She wanted DaShawn's hands on her. Inside her. But did she still love her? Did she ever? Was it love she had felt or simply desire?

"Yes or no, Rashida?" DaShawn held her by her shoulders then released her. Tilting her chin up, she forced her to look her in the eye. "Do you love me?"

Rashida brushed DaShawn's hand away. She longed for her touch, but experiencing it was too distracting. She couldn't think. All she could do was feel. All she could do was want. Her body ached with need. How, after everything that had happened, could DaShawn still make her feel this way?

"This is pointless. Even if I said I had feelings for you, what would come of them? We can't ever hope to—"

DaShawn didn't let her finish. "Do you love me?" Lit by a fire from within, her eyes blazed in the moonlight. Rashida felt the heat.

"Yes," Rashida cried from the depths of her soul, angry with herself for not being able to get over DaShawn and angry with DaShawn for not letting her try. "Yes, I love you."

DaShawn's smile lit up the night. "I love you, too. Let me show you how much."

DaShawn reached for her, but Rashida raised her hands to keep her at a safe remove. DaShawn's shoulders slumped.

"You don't trust me."

Tears streamed down Rashida's cheeks. "No." The word nearly lodged in her throat.

"What will it take to make you change your mind?"

"Time. I need time."

"I'll give you all the time you need. I'll jump through any hoop you put in front of me. Take any test you decide to give me. Just tell me it's not too late for me to undo the damage I've done. Tell me we can still be together."

Rashida shook her head. "I can't tell you what I don't know."

A series of powerful percussions shook the earth. Fireworks streamed across the sky. Rashida looked up at the colorful harbingers of a new year. DaShawn's arm slipped around her as they watched the awe-inspiring pyrotechnics. Instead of pulling away, Rashida leaned into the embrace. A sense of calm settled over her. The peace she had traveled thousands of miles to find was here in the arms of the woman who had taken it away.

"I love you, DaShawn," Rashida said when the last sparkler finally faded from view, "but is it enough?"

DaShawn wiped her tears and held her face in her hands. "Baby, it's all we need."

DaShawn leaned to kiss her, but Rashida pulled back. She had trusted DaShawn once, but her trust had been woefully misplaced. Was she about to make the same mistake all over again?

She searched DaShawn's eyes, looking for a sign she was being less than genuine. DaShawn didn't look away. She didn't try to hide the way she once had. She met Rashida's gaze. Invited her to look deeper.

"What do you see?"

Rashida placed her hand over DaShawn's heart, certain she was making the right decision. Certain she could trust DaShawn with her mind, her body, and her soul. "I see someone I want to spend the rest of my life getting to know."

DaShawn's defenses dropped. Raw emotion played across her features as she finally showed who she really was. This wasn't a performance. This was a revelation. An introduction.

"I'll make sure you don't regret a single moment."

And she did.

About the Author

Mason Dixon lives, works, and plays somewhere in the South. She and her partner enjoy grilling, traveling, and fighting for control of the remote. *Date with Destiny* is her first published novel. She can be reached at authormasondixon@gmail.com.

Books Available from Bold Strokes Books

Date with Destiny by Mason Dixon. When sophisticated bank executive Rashida Ivey meets unemployed blue-collar worker Destiny Jackson, will her life ever be the same? (978-1-60282-878-0)

The Devil's Orchard by Ali Vali. Cain and Emma plan a wedding before the birth of their third child while Juan Luis is still lurking, and as Cain plans for his death, an unexpected visitor arrives and challenges her belief in her father, Dalton Casey. (978-1-60282-879-7)

Secrets and Shadows by L.T. Marie. A bodyguard and the woman she protects run from a madman and into each other's arms. (978-1-60282-880-3)

Change Horizon: Three Novellas by Gun Brooke. Three stories of courageous women who dare to love as they fight to claim a future in a hostile universe. (978-1-60282-881-0)

Scarlet Thirst by Crin Claxton. When hot, feisty Rani meets cool, vampire Rob, one lifetime isn't enough, and the road from human to vampire is shorter than you think… (978-1-60282-856-8)

Battle Axe by Carsen Taite. How close is too close? Bounty hunter Luca Bennett will soon find out. (978-1-60282-871-1)

Improvisation by Karis Walsh. High school geometry teacher Jan Carroll thinks she's figured out the shape of her life and her future, until graphic artist and fiddle player Tina Nelson comes along and teaches her to improvise. (978-1-60282-872-8)

For Want of a Fiend by Barbara Ann Wright. Without her Fiendish power, can Princess Katya and her consort Starbride stop a magic-wielding madman from sparking an uprising in the kingdom of Farraday? (978-1-60282-873-5)

Broken in Soft Places by Fiona Zedde. The instant Sara Chambers meets the seductive and sinful Merille Thompson, she falls hard, but knowing the difference between love and a dangerous, all-consuming desire is just one of the lessons Sara must learn before it's too late. (978-1-60282-876-6)

Healing Hearts by Donna K. Ford. Running from tragedy, the women of Willow Springs find that with friendship, there is hope, and with love, there is everything. (978-1-60282-877-3)

Desolation Point by Cari Hunter. When a storm strands Sarah Kent in the North Cascades, Alex Pascal is determined to find her. Neither imagines the dangers they will face when a ruthless criminal begins to hunt them down. (978-1-60282-865-0)

I Remember by Julie Cannon. What happens when you can never forget the first kiss, the first touch, the first taste of lips on skin? What happens when you know you will remember every single detail of a mysterious woman? (978-1-60282-866-7)

The Gemini Deception by Kim Baldwin and Xenia Alexiou. The truth, the whole truth, and nothing but lies. Book six in the Elite Operatives series. (978-1-60282-867-4)

Scarlet Revenge by Sheri Lewis Wohl. When faith alone isn't enough, will the love of one woman be strong enough to save a vampire from damnation? (978-1-60282-868-1)

Ghost Trio by Lillian Q. Irwin. When Lee Howe hears the voice of her dead lover singing to her, is it a hallucination, a ghost, or something more sinister? (978-1-60282-869-8)

The Princess Affair by Nell Stark. Rhodes Scholar Kerry Donovan arrives at Oxford ready to focus on her studies, but her life and her priorities are thrown into chaos when she catches the eye of Her Royal Highness Princess Sasha. (978-1-60282-858-2)

The Chase by Jesse J. Thoma. When Isabelle Rochat's life is threatened, she receives the unwelcome protection and attention of bounty hunter Holt Lasher who vows to keep Isabelle safe at all costs. (978-1-60282-859-9)

The Lone Hunt by L.L. Raand. In a world where humans and praeterns conspire for the ultimate power, violence is a way of life… and death. A Midnight Hunters novel. (978-1-60282-860-5)

The Supernatural Detective by Crin Claxton. Tony Carson sees dead people. With a drag queen for a spirit guide and a devastatingly attractive herbalist for a client, she's about to discover the spirit world can be a very dangerous world indeed. (978-1-60282-861-2)

Beloved Gomorrah by Justine Saracen. Undersea artists creating their own City on the Plain uncover the truth about Sodom and Gomorrah, whose "one righteous man" is a murderer, rapist, and conspirator in genocide. (978-1-60282-862-9)

Cut to the Chase by Lisa Girolami. Careful and methodical author Paige Cornish falls for brash and wild Hollywood actress Avalon Randolph, but can these opposites find a happy middle ground in a town that never lives in the middle? (978-1-60282-783-7)

More Than Friends by Erin Dutton. Evelyn Fisher thinks she has the perfect role model for a long-term relationship, until her best friends, Kendall and Melanie, split up and all three women must reevaluate their lives and their relationships. (978-1-60282-784-4)

Every Second Counts by D. Jackson Leigh. Every second counts in Bridgette LeRoy's desperate mission to protect her heart and stop

Marc Ryder's suicidal return to riding rodeo bulls. (978-1-60282-785-1)

Dirty Money by Ashley Bartlett. Vivian Cooper and Reese DiGiovanni just found out that falling in love is hard. It's even harder when you're running for your life. (978-1-60282-786-8)

Sea Glass Inn by Karis Walsh. When Melinda Andrews commissions a series of mosaics by Pamela Whitford for her new inn, she doesn't expect to be more captivated by the artist than by the paintings. (978-1-60282-771-4)

The Awakening: A Sisters of Spirits novel by Yvonne Heidt. Sunny Skye has interacted with spirits her entire life, but when she runs into Officer Jordan Lawson during a ghost investigation, she discovers more than just facts in a missing girl's cold case file. (978-1-60282-772-1)

Murphy's Law by Yolanda Wallace. No matter how high you climb, you can't escape your past. (978-1-60282-773-8)

Blacker Than Blue by Rebekah Weatherspoon. Threatened with losing her first love to a powerful demon, vampire Cleo Jones is willing to break the ultimate law of the undead to rebuild the family she has lost. (978-1-60282-774-5)

Silver Collar by Gill McKnight. Werewolf Luc Garoul is outlawed and out of control, but can her family track her down before a sinister predator gets there first? Fourth in the Garoul series. (978-1-60282-764-6)

The Dragon Tree Legacy by Ali Vali. For Aubrey Tarver time hasn't dulled the pain of losing her first love Wiley Gremillion, but she has to set that aside when her choices put her life and her family's lives in real danger. (978-1-60282-765-3)

The Midnight Room by Ronica Black. After a chance encounter with the mysterious and brooding Lillian Gray in the "midnight room" of The Griffin, a local lesbian bar, confident and gorgeous Audrey McCarthy learns that her bad-girl behavior isn't bulletproof. (978-1-60282-766-0)

Dirty Sex by Ashley Bartlett. Vivian Cooper and twins Reese and Ryan DiGiovanni stole a lot of money and the guy they took it from wants it back. Like now. (978-1-60282-767-7)

The Storm by Shelley Thrasher. Rural East Texas. 1918. War-weary Jaq Bergeron and marriage-scarred musician Molly Russell try to salvage love from the devastation of the war abroad and natural disasters at home. (978-1-60282-780-6)

Crossroads by Radclyffe. Dr. Hollis Monroe specializes in short-term relationships but when she meets pregnant mother-to-be Annie Colfax, fate brings them together at a crossroads that will change their lives forever. (978-1-60282-756-1)